"So, you are Calista?"

"I am this year." She laughed at the confusion that must have shown on his face. "Do names matter to you?"

He frowned at the odd answer. The idea that she was someone else completely didn't sit easily on his conscience. "Yes, names are important."

"Then if you don't care for Calista you should pick another." She lifted her hand and twisted it in the air. "Names are like hats. They must suit the situation or be exchanged with no regrets or excessive sentimentality. A much-loved, jaunty riding hat has no place in a ballroom, for instance. I'll answer to any name you care to call me."

Constantine sat back in shock. He didn't believe he could do that easily. "Have you no name at all?"

She smoothed her gown with dainty fingers. "I've had many. None that I'd care to claim."

"That's absurd."

Her eyes grew shuttered. "The world is absurd. I didn't make it that way. I just try to live in it peacefully."

Heather Boyd

Hunting the Hero

Wild Randalls

4

Dedication

For readers and fans of the Wild Randall series. Thank you so much for your patience and impatience as you waited for this book and for Rosemary. Here she is -- the one that got away. Enjoy!

Chapter One

The devil chased away the daylight as Constantine urged his horse to take him far from his responsibilities and into the arms of willing debauchery. He thundered down the lane, running away from his guilt and toward the distant manor house outlined by the falling sun.

His heart pounded as it always did when he rode, keeping time with his mount's hooves upon the earthen road beneath them. But it was more than just the thrill of being free that filled him with anticipation. Today he had made a decision. Tonight he hoped to forget. Constantine crested the rise and slowed his horse to a trot as the remote manor house loomed before him. The place had no name but was widely known for its warm welcome. What else could you expect from a bawdy house perched high on a hill?

He swung off his mount as two liveried footman hurried toward him, one intent on his horse, the other upon him. "Your name, sir?"

Constantine experienced a pang of uncertainty, then brushed it aside. "Lord Grayling."

The bewigged footman bowed deferentially. "Welcome to the House, my lord. If you'd be so kind as to come this way, Mrs. Cohen will be only too happy to accommodate your every need this evening."

It wasn't Mrs. Cohen's accommodation Constantine required,

but one of the younger courtesans in her employ. Perhaps they could banish the memory of his late wife from his mind, along with his part in her death.

Once inside, the footman took his riding crop, hat, gloves, and caped coat away, leaving him free to stroll about the elegantly appointed lower hall unimpeded. Spartan but elegant. So far the rumors were true. Mrs. Cohen had been much sought after in London during her youth, but as age had lessened her appeal, she'd retired to the countryside to groom others for men's pleasures. He'd never met her, but the stories of her establishment were legend. They said a man could buy any pleasure for the right price.

Before he'd gone too many steps, an older woman long past the first blush of youth, but still lovely, appeared. "Mrs. Cohen?"

"My Lord Grayling. What an unexpected surprise. Welcome to the House."

Constantine was well prepared for this adventure. He reached into his coat pocket and handed over the expected funds. "A token of my appreciation."

The madam's expression eased into extreme friendliness and another footman appeared with a glass of wine balanced upon a gleaming silver tray. "You must be thirsty from your long ride. I trust your journey was uneventful."

"It was," he assured her, unsurprised that she knew he'd traveled some distance to arrive here. He wouldn't be shocked to learn the woman knew the location of every gentleman of consequence within a fifty-mile radius of her establishment, as well as the state of their pocketbook and their love life. She was in the business of providing a service where it was most needed.

Constantine took the glass and sipped. A remarkably fine vintage filled his mouth and he nodded. "Perfect."

The madam sent the footman away and gestured to an adjacent room. "I think you will find exactly what you require in this direction. Dark or pale, full-figured or slim. The House prides itself on ensuring a gentleman's pleasure."

Constantine nodded. He was tired of spending his nights alone with only his guilt for company. He was weary of mourning the life he had lost.

At the threshold of the saloon—a room soaked in red velvet

and supple limbs—he saw the ladies of the night reclined in shimmering, half-undone gowns as they listened to the strains of Bach adequately played by another of their number. A few gentlemen, some with vaguely familiar faces, graced the room, all engaged with willing women perched upon their laps.

The scene was one he had viewed before his marriage but found little pleasure in now. He wasn't one for public spectacles. Private pleasures were all he desired tonight. It was simply a matter of choosing a face with an appealing body and then losing himself in desire.

He scanned the room, searching for a face and form that would inspire him and satisfy his hunger. A leggy blonde sat alone and unoccupied for the moment. The madam noticed the direction of his gaze and provided her name. "Solange."

A rare jewel. Constantine doubted names held any accuracy in this place. With any luck she'd be willing, pliant, and easy on the senses of a man who'd come for distraction. He'd begin his quest there.

He strolled forward and limpid eyes flowed over him, caressing without touching. A prelude to intimacy to come. Her lips lifted into a smile as she rose to her feet, gliding toward him with smooth steps. When she held out her gloved hand, he kissed the back as if she were a dear friend.

"Welcome," she said, her voice soft and easy on the ears.

Constantine smiled in response. "Grayling."

Her hands touched his arm in a gentle caress, luring him toward her body, attempting to beguile, subtly at first. The smallest whisper of anticipation coursed through him. Perhaps a rare jewel would be enough? Perhaps Solange could provide the pleasure he sought. Yet even as he formed that thought, another filled him. Solange was lovely, but would she provide him with the challenge he craved?

Would she bend to his will completely, allow him to satisfy his needs even if it left her wanting? Would she dare to complain about his selfishness? There was no way to predict the outcome.

What Constantine missed most was the chase of love and passion. The hunt and claiming of victory. He'd had that once, so he knew what he missed and wanted tonight. A woman whose passionate nature could keep pace with his.

Solange leaned close to whisper in his ear. "Shall we sit and listen for a while, my lord?"

Constantine didn't particularly care for the music, but the performance would give him time to consider whether Solange would suit. "Of course."

She grabbed his hand and guided him toward an empty corner settee. Constantine followed her and after he'd sat, allowed her to press another glass of wine into his hand. While he sipped, Solange's nimble fingers stroked the top of his thigh. But the soft touches failed to arouse. That whisper of desire he'd felt at first sight had vanished as if it had never been. Constantine cursed under his breath.

After a short period, Solange turned her attention from the pianist and caught his eye. Her hands glided up his inner thigh to tease him with the promise of later pleasures. As she leaned close to nuzzle his neck above his cravat, he realized nothing had changed. He was no more aroused by her touch than he had been when he'd set off for the brothel that evening. Even when her fingers skimmed his chest and then tangled in his hair, he had no reaction whatsoever. The gentle kisses she bestowed to his jaw were persistent, but not enough to arouse. If he got her to the bedchamber, he feared neither one of them would be happy.

Constantine concentrated on everything else but what she did. Solange's ministrations had not banished his wife far enough into the past to allow him to lose himself in the moment. He wanted to forget he'd loved his wife. He wanted to banish the guilt that haunted him.

He glanced beyond Solange's shoulder to see who else lingered in the room. He'd choose another. Someone he hoped had enough mastery to cure him of his longing for the perfect life he'd lost.

There were three other unattached women in the room, but as he inspected them, they failed to stir him any more than Solange had. Perhaps he should have gone to London when Rothwell had suggested it. A few weeks of debauchery in the company of a trusted friend might have been better than the pleasures afforded by this private country house. It was just his luck that his situation prevented him from visiting the capital just now.

A flutter of pale skirts caught his attention as a slight woman paused in the doorway of the saloon. A slim figure appeared, deep black hair carelessly tumbling around her head as if she'd stumbled from bed and could just as easily return to it. She claimed his complete attention and he couldn't look away from her whiskey-brown eyes. Their eyes held as the plunking of the pianoforte dimmed.

Small limbs, perfect skin, and a smile that wasn't the least sincere.

For a moment he couldn't breathe. Whoever she was, she made no attempt to join them, no attempt to tempt him or any other man in the room. But she had done the impossible with one haughty glance. She had made his pulse riot.

When she moved on, Constantine continued to stare at the vacant space where she'd stood, waiting for her to come back into view. He'd never been so mesmerized by a woman before. The shock of being instantly aroused to the point of pain took a moment to sink in. She was just a slip of a girl really. Barely grown enough to be in a place like this, let alone have that effect on him.

Yet with one glance, an invisible hand had closed around his privates and urged him to follow.

Constantine extricated himself from Solange's clinging grasp, ignoring her huff and pout as he handed her his wine glass and excused himself to get a second, longer look at the dark-haired girl.

The hallway was empty, and as he looked down the hall trying to decide where she might have disappeared to, he cursed his foolishness for chasing after a light-skirt who'd made no effort to attract his attention.

As he took a few steps away from the pianoforte's tapping, he detected voices speaking urgently not too far away. Mrs. Cohen's voice he clearly heard coming from a nearby room, followed by a quieter response from someone else. A door stood ajar and he eased closer to it.

As he neared the doorway, Mrs. Cohen burst out angrily, "What do you mean you're not needed? Tonight is always our busiest night."

Constantine peeked through the gap, noting the dark-haired girl was indeed tiny when compared with the madam of the bawdy house. But she had the courage to stand up against a madam who could very likely throw her out into the cold Wiltshire winter without a moment's hesitation or regret.

The madam glanced over her shoulder and he ducked back out of sight before he was seen. He might be impatient for an introduction so he could dismiss his curiosity soon after, but he was interested in their argument too. It was not every day a man overheard an honest conversation in a place like this.

"I refuse to listen to Mallory's dull playing for one more night," the dark-haired girl muttered in a smooth, sultry voice that belied her tiny appearance. "She hasn't the talent to entertain the whole room and your busiest night is always filled with the same faces."

"Lord Grayling has come and needs to be entertained," Mrs. Cohen answered in a shocked tone.

On hearing his name, Constantine eased close to the door and peeked through the crack again. The dark-haired nymph stood with her back to the fire, rubbing her hands together as if she was chilled through. Judging by the sheer drifts of muslin wrapped about her that revealed the slim curves of her hips, she very well might be.

"If Solange is the sort to tempt him, then I'm sure he will be well satisfied," she said, her tone dripping with contempt. Her shoulder lifted a touch as she dismissed him out of hand. "Lord Squires is always expected at ten. He usually asks for me."

Mrs. Cohen drew closer. "Squires would be nothing compared to Grayling in your bed. If you would but listen to what was said of him you would not be so dismissive. How can you not accept the challenge of stealing him away from Solange?"

The slim woman turned, eyes narrowing in suspicion. "Gossip is seldom accurate and for a madam who should want peaceful relations between her employees, you certainly are stirring the pot of late. Why would you want me to captivate Lord Grayling so well that he sets aside that insipid creature? It's hardly a fair challenge."

Constantine choked. They were discussing him as if he were a prime piece of beef. He clamped his lips together and fought to remain silent.

The madam shrugged. "Solange is getting above herself."

A deep throaty laugh left the smaller woman's throat, forcing Constantine to revise his initial estimate of her as someone young and inexperienced. "And that shall never do," she purred. "Very well. I shall do what I can to lure the handsome lord into my bed just so you may prove your point and give Solange the setdown she deserves." She studied her fingertips by firelight. "I think as a reward I should have another trinket, one for my fingers this time."

"You and your gemstones." Mrs. Cohen wagged an excessively bejeweled finger at the tiny woman. "Only if you succeed, Calista. Only if he is sated and comes back for you another night, then I'll give you half his fee too."

A devilishly wicked smile twisted the dark-haired girl's lips, turning a formerly remarkable face into the most arousing sight he had ever beheld. Those lips and whiskey-brown eyes were so damn expressive. What would she look like as they made love? He adjusted his trousers. Damn woman could even affect him through the crack of the door. Her sudden throaty laugh sent chills racing down his spine. "Oh, I'm sure Lord Grayling's seduction is well in hand. Trust me on this."

"What would I do without you?" Mrs. Cohen murmured, genuine affection softening her voice. "These are powerful men and must be looked after as if they were made of glass."

"Not glass, Linnie. Something much, much warmer." Calista's gaze shifted to the doorway where he hid. Her lips lifted into a cunning smile as if she knew he was there, listening while they planned his seduction. "I've been at this for a long time now and I know what men want. Trust me."

The challenge was boldly made. All men wanted the same thing from a woman, didn't they? No demands but on their body, no conversation save for what they expected in bed. There was no doubt her experiences had made Calista overconfident, too. But his curiosity was roused and he was determined to find out more about her.

Constantine moved until he stood openly in the doorway, nudging the opening wider so he could view the entire room. Before him, Mrs. Cohen towered over the woman called Calista who didn't reach higher than his chest. Constantine was drawn to the stubborn, smug glint in Calista's eyes. They sparkled with the thrill of her dare.

Her gaze dropped to his groin and her lips curved into a satisfied smile. Damn woman. She thought she'd won already. However, he'd show her he could hold his own when it came to pleasure. There was no point pretending he was unaware of her game.

He moved into the room and cleared his throat. "An introduction, Mrs. Cohen?"

Mrs. Cohen spun about quickly, her manner changing to one of deference. "Lord Grayling. I did not… I was led to believe you were otherwise occupied."

Cohen sent Calista a furious glance. Was the girl in trouble with her employer for failing to inform her that a guest was listening to every word they said? He hoped the punishment would not be too severe. "So I overheard." Constantine smiled winningly at the madam. "However, I believe there is a trinket to be won for a successful seduction. Do you place wagers involving all your patrons? The gentlemen who recommended your establishment will be interested in that tidbit."

Mrs. Cohen pressed her hand to her brow. "No, never."

Calista strutted forward, hands on her hips, haughty glint firmly in place. God, she had nerve. The bold move placed her between him and the bawd as if the larger woman might need her protection. "This was a private conversation, my lord."

"About me."

She shrugged as if the matter were of no importance. "Wagers are placed in any number of places and at any time about many things. Do you take offence to each and every one?"

"I never said I was offended. I just doubt your ability to do as you claim."

Calista's lips pressed together as if she was annoyed by his skepticism regarding her prowess in the bedroom. A wild impulse to laugh at her vexation rose in his chest. This woman did not like her claims to be challenged. That made him all the more determined to spend the night in her bed purely to see the lengths she would go to win her pretty bauble from the madam.

Her eyes narrowed to slits. She might be tiny but perhaps she wasn't as delicate as he'd first thought. Calista was no young miss but a mature woman, one who might have extensive experience in dealing with demanding men. Would she enjoy the challenge of her work, too?

She stepped forward and held out her bare, ringless hand to him. "Calista, my lord."

He took her hand, noting the coldness of her slim fingers as he kissed the back of them. "A pleasure."

He released her hand even while imagining that cold grip wrapped around his limbs and other parts. How long would it take to warm her until her skin glistened by firelight? He knew several ways to build a heat quickly, and a romp in between the sheets was certainly the most appealing.

"A pleasure, certainly." Calista circled him, her hand sweeping over his bottom in a fleeting caress. He withheld a groan, determined not to betray how deeply she affected him. "Not yet, but soon," she said.

The dark-haired woman raised a brow, as if daring him to disagree with her. For reasons he couldn't fathom, he accepted her silent challenge. It wouldn't be him to cry for mercy at the end of the night. She would be the one asking him for pleasure to cease. He held out his hand. "Very soon."

Amusement twinkled in her eyes and after a moment Calista placed her cold, slender hand in his. "Do you really believe you can handle me, my lord?"

He gripped her tightly, feeling the bones of her hand shift within his. He relaxed his grip but didn't dare let her go. "Oh, yes. I do."

Chapter Two

—◆—

Sinfully beautiful men were Meredith Clark's weakness, especially ones who didn't notice the spell they cast over their captive audience. Known only as Calista in the secluded country brothel, Meredith Clark breathed deep, scenting the clean skin and earthy fragrance of Lord Grayling as he filled her starved senses. Her job might be to please those who came into her arms and bed, but gaining a little pleasure for herself in return was always an unlooked-for treat.

"I believe I shall leave you in Calista's capable hands, my lord. Do be sure to ring if you require the slightest embellishment to your night," Linnie murmured, casting Meredith a look that warned she'd better not leave him wanting for anything. The madam departed soundlessly. Grayling barely acknowledged Linnie's departure. He remained apart and returned Meredith's frank stare.

Meredith's pulse quickened. Grayling was handsome and had an air of command. A fallen angel sent to lure any good woman to ruin. Not that Meredith's ruin was possible or even probable now. She'd fallen as far as she could already without being forced to beg. Yet when she looked Grayling over from head to toe, the idea of begging this man for anything involving pleasure held an appeal she could not dismiss easily. Men of his caliber rarely came her way.

Grayling's eyes flowed over her from the top of her head to dainty, pointed slipper. Not a new situation. A whore was always leered at and she was prepared to be pleasing no matter the circumstances. Meredith looked her best tonight. The cream color of her fine muslin gown left few surprises for a gentleman's imagination to fill. She enjoyed seeing their stunned, almost slavering, expressions. The majority of her gowns were little better than tissue.

However, for the first time in quite a long time, Meredith couldn't help feeling just a little overcome by a man's scrutiny. Even if she was dressed in the primmest of gowns, she was rather afraid Grayling would unnerve her. There was an intensity in his gaze that most others of his class lacked. A surety that he was entitled to what he saw and touched and one would like being his property. Crave it even.

Meredith reprimanded herself for becoming so distracted by her quarry. Handsome men were also trouble. She gestured to the far table, cluttered with bottles of spirit and expensive glassware, ignoring the way her body demanded she make him hers immediately. "May I offer you refreshment, my lord?"

His lips pursed momentarily.

Surely he didn't believe she wanted him too foxed to be of any use in bed? Where was the challenge in that? Many a whore used that trick to lessen their client's desire, but that certainly wasn't her plan for Grayling. Meredith reached for a bottle and squinted at the label to be sure she held the right one. "Linnie has a fine brandy if you prefer that over the wine you were served on your arrival."

She flexed her fingers around the neck of the bottle as she showed him what she held, watching his eyes widen and the bulge in his breaches grow as she observed him.

Grayling shook his head as if to clear away the fog of lust but then barked a laugh. "Thank you. I do prefer brandy to wine."

Meredith withheld a grin of triumph, pleased that she'd guessed correctly about him. There had been the faintest hint of brandy beneath the cologne that cloaked him. A man of his power would not sip wine when he wanted enjoyment. The way Grayling watched her was bold and demanding. There would be no half measures for him. What would he expect in bed? Her pulse raced with possible choices. She could think of any number of interesting ways to keep Lord Grayling occupied this evening and she was rather pleased to have rescued him from Solange's uninspired passions.

The heat of his hands, for instance, would be put to better use wrapped around her naked flesh. She shivered at the memory of his warmth and turned back to the task of pouring drinks, surprised that she was looking forward to the evening ahead more than she usually did.

And it wasn't just the bet she had made with Linnie, although an expensive bauble for her fingers could fetch a pretty penny one day should she need it. She had her future to think of. Getting Grayling to return a second night, and thereby earn half his fee, was another inducement to captivate him. But still. There was something about him that made her believe she'd remember him long after he'd gone. Tonight she might find a memory to treasure on the lonely nights ahead.

She served Grayling Linnie's finest brandy, a smaller portion for herself, and returned to the earl, allowing their fingers to brush his with seeming innocence. She raised her glass. "A toast."

His dark brow arched farther to show his surprise.

"To the esteemed lords of England, Ireland, and Scotland," Meredith murmured. "May they all be as blessed as you in looks and in intelligence and find their own pleasure before the night is through."

After a moment, Grayling offered up a smile that spoke of embarrassment, amusement and grudging respect. He drank to her toast. "You are very good," he murmured in a voice so deep and dark that she shivered.

"Oh, the best you've never had," Meredith replied in as daring a manner as she could manage while simultaneously restraining her own amorous tendencies. It was hard to know who was seducing whom right now because she had the astonishing urge to claim the man as if he were her own personal toy.

"Modest to a fault." He laughed and gestured to a nearby chair. "Would you care to sit?"

Meredith beamed at his gallantry and took a place on the settee closest to the fire. At this time of year, she could never manage to ignore the chill of the night. Besides, the settee would allow for greater intimacies to spring up between them. An innocent touch, the seemingly random brush of her limb against his as she appeared engaged in his conversation while planning the next part of his seduction. This would be so easy and she would have her prize come morning.

Grayling seated himself in a spindly wooden chair across from her, spoiling her plans for a direct, hands-on seduction. He sat back, one leg crossed over the other, the fabric of his breeches straining to reveal well-muscled thighs. Her mouth watered. Her body pulsed. The polished boot attached to his upper leg swung back and forth in a hypnotizing dance that kept her attention fixed on his large body.

She blinked and dragged her gaze back to his sparkling green eyes, which were again filled with amusement at her expense. She did her best to keep her irritation hidden. Grayling's seemingly innocent smile was utterly fraudulent. He'd sat apart just to upset her plans for unfettered success. She'd have to be much cleverer in her methods if she was going to have her way with him. And wicked it would be.

Meredith thrilled at the challenge of a reluctant bed partner. In her line of work, men rarely played hard to get. Most were always willing and eager to get to the end without fighting for the best of the moments before. She hadn't met a man equal to the challenge in a very long time. Tonight might even be fun.

Determined to intrigue him, even from a distance, Meredith eased back in the chair, leveling him with an amused smile. She widened her knees slightly, just enough that he'd notice the movement of her gown pulling tight across them. As she hoped, his gaze dipped to the light gown covering her thighs. He couldn't see anything now, but he would surely remember the way the fire had revealed the outline of her body as he'd spied on her and Linnie talking earlier through the crack in the door. "Tell me of yourself, my lord. Do you enjoy the hunt?"

His eyes rose slowly, sparkling with mirth. "Very much. I keep hounds and host a gathering every year on my estate."

That hadn't been what she'd alluded to with her comment, but if he wanted to play the part of a reluctant lover then the least she could do was humor him. She'd learned to be always obliging to those she wanted something from. Grayling was her guarantee of further riches. "Is the event very well attended?"

His legs unfolded and he set both feet out before him. His eyes lost their merriment as he crossed his arms over his chest. "Everyone who is invited finds their way to Stanton Harold Hall. Getting them to leave is another matter entirely."

Curious about his change of posture, a defense if ever she saw one, Meredith's fingers rose to toy with the neckline of her gown. The slow movement drew his attention but did nothing to soften his pose. "I imagine you to be such an agreeable host, so willing to see to their every whim and need, no matter the inconvenience, that your guests cannot bear to be parted from your company."

His expression grew skeptical. "They come for the food, the wine, and to gawk."

"People always covet what other people have." Meredith saw no harm in it and frequently admired the pretty gems other ladies wore with no ill effect. But she'd never met someone who was vocal about their dislike of being looked upon. Given his looks, Grayling should be used to such attention. In fact, Meredith could not tear her eyes away from his person for any length of time. When she'd spotted him in the drawing room with Solange draped all over his lap, she'd been unaccountably aggrieved. As if Solange deserved such a man.

She let her hand still, fingertips resting lightly on the skin of her upper chest, and slowly drew a line down toward her bodice. "Is your home very beautiful?"

She dipped her fingers beneath the fine cloth and drew them back and forward, teasing her fingertips with the soft sensations. Grayling's eyes tracked her every movement.

"No."

She smiled at his blunt confession. The absence of boasting was intriguing. Most men she met couldn't wait to embellish on the wonders of their lives. The size of their estate, the esteem of their connections. Grayling told her nothing about his life beyond cursory detail. Meredith found that utterly fascinating.

She slid her hand lower until it would appear to her companion that she was about to cup her own breast. His eyes narrowed, focusing on her intent. She laughed softly at his response. Meredith was tempted to show him just how bold she could be, but she wanted to leave some surprises for later. "Come now, surely a place named Stanton Harold Hall has something to recommend it? Even if you take such beauty for granted."

His eyes grew shuttered, his gaze fell to the floor between them. Silence thickened but then raucous laughter just outside the door jerked his head up and around.

Solange and her replacement companion, the lanky and exuberant Mr. White, burst into the room. That they were kissing quite passionately without noticing they were barging into an occupied room set her teeth on edge. A vase was almost knocked over in their exertions, a chair pushed aside in their haste to disrobe. The occupants of the house might be among the lowest in society, but other people did not always enjoy viewing the more earthy aspects of their trade. When she glanced at Grayling, she saw his jaw had clenched at the intrusion. He wasn't one for public displays then.

Solange deserved a good paddling for her interruption. Meredith had to content herself with glaring instead.

"Oh, I'm sorry Calista! I didn't know you had a visitor." Solange glanced between Meredith and Lord Grayling and then giggled behind her hand. "I see I wasn't interrupting anything important. May I offer my company, my lord? Wouldn't you prefer someone still in the first bloom of youth?"

Mr. White appeared shocked to be so quickly cast aside in favor of another. Linnie would be furious if he never came back to the House. Meredith had to act quickly to ensure the young man was not slighted. Mr. White had a reputation for vigor that many women in the House rather enjoyed, save Solange. Meredith had a better partner in mind for him.

She rose to her feet, stretching to the limit of her five feet two inches, and stepped forward until she stood beside Grayling's chair. And how dare Solange hint that she was too old? It wasn't only youth and easy agreement that men wanted. Some men liked more of a challenge than Solange presented. She'd lift her skirts for the vicar if he so much as smiled in her direction. Solange would pay for the interruption tomorrow morning, bright and early. A good ten strikes of Linnie's paddle could go a long way to restoring the pecking order in the house. Calista was the house's diamond, the one every man longed for. Solange was lower but with aspirations she couldn't hope to attain. The stupid little fool had yet to learn her place. "Go back the way you came and find another room for Mr. White. If you lack the imagination to entertain him, then I'll send Mallory to him. She was saying just the other day she wished for a long ride."

Although Mr. White blushed, he didn't deny Meredith's suggestion appealed to him.

Grayling turned away from the interruption and lifted his face to Meredith's as he brushed his left hand across her bottom lightly, proving he wasn't the least bit interested in the discussion. The sensation just about took Meredith's breath away. Every nerve in her body was aflame. One touch and she'd turned to butter on a hot day. She fought to remember what she was doing while fully aware her reaction to Grayling was a new experience.

Meredith took a deep breath, fighting the urge to press her rear into his hand, and glared until Solange realized she should leave. The twit nudged her companion until he cleared the doorway. "Excuse us, Calista."

The doors banged shut with a thump. Meredith glanced at her companion, surprised to find her hand resting on Grayling's shoulder. She stroked the broad expanse, feeling the subtle shift in his body toward hers. Warmth poured off him in waves. She grinned at him as he brushed lightly over the crest of her bottom, pleased that he would be hers eventually. Proximity obviously produced a similar arousing effect on him. His breeches were positively straining at the seams.

Any tentative doubts about the night ahead vanished. If Grayling was going to keep a distance in the beginning, then so be it. His touch gave her all the assurance she needed to accept the slower pace of his seduction. He would come closer eventually and then she would win. All she needed to do was find the right inducement.

The challenge to please them both had begun. The winner would take all.

Chapter Three

---◆---

The hand resting on his shoulder had more effect than Constantine dared let on. Calista set his senses on fire. He'd never reacted to a woman like this before. Not even to his wife, whom he'd treasured as the love of his life. Augusta had been a gentle soul. A refuge from the troubles of life and the perfect companion to his nights. They had married by arrangement, but prolonged intimacy had made them true partners. Augusta had been the one to encourage him to explore his darker passions in their marriage bed as the years of wedded bliss increased.

But Augusta had never made him feel as unbalanced as this. His reaction to the woman grinning down upon him triumphantly was nothing like what he'd expected. He worked to bury his lust. "I have an excellent cook and my housekeeper dotes on all my guests." He continued as if the interruption had never occurred. He needed time to restore his equilibrium and commonplace conversation would give him that.

Her fingers slipped from his shoulder as she turned, but then her other hand rose to replace it. "Who acts as your hostess?"

Her fingers crept into his hair, just above his cravat, and gooseflesh chased down his spine and legs. He swallowed quickly. "A very good friend. She has a talent for making everyone feel at home and wanted. I'd be rather lost without her, honestly."

"She sounds perfect." The whore's touch slipped from his hair as she glided across the room. Calista stopped before the fire, staring down into the flames. The flickering firelight revealed the slight parting of her slim legs. "Why are you in a brothel rather than with this paragon?"

Constantine shifted in his chair to accommodate his expanding dimensions and pondered what to say of Lady Farnsworth's place in his life. A truer friend he'd never met. Arabella, his late wife's good friend and confidant, was a beautiful widow who lived on a property bordering his. But she didn't view Constantine as a potential husband or even a lover. When his wife had died unexpectedly two years ago, Arabella had smoothly stepped in and propped him up with a light touch and astonishing disregard for potential gossip. They'd never even so much as kissed in greeting, but she came to his house several times each week to jolly him from his bad mood and to cheer his daughters. "It's complicated."

"Relationships between men and women often are but rarely need to be." Calista spun slowly around and the flickering firelight behind her outlined her tempting curves to perfection, and the impact to his lust grew. To his considerable discomfort, their game, a dance of a few light touches so far, had the power to arouse him very easily.

She thrust her hands behind her, toward the flames to warm them, most likely. He'd never met a woman with such cold hands. But the pose also forced her breasts into prominence, revealing nipples swollen to hard points. Unable to maintain a distance, Constantine rose and crossed the room to stand before her, keeping a short space of air between them. The heat from the blazing fire battered his face. He blinked slowly until he grew used to the warmth and then studied the small woman in greater detail. Her eyes were alight with anticipation. She desired him too.

He'd chosen well. He couldn't wait to get a bed at her back. "Shall we retire for the night?"

Her eyes glinted brightly. "As you wish, my lord."

The compliant tone was completely false. He doubted Calista was finished turning his world upside down this evening, but he'd prove he was more than willing to keep up. In fact, he might just take the game further than he'd originally intended. What would she do if he held off his release, fought the inevitable end to pleasure as long as he possibly could?

He didn't like his chances but he was definitely determined to try, just to keep her on edge.

Calista smiled, far too pleased with herself, and gestured toward the door. "Please, follow me."

Bemused, he trailed behind her like an obedient puppy to the door, opened it, and then strolled after her as her shorter stride practically ran for the staircase. He kept his gaze fixed on her dark, curled hair, then noted the smooth, unblemished skin of her nape, the firm shoulders beneath, and the determined strut to her walk.

His state of arousal ebbed a little and he breathed a sigh of relief. However, when she looked over her shoulder to ensure he followed up the stairs, his length thickened beyond his power to recall it. Damn those eyes. She'd made him as lusty as an adolescent youth.

After a few steps along an upper hall, Mrs. Cohen appeared. Her glance flickered over him briefly. "The end room for His Lordship."

Bedroom or barn, Constantine couldn't care less where he spent the night as long as Calista was with him. However, his companion hesitated beside the madam, a scowl replacing her earlier serenity. "You promised not to assign that room to me again."

"Yes, well, His Lordship deserves the best the house has to offer. All of it."

Calista's face grew tight with frustration. Eventually, she got herself under control and replaced her frown with an insincere smile that failed to reach her eyes. She gestured ahead and Constantine eagerly went where she sent him.

He opened the door and allowed Calista to pass by, unmolested for the moment. With rather more relief than necessary, he locked the door to give them the privacy he craved and looked around. Lush red velvet, dulled and slightly aged by the daytime sunlight that would stream through a pair of east-facing tall windows. At night he could see nothing beyond their reflections in the glass, but by morning it should boast a pretty view of the valley beyond.

He was puzzled by his companion's dislike for the room. As

far as he could see, the bawd was being truthful about the room's superior appointments. Perhaps Calista had no love for red velvet.

Noticing the tense set of her shoulders and her hands clutched together as if she was cold again, he strode to the fire and added enough fuel to increase the warmth of the room. He didn't want her to become even more chilled when he removed her clothes. The idea of her naked and covered with distracting gooseflesh wasn't at all what he wanted for the night.

Grasping, sweaty passion would be preferred.

When the fire had flared to greater heat, he dusted off his hands and faced Calista. Her name meant most beautiful. In his opinion the name didn't suit her because there was so much more to her appeal than her appearance. The mischief leaping from her eyes had blinded him to all others.

She drew closer, a teasing smile on her lips. "Thank you."

Constantine placed her before the fire. "For what?"

"For sparing me from embarrassment in front of Linnie earlier." She rubbed her hands together and held them out to the flames. "You were my hero not to refuse my challenge."

A smile tugged at his lips. He was the sorriest of heroes, but if she wanted to view him that way for one night, who was he to stop her? When her hands shifted to caress him instead of the fire's heat, he motioned to a small settee. "Will you sit and continue our conversation?"

For a moment he thought she might object and encourage him toward the large bed standing behind her, but she eventually inclined her head. "Hmm. A gentleman through and through."

He bowed to her, a laugh bubbling up inside him. His thoughts were far from genteel. She made him want to be very, very wild. "I try to be."

Acting rather more reserved than her earlier behavior indicated she might once they were alone near a bed meant to be rumpled, Calista perched on the edge of the seat as daintily as any well-mannered lady of society. The prim posture was so utterly perfect for her that he was not surprised to be spellbound again. He'd always enjoyed the company of elegant ladies and Calista was a study of contradictions. Lusty and prim, haughty and laughing. It was almost as if she were many women rolled into one.

He sat at her side. "Have you been here long?"

"Almost a year now." She shrugged. "I never stay long in any one place. You?"

He couldn't help but smile. Her pretense that she didn't know anything about him was unnecessary, but endearing. "This is my first visit, but I have lived in Wiltshire my whole life. Where are you from?"

She glanced away. "Many places. The details are unimportant."

His wife had once complained that he stuck his nose into other people's private affairs far too often. Like many in society, he enjoyed a good story. It wasn't his place to ask, but he couldn't help but be intrigued by the woman he wanted to bed. He offered a wry smile to his companion. "So, you are Calista?"

"I am this year." She laughed at the confusion that must have shown on his face. "Do names matter to you?"

He frowned at the odd answer. The idea that she was someone else completely didn't sit easily on his conscience. "Yes, names are important."

"Then if you don't care for Calista you should pick another." She lifted her hand and twisted it in the air. "Names are like hats. They must suit the situation or be exchanged with no regrets or excessive sentimentality. A much-loved, jaunty riding hat has no place in a ballroom, for instance. I'll answer to any name you care to call me."

Constantine sat back in shock. He didn't believe he could do that easily. "Have you no name at all?"

She smoothed her gown with dainty fingers. "I've had many. None that I'd care to claim."

"That's absurd."

Her eyes grew shuttered. "The world is absurd. I didn't make it that way. I just try to live in it peacefully."

How could she be so jaded, so dismissive of sentiment? She hadn't the experience for such ennui. Or had she? On an impulse that defied good manners, he captured her face in one hand and studied it. Smooth, flawless skin, delicately arched, dark brows, but the brown eyes beneath held a world of weariness no fledgling woman should ever know. She was quite a bit older than he'd first imagined. "You've a face that confounds the passage of time. I took you for a young girl, not a mature woman, when I first saw you."

Her brow rose, her lips twisted into a smile of amusement. "If you prefer very young girls I am sure Linnie will only be too happy to acquire one for you and provide me with another challenge."

He turned her face this way and that. "That is not what I meant and you know it. When I look at your face, I see innocence, but your eyes say otherwise. How old are you?"

Her smile dropped away in an instant. "Old enough to wish men would not ask for the recounting of my years."

A reluctant smile tugged at the corners of his mouth at her answer and he let go her face. Women were often considered on the shelf at nineteen. He judged the days of her being a blushing debutante were long gone. "Old enough, then. I shall ask no more about your age."

He sat back, seeing her with new eyes. A fine, compact body, firm and supple. A sweet handful of pleasure to be had for one night. However, she was honestly dishonest about the things that mattered most in his society. And still, the idea of bedding her only increased in appeal. She was nothing at all like his wife. He would certainly be exploring new territory.

The woman leaned back in the settee, a smile playing on her lips. "From what I've gleaned of you this evening, I expect you to be very demanding in bed."

Constantine started, rather shocked to have a woman come straight out and say she saw through his attempts at moderation and control. But then he deduced Calista meant to keep him on edge, prevent him from settling into any sort of easy comfort with her. What a devilishly crafty bit o'muslin she'd turned out to be. "Does that bother you?"

The woman rose, lifted her skirts to kick off her shoes, and then straddled his thighs. The warmth of her limbs penetrated his and he set his hands to her hips to hold her steady. Her fingers toyed with his hair and she pushed it this way and that with a critical eye. "That you are hard to please is a challenge to make our association more pleasant. I do not expect you to be gentle with me if you do not wish to be. I'm not fragile. You cannot hurt me."

Guilt returned to sink its claws into Constantine's soul. A man could easily hurt a woman in ways he never imagined in the beginning. He shifted beneath Calista, doubts crowding his mind. For a small woman she was remarkably hard to ignore. Would he be able to control himself when he had her completely at his mercy? Surely he would not become so addled with lust that he'd neglect to withdraw when he should. He brushed a few strands of hair back from her eyes. "I would not mean to hurt you, but it is possible. You should hold me accountable for my actions if I cause you lasting harm." He swallowed past the lump in his throat. "If I should get a babe on you, please send word to me. That's why I want your name."

She shrugged and then fiddled with his cravat pin. "As I said, names are unimportant. It is unlikely I will conceive when I never have before." The matter-of-fact pronouncement of her barren state eased his mind somewhat. If she never conceived his child, then he would be free from further guilt and worry.

He lifted his chin as Calista removed his cravat. When she leaned forward, brushing her breasts with seeming innocence across his cheek as she stretched to lay the white fabric over the back of the couch, he held back a groan. The woman was an unbelievable tease. When she resettled, she was much closer.

Constantine slid his hands around her back, holding one exactly on the bumps of her lower spine. He massaged a small circle. "Were you ever married?"

"Good Lord, no. Why on earth would I want a husband?" Her brow rose and she wagged a finger in his direction. "Oh, you're still fishing for a last name with which to categorize me. Names are restrictions meant to confine us to one situation. It's not the same for men. They may behave however they want. A man may have a reputation as a seducer without censure. Far different if you're a woman and lacking the burden of a husband or even a prior one to add the slimmest veneer of respectability."

No name and no prior husbands. Intrigued even further, Constantine slid his fingers lower, taking his time, determined to seduce Calista into revealing more of her inner thoughts without her realizing it. He grasped her bottom firmly. "So you have never been tempted by a man before?"

Her nails scraped over his skull, causing gooseflesh to cover him again. "Tempted, yes. Many times. But not foolish enough to want to keep one around for long."

He moved to stroke her covered thigh, then teased his way beneath her gown, eager for the night to culminate and for Calista to want him as he wanted her. "So who are you? Really?"

"A woman in need of a handsome man to please her." She laid her fingers across his lips to silence his next question and then brushed them across the surface until his skin tingled. "Close your eyes, my lord. You've all night to prove you're the one."

He obeyed her as a thrill of excitement filled him. Finally, a woman who could challenge his senses and one who might leave him panting for more. They hadn't even kissed and he was burning. He drew her tightly against him, more aroused than he'd been in all the years since his wife's death. He pressed his lips to hers, pleased when she responded with a soft moan. Her tongue tangled with his in a slow, seductive dance and when he drew back, he half believed her insinuation that he might not be fully prepared for her. Yet his erection pressed against his trousers, proving at least one part of him was up to her challenge.

Chapter Four

---◆---

Meredith rubbed herself against Grayling's warmth, eager for his touch. His lips skimmed hers softly until she couldn't bear the slow pace he'd set. She cupped his head and devoured his mouth recklessly. She couldn't remember the last time she'd been this eager for a lover.

The rip of fabric brought a chill to the skin of her upper back and she smiled against his deliciously sinful mouth. Unfettered passion was more to her taste. She rather enjoyed an impassioned man who took what he wanted, rather than someone who waited for permission.

Grayling's hand skimmed the newly exposed flesh and made her shudder. To be wanted so well, to have the exact same desire created in herself was not in the realm of her experience. Her lovers paid to be desired. Meredith wouldn't have to fake any part of her response tonight.

She teased Grayling's shirt collar from his neck and kissed the corded flesh, surprised to find his skin tanned rather than pale as many Englishmen were beneath their fine clothes. She licked the flesh she'd uncovered and nibbled gently beneath his ear with her teeth. An image of him shirtless, striding in the summer sun toward where she lay beside a brook, filled her with yearning. To make love by day, outside in clean air, with no one grunting nearby as often happened here, had been a fantasy of hers for the longest time. But at her age, she had to admit that candlelight was kinder to the complexion than the brighter light of day.

One day she would do everything she'd denied herself.

One day she would just be.

Grayling caught her hair in his large hand and turned her face back to his. He kissed her—long, searing kisses that tempted her to forget the role she must play. His tongue plundered and took, giving Meredith chills everywhere. There was a rightness to being in his arms that she'd longed for without even knowing what she'd missed. She was safe and warm and tempted beyond reason. Returning to the world she lived would be hard to do on the morrow.

Another tug and her sheer gown split in two. Poor Linnie would be cross about the repair necessary, but Meredith was not unduly alarmed. She'd taken Grayling's measure the moment she'd laid eyes on him.

The bodice gaped, revealing the fine silk chemise and corset binding her. Grayling caught her hands from about his neck and drew them before his chest. He tugged until her sleeves pooled at her wrists and urged them free of the confining material. His grin as he flung her destroyed garment away was wide.

"Pleased with yourself, my lord?"

He pressed his head to hers, grin growing wider if that were possible. "It was in the way."

As she stared into his eyes, the urge to laugh and wrap herself tightly about him and never let go grew stronger. Meredith didn't cling. Not even during intimate relations. It was easier to give her body to her clients if she kept part of herself at a distance. The lovers she met with would leave and some never returned to see her again. It was better to accept that from the beginning. However, with Grayling, she was in danger of forgetting her own rules. She would set herself up for disappointment if she expected more than a quick fling with him.

Chagrinned by her dissatisfaction with that, she lowered her eyes to his wide chest. Grayling chased her gaze, cupping her face and lifting it until she had no choice but to meet his bright green eyes. What she saw stirred her fears. Grayling might want more than she was prepared to give—her complete surrender to his lovemaking. Meredith couldn't give herself over so thoroughly into his hands without losing what was left of herself. She had to keep the upper hand no matter what happened between them.

———◆———

The moment when desire between them had been completely honest faded. Constantine cursed under his breath at the shuttered, caution-filled eyes staring at him. He wanted her. She wanted him. Everything had been going well between until he'd pushed, until he'd looked deeply into her eyes, searching for the real woman behind the disguise and detecting the doubts and evasions filling them.

He kissed the woman in his arms, aware that Calista's responses were measured to please him rather than herself. The woman who had flirted with him shamelessly, the one he'd begun kissing with unrestrained passion, had flickered to life briefly and then hidden herself away. He didn't understand why she would hold back when he only wished their pleasure to be mutual. Even if he paid for her time, he would not leave her used and discarded. It wasn't in him to be so selfish.

He pulled Calista closer against him and struggled to his feet. Her legs, bare of all but her fine silk stockings, wrapped tightly around his waist as she held on to him so she wouldn't fall. When he secured his grip on her, he smiled. Her compact form made such maneuvers very easy. He kissed her quickly, afraid she'd beg to be set on her own two feet, and began to twirl slowly about the room as if they were dancing in a crowded ballroom. The room didn't allow too much spinning, but when he hummed, she joined in too.

He passed the mirror, catching their reflection. Except for his missing cravat, he was still completely dressed. Only the woman in his arms was delectably indecent. The slim legs tightened about his waist; her hands twined in his hair and tugged. He closed his eyes and forgot about everything but the feel of her slim warmth against him.

As the spinning began to unbalance his mind, he backed her into a bedpost and when he was sure she wouldn't fall, he struggled to free himself from his coat. The broadcloth slipped from his shoulders with Calista's help; his waistcoat sailed across the room. Calista herself tugged his shirt free of his breeches and pulled it over his head.

He captured her again and eased her back into his arms, but her hands were everywhere, sliding over his chest and shoulders, driving him mad. The cool touch did nothing to dim his ardor. He wasn't sure what would. He spun slowly around the bed and gently laid her down. Dark eyes brightened to brilliant watchfulness, lips red and full from his kisses parted. Her tongue darted out, coating her lower lip with moisture.

His cock ached, his balls drew up tight.

Constantine deliberately turned his back on the provocative sight to regain some semblance of control as he removed his boots. When he turned back, Calista had drawn her feet up onto the bed, knees bent, chemise teasing her upper thigh. As he stared, she caught the edge of the garment and slowly worked the fabric higher, tempting him with what lay beneath.

Constantine jerked her legs straight, straddled her tempting thighs, and went to work on the front-laced corset. The quicker he had her free and unclothed, the better. Temptation needed to be equal in this bed. The cords proved a little difficult, but he considered that his hands would have performed better were he not so bloody aroused.

When the laces came loose enough, he barked, "Get undressed."

Constantine rolled off her and stripped himself of his clothes. He had one last rational thought before he climbed back onto the bed. He dug into his inner coat pocket and removed the velvet pouch containing a condom and tossed it beside her head.

In the interim, Calista had done as he'd requested. Her bare skin glowed with health, pert, small breasts jutting up proudly, nipples erect, either from desire or from a chill. He reached out a shaking hand and covered one, pleased at the hiss of pleasure that escaped her lips. Just enough to fill his hand.

She tugged him closer and he happily complied, covering her small body and settling his hips between her spread thighs. The temptation to plunder, to take what he needed, was there in the back of his mind, but when he met Calista's gaze, he knew there were no shortcuts to take. Not with her. He needed her to want him without reservation again.

At her urging, a firm grip pressing his head down, he peppered light kisses around her uncovered breast. He brushed the distended nipple lightly at first before drawing the peak into his mouth. A soft moan filled the room. A sound he didn't believe was contrived. Although Calista held his head in place at her breast and the increasing pressure was a certain sign he wasn't to stop anytime soon, he escaped her clutching limbs and rolled the bulk of his weight onto the counterpane. He didn't want to crush such a delectably tiny woman. And he certainly didn't want to rush to join with her. For now he was content to arouse her.

Calista arched her back, pushing her breast harder against his mouth. He eagerly teased and tugged on her firm flesh, enjoying her moans of abandonment as his due. Making love was something he took pride in. Making a woman beg for her release, his ultimate goal.

When he drew back to caution her to patience, she flung him onto his back and straddled his body. Taking control of him and his desire again was clearly her plan. Her hands, fingers spread, swept over his chest possessively. He loved the way she touched him as if storing up the memories for another time.

"Cheeky wench," he murmured, rather pleased that she would not let him have his own way all the time. Later, he would use his greater strength to keep her where he wanted her.

She grinned at him. "Would you rather I lay still on the bed?"

When she bit her lip and leaned close as if to kiss him, he bucked his hips beneath her, settling her sex over the softness of his belly. "Hell, no."

Already he could feel her moisture coating his skin. Was she always this aroused by her clients or was he the lucky recipient of her exceptional passion?

"What we have is perfect," he told her honestly. "Stay right where you are, my lovely."

Yet Calista could not be still no matter how tightly he gripped her hips or breast. She rubbed against him like a cat against the object of her affection, butting the head of his cock with her pert bottom and rubbing her breasts against the hair on his chest. The sensations were both amusing and arousing and he couldn't imagine the night progressing in any other manner. Calista would fight his plans for slow pleasure with every hot pant of breath. Did he really want to wrestle to keep her off his cock if she wanted it so badly?

There *were* more hours in the night to make love to her again, and again. There was no chance he wouldn't want her more than once tonight.

He squeezed one full orb tightly in his hand and searched for the velvet pouch he'd tossed onto the bed. Calista's smile dimmed and then vanished as he fished out the length of gut that most men claimed prevented the spread of disease. That wasn't the reason he'd brought one, but he didn't want to spend the time explaining his beliefs of why such a measure was necessary.

The first time he'd fitted the condom had been rather awkward. He'd tested the purchase at home to be sure he applied it correctly without fumbling. He had no qualms over wearing one tonight. It was in Calista's best interests and would ease his mind. Without this, he would worry. He might fail to find release.

Calista dismounted his body, coming to sit at his side on her hands and knees to watch. She said nothing as he lowered his hands to fit the thing to himself. The pliant tube wasn't particularly attractive, and the pale pink ribbon required to tie it firmly in place seemed absurd. But the shopkeeper in London had suggested they were essential for a sensible widowed gentleman in search of fleeting pleasure. He didn't want to take any chances.

Under her scrutiny, he fumbled with the job of tying the ribbon. Her hand touched his thigh and then she took the ribbons from his hands, tying it securely. When her gaze rose to his, the expression in her eyes caught him off guard. Laughter or any form of passion had left her eyes. The flat expression staring at him made him feel like an utter bastard. "It's a sensible precaution," he told her.

There wasn't anything she could say to change his mind. He'd chosen this brothel and planned for every eventuality. He caught her face in his hand and brought her against him to kiss, determined to bring her back into the safe haven of mutual desire.

She stretched out over him, rubbing her body seductively against his skin. Unhappy that her touches had lost their strength, he rolled them so he lay above her and started to woo his lover all over again. It was then he noticed the condom was loose. His cock has grown limp within the ribbon-tied protection and it was in danger of falling off.

Constantine buried his face in the crook of her neck. Damn

universe was conspiring against him, keeping him from getting what he wanted. Frustrated, he reached down to remove it, tucking it beneath a pillow on the bed for later use. Perhaps his first plan had been the better one. He would come only once and wait as long as he possibly could. He didn't even need to be inside Calista's body to do that.

He eased down her body, pressing kisses over her soft belly and into the dark curls nestled below. He inhaled, loving the scent of her arousal. Eager, he forced her legs apart and held their sleek strength in his hands. He touched her sex gently with his fingertips, parted her folds and admired the effect he'd had on her body. She was so wet and ready. If not for his traitorous libido, he'd already be plowing her body thoroughly by now.

Calista moaned, a sound he did not believe manufactured for his benefit. He slid a hand from her thigh and caught one lower lip in his fingers and pinched. He parted her slowly, noticing the thigh he still held firmly trembled. He blew a soft breath over her sex and she gasped.

Pleased to have her with him once more, he teased her nubbin with firm stokes, making sure to spread her moisture as he worked. She shook when he eased a single finger inside her body and slowly withdrew it again.

"Is that the best you can do?"

He glanced up her beautiful body and set his chin on her curls. "Is that not enough?"

She raised her head, one perfectly curved eyebrow raised. "If that is the sum of your prowess, I should have let Solange keep you."

Constantine pressed his closed mouth to her curls and hummed, knowing the sound would vibrate through her skin and bring her pleasure. Her hips lifted toward his mouth and he shifted, flicked out his tongue, and brushed over her nubbin. "More of that but harder," she begged.

Since her desires matched his, he settled more comfortably and learned all the ways to make Calista moan. She had quite a range of sounds but the one he found the most arousing was when she scolded him by name for failing to do exactly what she wanted. He focused all his intent on her pleasure, reveling in the mewling cries that filled the room. To add to her desire, he carefully added another finger to her drenched pussy.

"Gray, don't."

He did the opposite. He eased his fingers deep and then withdrew, massaging her as he wished to do with his bare cock but couldn't. It didn't take long before Calista clenched tight around his fingers, arched her back up from the bed, and screamed incoherently.

When her thighs released him, he slipped from the bed, washed, then returned and climbed onto the bed again. Sated, sleepy eyes blinked up at him. He tweaked her nose and drew the bedding between them down as far as he could. "Are you cold yet?"

She nodded and he eased her boneless limbs under the covers. Calista hesitantly cuddled against him and Constantine nestled her closer, guessing she became chilled quickly. His cock remained at the ready, but his urgency to fuck Calista had ebbed. Touching her, bringing her pleasure, had been enough for now.

The silence soothed but after a while it wasn't enough. He caught a strand of her dark hair and twined it around his finger. "Have you been to London?"

Calista's cheek shifted onto his chest, her leg draped across his. "No. I've never been to the capital."

"I should think you'd enjoy it immensely. There is always something to see and plenty of pretty baubles to be bought."

A chuckle left her. "If one has the time and money to afford them, perhaps. But I'm much too busy entertaining wicked lords in my bed right now."

Constantine cursed under his breath. For a moment he'd forgotten the exact nature of his lover. She couldn't just decide to go to London for the pleasure of it. But he could imagine her there, eyes sparkling as brightly as any bauble worn round her throat. She would undoubtedly enjoy the pretense of the opera and Theatre Royal. A shame she could not go unless…

His thoughts fled when her hand drifted lower and curled around his length. The tight, possessive grip took his breath away. When her head disappeared beneath the sheets, he struggled to escape. No woman had done this in a very long time. His wife had not particularly liked to pleasure him in this manner.

Calista's throaty laugh filled his panicked ears. Her tongue licked the head. His pulse exploded as she kissed him, caressed him and took him into her mouth. Constantine flung the covers back to expose her. She knelt at his side, long hair fallen haphazardly to caress his belly and thigh. But her mouth, that gloriously mesmerizing mouth, had him firmly under its spell.

Her cheeks hollowed as she sucked and his world narrowed to that one spot. Calista pumped her hand slowly, licked and kissed and sucked until he couldn't hold back. He swept her hair over her shoulder so he could see every move she made. She lifted her head. "I take it this pleases you, my lord."

For an answer, he pushed her head back down. "You damn well know it does so don't stop." When she took him back inside her mouth and tongued the sensitive head, he near exploded. What had he done to be so damn fortunate?

The speed of her hand increased, the suction of her mouth grew stronger. Constantine levered up to touch her cheek, prepared to lift her from him at the moment of release. She twisted her head slightly, away from his touch. He frowned. She couldn't mean to… No woman did.

When she shifted between his legs, pushing his limbs wider to cup his balls, he groaned. Calista was too damn dangerous for her own good. His balls tightened, drawing up tight. His cock ached and when he exploded he didn't call his wife's name. He said Calista instead, because he couldn't think of anything beyond the woman in his bed.

Chapter Five

---◆---

Meredith studied the young woman opposite her. "Now curtsy, glance at me shyly from beneath your lashes, and rise. There. Captivating. The gentlemen you meet will not take their eyes from you."

The young woman she was tutoring in the intimate arts had come a long way from her rather shy beginnings and should, if she was diligent, exceed her teachers in every way.

"Are you sure I'm doing it correctly?" Oralia, the name the girl had assumed from the day of her arrival, worried at her lower lip, giving it a pretty pink glow. "Solange says…"

"Solange has all the subtlety of bull in a china shop. Men do, in fact, know when a woman is being insincere. What you just did so innocently with your lip will enthrall the gentlemen you meet." Meredith patted the cushion beside her and the coltish young girl forgot her training and practically leapt across the room to sit at her side.

Oralia fussed with her gown. "That was pretty?"

"Very appealing." Meredith smiled at the girl's uncertainty. It had taken Meredith far longer to learn how to make the most of the cards that had been dealt to her. She intended to make sure Oralia would not make the same mistakes. She could rise as far as she dreamed if she went about the matter sensibly. "The gentlemen who come to us may believe they come for one reason alone. Sex. But they don't always want it immediately when they arrive. Sometimes gentlemen like to talk, to be teased, and to be tempted before the inevitable happens. Improving your skills in conversation is vital to doing well and being sought after. Men are *very* fragile creatures. They want to be thought of as desirable and intelligent. They want to believe the fantasy that you only have eyes for them."

"Of course we do," Grayling said from the doorway. "No man wants to be chosen solely for his pocketbook."

Meredith glanced up in surprise and quickly stood. She dropped into a curtsy, rather alarmed that Grayling had overheard her assessment of men. "My lord, I wasn't informed of your arrival."

When she rose, his smile was smug. "I asked to surprise you and I'm glad that I managed it. What a fascinating conversation to stumble upon."

He strolled into the room and lifted the hand she held out to his lips. The kiss he pressed to the back was so warm she caught herself swaying toward him.

"You were successful. I am very surprised."

Grayling glanced at the young woman she had taken under her wing. "Would you care to introduce me?"

Meredith quickly gathered her scattered wits. Where was her mind? This was the perfect opportunity for Oralia to interact with a superior gentleman. If something came of it, a spark of desire, then Oralia could begin work at the House.

Meredith pushed aside the sudden pang of resentment while she performed the introductions. Oralia performed an adequate curtsy, glanced up at Grayling from beneath her lashes, and did everything perfectly. Meredith eased back from the pair to give them privacy to speak, trying not to listen too closely for any hint of teasing in the conversation which might signal Grayling's interest in the young woman. Oralia was very pretty. And young.

Grayling leaned in her direction, caught her arm, and dragged her back against his side. "Not done with you yet."

Despite her surprise, she could feel her face warming. "Oh?"

His eyes lit up with mirth. "Your protégé has asked a question I cannot answer."

She frowned at Oralia, noticing the girl's awestruck expression as she stared at Grayling. Such puppyish devotion had no business for a woman in this trade. "Well?"

The hard edge to her question brought Oralia's mind back to the room. "I asked His Lordship if he had a mistress. He said you would know."

"I…" Meredith faced Grayling. He appeared decidedly pleased by her speechlessness. She shrugged haughtily. "Not that I've heard. But then my acquaintance with Lord Grayling has been brief. He could have a harem and I'd have no idea."

"A harem?" He shook his head and clucked his tongue in disapproval. "No, no. I should only need one woman."

Meredith tensed at the delicate subject they were discussing. After only one night in Gray's arms, he should not be considering that he needed a mistress. He couldn't possibly be dissatisfied with their arrangement or he would not have come back. She met Millicent's gaze. "Perhaps you would like to see to His Lordship's comfort."

At the reminder of the first rule of the house—satisfy a guest's every need—Oralia's training came to the fore. She encouraged Grayling to sit, brought him brandy, and generally hung on his every word. When her hand landed on his leg with seeming innocence, Grayling sighed heavily and removed it. He shifted his gaze to Meredith. "I'm not here as part of her training."

"Of course not." Meredith pressed her lips together over a laugh. "But Oralia needs the practice. No harm."

"Only to my good mood." He faced Oralia and pushed away the hand that had crept back onto his thigh. "A pleasure to meet you. I can see you've lapped up Calista's training very thoroughly, but remember to be yourself. There is only one Calista, and I should like to be alone with her now if you don't mind."

Oralia's grin grew sly as she glanced between them. "Very well, my lord. Perhaps I shall see you on another visit."

"I doubt that," Gray muttered softly.

But Meredith heard and found his assertion rather pleasing. "Let Linnie know I said you are ready to have your gowns chosen, my dear."

"Oralia," Grayling said, "do make Mrs. Cohen aware that Calista has earned the rest of her wager from last night."

With the promise of pretty things in her future and a message from a patron to deliver, Oralia bounced out of the room with a decided spring in her step.

Grayling scowled. "She should be at home under the watchful eyes of her parents."

Meredith heaved a heavy sigh as she listened to Oralia's running steps. "That would prove difficult as they were the ones who tossed her out like kitchen scraps."

Grayling patted the cushion beside him. "She was seduced, I take it."

Meredith shook her head and remained where she was, remembering the terrible state in which the young girl had arrived. Every door had been slammed in her face. "Raped, by several village boys. Her parents couldn't get rid of her fast enough."

Grayling shifted uncomfortably in his chair. "Is that what happened to you?"

"No," she said flatly and moved to refill his glass. She struggled to keep her voice level and devoid of resentment. "But situations like Oralia found herself in happen all the time. Luckily, Linnie came across her soon after the incident and brought her here. I'm proud of her progress. At first, she wouldn't even glance at the footmen without shaking."

"No tremble in her hands when she touched me," he told her.

Meredith raised a brow. "I noticed that."

"And I noticed you watching and pretending not to." He placed his glass on a nearby table. "What game are you playing now? Are you bored with me already?"

"No," she answered truthfully. But his question made her uncomfortable. In fact, she feared herself in danger of making a superior fool of herself. She shrugged, hoping the gesture conveyed a practical response rather than an emotional one. "But if you'd have shown the least bit of interest in Oralia, I would have left the room."

He pressed his lips together firmly, sucked in a breath, and when he let it go he held out his hand. "Come here," he said softly, a hint of steel in his voice. The same tone he'd used last night in bed. She trembled because that voice had the power to make her forget everything but pleasing him.

Meredith slowly moved closer and then let out a small shriek as Grayling tugged her onto his lap. His hand covered her breast.

"Not one bit of interest. The only woman I want today is in my arms right now."

He kissed her lips, sucking gently on the lower one before a growl left his chest. "Don't ever do that again. I'm not a plaything for your associates."

Despite the warnings in her head, Meredith threaded her arms around his neck and clung to the dangerously tempting lord. "No?"

"No."

Before she realized what had happened, she was flat on her back beneath him. She blinked up into his frowning face.

He brushed his warm fingers over her cold cheeks. "Do you never stay warm?"

It was impossible to shrug in this position, so she settled for wrapping her arms around his waist, beneath his coat, soaking in his remarkable body heat. "I've always been susceptible to chill."

He fingered her thin gown. "This isn't sufficient. Come, I have gifts for you."

"Where?"

"Wherever the footman took the parcels. I imagine a single question will be sufficient to locate them." He stood. "Although, seeing you like this has given me other ideas for the afternoon."

With a decidedly wicked grin, Meredith smoothed the wrinkles from her gown. "I hadn't expected you so early."

He shrugged. "My daughters have gone to stay with the friend I mentioned for a few days and I had nothing else pressing to do for the estate. I thought to spend the night with you again, if you are agreeable."

A small bubble of happiness crowded her lungs, making speech impossible for a time. Eventually she convinced herself she was overreacting to the news and hurried into the hall. A footman loitered nearby. "William?"

"His Lordship's gifts were taken upstairs. Mrs. Cohen felt the room you used last night would suit today as well."

A deep, rumbling laugh echoed behind her as she made her way upstairs. Each step toward that large bed brought fresh doubts about further association with Grayling. She might just be in danger of truly liking him.

At the door, she glanced over her shoulder. Gray's attention was fixed on her rear. As she crossed the threshold, she made sure to sway her hips in an exaggerated fashion. He laughed again and slammed the door shut behind them before hurrying to toss more fuel on the fire to drive the chill from room.

The bed was covered in brown-wrapped parcels. One even had a pretty pink bow. Puzzled, she pulled on the ribbon to open it. A white fur wrap spilled out and she gasped at the extravagant gift. She'd expected another sheer dress to replace the one he'd destroyed, not a garment suitable for the outdoors. She peeked at him as he settled on the far side of the bed. His gifts were rather lavish given they'd only met twenty hours ago. Unable to resist, she pulled the fur against her cheek, feeling the rich warmth drive the chill from her skin. "However did you manage this?"

"I had a word to the abbess before I left this morning. She was kind enough to give me directions to your modiste. I confess, I may have gotten carried away, but at least I will have the satisfaction of knowing you should be warm in my absence."

"Are you going somewhere?"

"Not yet."

Meredith glanced at the other parcels and, feeling as if the best Christmas ever had come early, quickly unwrapped them all. Grayling had replaced her torn gown with a blue velvet carriage dress complete with stiff, high ruff, provided a matching deep muff to the wrap, and a completely practical pair of half boots. "I appreciate the gifts, but why should you do such a thing?"

He glanced away to the fire. "Do you not like them?"

"I love them, but it's not fair to accept so much on such short acquaintance."

He rose and moved to stand behind her. "Yes, you can, because I intend to get to know you very well indeed."

He undid the first button on her day gown and continued until she was standing in only a shift and corset, shivering. Yet instead of the ravishment she expected, he dropped the new gown over her head. The heavy velvet warmed her instantly. The higher neckline caressed her upper back and drove away her chills. The gown wouldn't be suitable to greet visitors to the House, but it was such a lovely shade of blue that she wanted to wear it every day.

She spun in a slow circle to show him how she looked.

"Thank you."

"Thank your modiste. Woman was only too pleased to help. She said you were her favorite."

Meredith smiled, but wariness filled her. She hoped the woman had not mentioned that when they'd first met, Meredith had gone by another name. Grayling didn't need to know more than one. Better to turn the subject from herself and back to him. "You mentioned you have children."

"Yes, three daughters."

She glanced at him, curious about their ages. They must be very young, or Grayling held his age extremely well. Did she need to know of his life away from the House? Uncertainty filled her. If he had children, then he had a wife somewhere. Meredith didn't need to know more than that.

His brow rose. "You have questions?"

"No. I just wanted to thank you again for the gifts. You are a very generous man."

He seemed about to say something but then shrugged his broad shoulders before stretching out on the bare portion of the bed. Meredith quickly moved her new possessions to a chair, shook out her old gown, and laid it on top. When everything was tidy again, she came to stand beside the bed.

Grayling had closed his eyes, feigning sleep. He looked sweet, not like the devil lover of last night. Meredith carefully climbed onto the bed and straddled his thighs. He cracked open an eye. The green sparkled with mirth. "Do you know one of the things that impresses me most about you? Your ability to read my mind. I was just thinking it would be nice to have your tidy little body draped across mine, and here you are. Tempting me to ruin another gown."

Meredith pressed her hand over the bodice. "Please don't."

He sat up, curling his arms possessively around her back. "Well, since you said please, I'll have to be content to burrow beneath it." His fingers skimmed up her leg. "Hmm, definitely warmer now." He leaned close to her ear. "I do enjoy making you hot for me."

He caught her gaze in his and she saw humor in his eyes. After a moment, she dug into his coat pocket to retrieve his condom. He sucked in a breath as she eased back from his lap.

The large bulge beneath his trousers awaited her touch. Meredith slowly unbuttoned his trousers, peeking at him several times from beneath her lashes. He caught his lower lip between his teeth as she took him in hand, and when she had affixed the condom to his length, he groaned loudly.

Meredith shifted position and, without preamble, slowly lowered herself onto his length. The sensations were not as pleasant as a bare man, but if he still brought the condom when he came to her, he must be serious about its use. When he was fully seated, he slipped his hand beneath her gown. She lifted slightly and his hand worked between them, clamped on his length, and kept the condom in place.

In most circumstances, the things were next to useless, often slipping free and becoming lodged inside the woman. With Grayling holding the base, however, slippage shouldn't be a problem. Meredith rode him carefully, rising and falling to build his enjoyment. He bit his lip again and she hoped he would not take long. Meredith found little pleasure with the condom between them.

"Devil take it, woman! Exactly what I need."

He clutched her to him with one hand and groaned against the skin of her neck. He shook in her arms and she cuddled him close, loving the control she had over him and planning his next surrender. She did love a man who didn't mind expressing his desires out loud. That made her job as simple and as good as it could be.

Chapter Six

—◆—

The patter of small scurrying slippers on tile greeted Constantine as he stepped into the conservatory at Stanton Harold Hall, chasing the location of his family. The indulgent soaking bath and a change of clothes had made him more presentable, but he was well aware he'd lost many valuable working hours today because he'd tarried overlong elsewhere.

He glanced about for his daughters among the shrubbery and his breath caught in his throat. Augusta? His wife stood bathed in bright sunlight in the conservatory she loved so much, hand raised to cup a flower close to her face as she inhaled. Her pale hair was twined about her head in elegant curls as if she was on her way to a party or fete and waiting for him to join her. A fierce pain pierced his chest and he swayed toward her, wishing to touch her.

Her head turned and instead of the fine patrician nose he remembered and loved, he glimpsed a Roman one that belonged on another woman's face. He shook his head to clear the vision and return to his reality. His wife was dead. He'd killed Augusta.

When he looked again, he saw it was Arabella, Lady Farnsworth, come to call.

She turned a puzzled gaze in his direction. "I was just beginning to doubt you'd return, Grayling," she murmured quietly.

He hurried down the shallow steps to greet her properly, glancing about for his children. When he couldn't see them immediately, he gave her his full attention. "A delay. Forgive me.

I'd have hurried if I'd known you were here and waiting."

She dipped an elegant curtsy to his bow and the longing for his wife faded to one of regret. Lady Farnsworth wasn't much like his wife save for the color of her hair and her slender height.

"I forgive you, especially when you appear in such good health," Arabella whispered as she glanced about the room. "Twenty. Here I come."

She held her finger to her lips and began to creep about the conservatory. "Found you," she cried as she pounced behind a potted palm.

His middle daughter, Maisy, giggled and glanced at him shyly before ducking down again. Arabella continued to creep about, and Constantine grinned. He'd stumbled into a game of hide-and-seek and had now to wait for its completion.

He eased closer to Maisy. "Good morning, Mischief."

At four, Maisy didn't understand what he meant, but that didn't mean she didn't cause him considerable worry for the future. Maisy was always up to something she shouldn't be, hence the nickname his wife had bestowed on her when she'd first started to move about, most often disappearing beneath the furniture. As usual, his daughter remained apart, hidden from view behind the potted plant.

He sighed and took a seat rather than press the issue of the lack of greeting. He just couldn't seem to gain her affection. Perhaps they blamed him for taking their mother away. His wife had been their whole world and he an interloper who stole her from them. His children showed their sadness in different ways.

When Arabella found his eldest daughter, she dragged Willow across the room by the hand and pressed her into the spot beside him. Not a giggle, greeting, or protest passed her lips. His eldest daughter had gradually fallen silent since her mother's passing. Constantine was well beyond worried about that. Arabella could only suggest patience.

She smiled across at him. "There now. That's a pretty picture."

"It is," he agreed, his gaze straying toward the potted plant Maisy still hid behind. She wasn't a silent creature. She just tended to disappear when he wasn't looking. "What other fun have you been having today, ladies?"

Arabella gestured to Willow. "Oh, lots of things. Willow can tell you all about it, I'm sure."

Willow remained silent, however, unwilling or unable to fill the gap with chatter. The girl's silence wasn't unusual. He just hoped she grew out of it soon.

Arabella glanced at where Maisy hid, a deep sigh passing her lips at his children's difficult natures. "Willow, darling, would you be a treasure and collect your sister so you can return to the nursery for tea with little Poppy? I'll come and see you all again before I go home. I promise."

Released from the necessity of sitting beside him, Willow obediently crossed to Maisy, grabbed her by the hand, and hauled her from the room without a backward glance. Their lack of ease around him wasn't something he could change. "Were they good for you?"

"They are always good for me because I do not demand they behave like perfect ladies. You know my opinions on that. Little girls need some freedom." Despite her words, Arabella pressed her hand to her brow and rubbed her temple.

"But they have worn you out?" Gray sat forward, hands on his knees. "Then you should be unhappy to know their last governess up and quit on me yesterday."

"I heard and am glad to see her gone. She never played with them at all." Arabella kicked off her slippers and tucked her feet beneath her as she had done countless times since he'd known her. Arabella wasn't one to adhere to the rules of proper conduct when she didn't believe it necessary or when no one was looking. Her lack of decorum made her a comfortable companion for a heartbroken man. "Have you placed an advertisement for her replacement?"

"That is my intention for this morning."

Her brow rose and a mocking smile twisted her lips. "Grayling, it's three in the afternoon. Where exactly have you been? When I arrived, Old Cunningham wouldn't even look at me to say he couldn't tell me of your expected return."

An uncomfortable flush swept over his skin. His nights of pleasure had extended far into the mornings after. To his considerable surprise, he had not been able to stop touching the fetching Calista as the sun rose. He had enjoyed another morning romp, feeding Calista breakfast from his own fingers before making love one more time. The fact that he'd lost his inhibitions so easily was a relief. Making love to Calista up to five times a night and snatching sleep between had been quite the surprise. As a consequence, his poor overused prick was rather uncomfortable now, nestled as it was in his snug, fitted trousers. The condom wasn't the best idea he'd ever had, yet he'd never experienced more enjoyable nights. He planned for them to continue and had paid plenty to ensure Calista was his alone.

Arabella swung her feet to the tile floor and peered at him. "You've met someone?"

He braved the likely rebuke and nodded. Constantine didn't want to keep secrets from his friend. She'd done so much to help him over the preceding two years that he didn't believe he'd like her to hear about his visit to a bawdy house from spiteful gossips.

Instead of a shocked, disapproving silence, Arabella clapped her hands together and grinned wickedly. "Do tell, who is she and when can I meet her?"

Constantine gaped. He'd expected outrage. Given he'd caught Arabella discouraging other unattached and available female guests at the last hunt from pursuing him, he was rather baffled. Had she simply meant to keep him from choosing from one of their number? He'd thought her interference was because she was against the idea of him finding Augusta's replacement. "You're not angry with me?"

She laughed heartily, a throaty sound that made him at once at ease and on edge. "Why should I be? You're a handsome man. Any woman would be proud to be yours."

He frowned. "Any woman?"

"Well, any woman besides myself and the ladies of your prior acquaintance." She shrugged. "We'd never make you happy."

"Ah," he said. But in all honesty he didn't understand why she thought as she did. Arabella was born the daughter of an earl, young and widowed, with startling good looks and abundant exuberance for life and society. He simply couldn't fathom why she hadn't looked for another husband. She'd had ample opportunities and interest.

Even he'd considered Arabella as a candidate for a lover briefly or even a second wife. She was fond of his children, and he found her intelligence attractive. However, after the first night with Calista, he wasn't finding the idea of pursuing Arabella or anyone else in the least interesting or pressing anymore. One day he'd consider the matter again. But not yet.

"So, the details if you please. I'm not leaving till I have her name."

"That could pose a difficulty." He laughed. "I don't believe a meeting would be very wise."

Arabella's eyes narrowed. "Is she one of my enemies?"

"Since when do you have enemies?"

Arabella shrugged and peered at him. "Don't be so easily distracted."

"I doubt she has even heard your name before." When Arabella appeared crushed, he rushed on. "She's not a lady, Bella. The furthest thing from one, in fact."

Instead of looking scandalized, Arabella appeared intrigued. "If she can turn your head around in such a short space of time, then I absolutely must meet her. I'm certain we'll become the best of friends. I can pass along all your secrets to give her the upper hand in your relationship."

Constantine rubbed a hand through his hair, wondering what Arabella could possibly know about him that could be considered a secret. Likely she was just teasing. "As enticing as that might seem to you, I don't believe you'd care for the connection."

"Very well," Arabella said, but her eyes hinted at mischief. "If you believe that to be the case, then I shall bow to your opinion for now. However, I should like to ask how it is if she is so beneath me that she caught the Earl of Grayling's eye?"

Constantine pursed his lips. "She's rather dishonest."

"And yet you smile so broadly this afternoon when you speak of her."

Constantine did his best to appear stern, but then he didn't think he pulled it off very successfully. There was certainly something about Calista that appealed to him. However, it was not her false name. When he went back to the House he would get the truth from her lips. He settled for a half-truth in answer to sum up his evening. "It's been a rather unusual week."

Arabella grinned widely and then looked around. "A sherry, Grayling. I need a drink to ward off my approaching disappointment that you will not share the particulars of your scandalous affair with your closest friend."

An affair? Was a tryst at a bawdy house labeled an affair if it took place only over several glorious hours a few nights in one week? As he led Arabella to his study to fetch the requested drink, he realized he intended to go back to the bawdy house on the hill many times. He intended to see Calista again and acquire her real name and connections. That certainly qualified as more than a passing interest.

Arabella touched his arm lightly. "You know, if Augusta could see that smile on your face, she would wholeheartedly approve of your choice."

Constantine almost lost the glass he held. He renewed his grip before passing it over. "I doubt that very much."

He quickly swallowed his sherry and refilled the glass.

Arabella glanced toward the door to check that no one lingered and then clutched his arm. "She would never want your misery to last forever. You have mourned her deeply, everyone knows how much, but it is time to look ahead to the future. Taking a mistress is an excellent first step. It's just a shame you didn't meet her sooner. Now you will have to go to Romsey for the wedding alone and hope she is not offended that you cannot take her with you for your sisters to meet."

Constantine winced. The timing for taking a lover was the absolute worst and Calista did not fit with his sisters' set. Given that, he wasn't keen to depart Wiltshire for Romsey. Surely there was plenty of time to meet the men his sisters intended to marry. The wedding wasn't for another week or so. He took a long sip of his brandy. He would stay and see where this affair headed. If an affair it was, then he'd need to set Calista up in a residence far away from the bawdy house. "Are you headed to Romsey soon?"

"I could not possibly miss this. London will be abuzz when the season starts and likely is already. I want all the details so I can be Her Grace's staunchest supporter when the knives come out. I'll be yours, too, when the time comes and you take another bride to give you the son you need."

Guilt tore into Constantine's gut and twisted the knife already lodged there. He never wanted to risk getting a woman pregnant again. It was selfish, but he might have no choice because he would need an heir someday.

Arabella patted his arm. "I see that look and I've told you time and again Augusta's death wasn't your fault. Stop blaming yourself."

"It's hard not to." He pressed the heel of his hand to his temple. "I pushed the issue."

"Nonsense. Augusta was determined to give you a son despite the risks." Arabella released him. "Please—she knew the odds were against her from the beginning. Now think of that remarkable new friend of yours and find a reason to smile again. Make her your mistress as quick as you can, spend enough time in her arms to lay your ghosts to rest, and begin again. I'm certain you could convince this woman to love you if you set your mind to it. If you love her, too, you'll have my complete support."

Constantine didn't know if that was wise. Calista lived behind a thick wall of secrets and lies. The lack of her real name really wasn't acceptable. Before any permanent arrangement could be considered, he'd have to have her name so he could be sure who her connections might be and if there was likely to be trouble from a long-term association.

Arabella excused herself to say a brief goodbye to his daughters while Constantine mulled over his reactions to Calista and whether it was wise to become more involved with such an honest liar. His lover, and he couldn't think of Calista in any other way, wasn't his alone. The bawd had hinted Calista was very important to the House when he'd paid for a week of her time in advance.

If he wanted Calista to be his beyond that, he would have to meet with the bawd and Calista again to negotiate terms. He'd do more talking than kissing this time and offer an enticing arrangement that would remove her from the brothel immediately. He almost laughed. There would have to be jewels involved in the negotiations. A house somewhat closer to Stanton Harold Hall to ensure he wasn't far from his daughters at night. He wasn't fool enough to believe that if Calista became his mistress he wouldn't wish to be in her bed every night.

Arabella's sultry laugh jerked his thoughts back to the present.

Shamefaced, he apologized for not noticing her return. "Forgive me."

"Oh, no. This is completely diverting. I've been gone half an hour and you're still standing in the same spot." Arabella wagged her finger at him. "Now I simply must meet her."

Chapter Seven

Meredith perched on a chair before the desk in Linnie's sitting room, curious about her curt summons and cool greeting. Usually they got along well. Meredith accommodated the clients' needs with little fuss and a welcoming smile. She couldn't fathom what was so urgent as to drag her away from her last-minute tutelage of the newest initiate of the House. Tonight was Oralia's debut. The girl was remarkably nervous.

Linnie focused on Meredith, and her steely-gray eyes, set in a face many a young girl would kill for at that age, bored through Meredith's head. "Are you sure Oralia is ready?"

Meredith nodded. "I've done all I can with her. Her behavior is still atrocious when she's weary, but her gait is smooth and her attention to her appearance improving. She should attract the gentlemen easily enough. She'll be an asset to the House, I assure you."

"She needs to be." The madam picked up a letter and tapped it on the desk. "This business thrives on being agreeable and available to any who come." Her lips pursed. "When I have one girl unavailable for a long period of time, it is bad for business. Very bad."

Unease straightened her spine. "It is my understanding that Grayling has paid handsomely for my time this past week?"

Linnie dropped the note and picked up another. She tapped it on the desk, too. "You, my dear, are as close to an exclusive arrangement as you have ever come with any gentleman caller in the past year. I have a note here from Lord Grayling. He's requesting your company for the next week exclusively. I also have one from Squires. It's time to make some difficult decisions."

Meredith frowned at the news that she had two gentlemen competing for her time. Grayling might be a fine lover, his appetite for touch as voracious as it was for conversation, but she had done little to encourage him toward a permanent arrangement. As for Squires, she was honestly not too concerned that she hadn't needed to entertain him.

She didn't want to belong to a man as if she were a horse to ride when he could spare a moment. As a mistress, she would be expected to entertain only one man. Meredith would rather it be Grayling in her bed, but she was aware that during the height of the season she could go months without seeing him. Meredith enjoyed intimacies far too much to remain faithful should a protector become distracted and not call.

She met Linnie's gaze. "I had suspected Grayling was starting to tire of visiting."

Linnie picked up the first note. "He's not."

A foolish burst of happiness filled Meredith. They'd made love only once last night and although he'd left her very late, he'd done so without waking her to say goodbye. They had talked for most of the evening. "If he's requested my company, then you know I will do everything I can to make him happy."

"T'is not just him that has to be made happy." Linnie's lips curved in distaste. "Someone must make Lord Squires happy, as well. Besides this letter, he's asked for you every night this week and was far from happy to be told you were claimed again."

Meredith looked at the madam squarely. "What would you have me do? Break with Grayling?"

The idea didn't appeal, but perhaps it would be best to avoid forming an unwise attachment to the man. She'd caught herself thinking of him far too often and planning for their next encounter. He seemed to know just what she needed to be happy in his bed. Out of it, he'd become a dab-hand at fueling the fires just to keep her fingers and toes toasty warm.

The madam's face grew pinched. "Grayling cannot be

dismissed. He has paid a pretty penny to keep you solely for his pleasure, but Lord Squires is in danger of taking his patronage elsewhere. I cannot stand to have him tup a streetwalker when he should have the best the House has to offer."

Meredith sighed. Deep down, she knew what the madam hoped she'd do: either speak to Grayling about a permanent arrangement, one that would see a handsome fee fill the House's coffers, or service them both, either honestly or dishonestly, if necessary. Either way, Meredith didn't enjoy the situation. She had grown comfortable meeting the demands of one man over several. But that was not the normal life under the bawd's rule.

She met Linnie's intent gaze. "I'll speak with Grayling tonight and do my best to convince him that he should share."

"Good."

The notes on Linnie's desk disappeared into the top drawer and she tipped her head toward the door, signaling that their conversation was over. Meredith left the room quickly, but anxiety filled her. She didn't anticipate her conversation with Grayling would go well. She needed to be ready with her arguments. She stepped into the room she'd been assigned, the red velvet bedchamber with the southern view overlooking the gardens, and surveyed the space. It might be the best that the house had to offer, but it lacked the little touches that made seductions all the more pleasurable.

She dug into the drawers and cupboards and extracted sweet-smelling herbs, perfumed oil to rub into her skin, and oddments to make the room look as if she really did sleep here at night. By day, Meredith shared a cramped room in the attic with another girl, the windows of which never ceased letting in blasts of cold air. Sleeping beside Grayling night after night was a little-known luxury in her existence. Very much like sleeping beside an agile furnace, too. She was always surprised to wake with his body wrapped around hers.

Meredith arranged a thick quilt over a chair by the fire, then made sure the brandy decanter was filled and the glasses were free of imperfections. Grayling was fond of touching the items she's strewn about the room; she guessed he assumed they belonged to her. He'd even combed her hair once, which she'd possibly enjoyed more than he had. The moment had been a soothing lull after sharing his bed. He'd even kissed her cheek as he'd left that morning.

With everything rendered rather homey, Meredith slipped out of her serviceable day gown, corset, chemise and stockings, and reached for the bottle of oil. She wasn't needed in the drawing room when Grayling came to call. She could greet him stark-naked and be perfectly sure he'd be happy about it.

She poured a generous portion of oil into the palm of her hand and applied it liberally to her arms and legs. The earthy scent of herbs filled her nose as she continued to smooth any dryness from her skin. The liquid warmed swiftly and she rubbed her belly and twisted to smooth the oil over her bottom and lower back. She was so wrapped up in imagining Grayling completing the task that she didn't notice the door opening until it was too late.

Squires leered at her nakedness. "Would you care for assistance with the rest, pet?"

Meredith turned slowly and reached for her robe. "Lord Squires. I didn't hear you knock."

"That's because I didn't. If I had, I wouldn't have the pleasure of seeing you so unguarded. I've never seen you so lovely. What were you thinking of to smile like that? Me?"

Grayling. Her every spare moment was filled with thoughts of the wicked earl. "Of course, my lord," Meredith said smoothly as she slipped into the thin garment. She wasn't particularly concerned with nakedness, but she didn't want to encourage Lord Squires when she was promised elsewhere. "It's good to see you again, my lord."

As she finished belting her robe tightly about her waist, Squires came closer and caught her hand. "Is it? I've missed spending time with you."

His grip tightened till it was almost painful. She did her best not to struggle, but it wouldn't take much more for her to do something that would have her expelled from the House. "And I've missed you, too. However, I must speak to Madam quickly. Would you excuse me?"

When she tried to leave, his grip on her hand remained firm. "Not so fast. There is something you need to understand."

Meredith sighed wearily. Where was Linnie or an idle footman when she needed their intervention? "I'm afraid I am otherwise engaged this evening. Surely Linnie informed you I'm promised to Lord Grayling."

His eyes narrowed and his grip tightened painfully until Meredith feared she'd cry out. The last time she'd spoken with Lord Squires, she'd heard the possessive tone in his voice and shrugged it off. Now, however, all those little warning signs were back and insistently telling her that Squires was a jealous man. She counted to ten slowly to keep her temper in check, but the man was in danger of having his hand broken.

"You'll be mine and no one else's. I'll see the bawd and settle terms so we can be on our way."

His arrogance astounded her. She wasn't a pet to buy. She had a say in whom she bedded and it wouldn't be Squires ever again. "On the contrary, my lord. I belong to no man."

She shook off his grip as the door opened. Grayling stepped inside, another parcel clutched in his hand but a furious expression on his face for a change. "I beg to differ. She's mine tonight and every night."

In the face of Grayling's presence, the smaller built Squires didn't appear so threatening. Yet he puffed up his chest importantly and put on a good show. "Miss Bower and I have a long-standing arrangement."

"Miss Bower?" Grayling's brow rose at the fraudulent last name Squires used. Grayling hooked his hand around the man's arm and dragged him to the door. "If she was so important, you should have made her your mistress long before this. As it is, you are too late. Now get out, and don't ever touch her or speak to her again."

Squires's arms and legs flew as he was tossed out on his ear into the hall. The door slammed shut and Grayling locked it for good measure. When he turned, he appeared anything but pleased.

Meredith went to him and stroked his arms. "Thank you, my lord. Your timing is as impeccable as ever. I was attempting to show him out."

Grayling folded his arms over his chest, forcing her to keep a distance. "Not very well."

Meredith snuggled closer, determined to ease him from his bad mood and give him the night he had paid for. "As well as any woman can. We cannot throw grown men out as you would. We must use the means we have available."

His smooth brow creased with deep frown lines. "You mean you've nothing to defend yourself with but the flutter of your lashes?"

Grayling would not be so concerned if he knew just how capable she was. Keeping him in the dark about her other skills was a simple matter. He wouldn't want to know. Just for the effect, Meredith fluttered her lashes, looking up at him with an utterly vacuous expression on her face.

A rueful smile crossed Grayling's lips and he unfolded his arms slowly. "You'll be the ruin of me."

Meredith laughed and slipped her arms about his waist. His warmth and scent filled her. She snuggled closer, pleased to feel a thickening lump pressed against her belly. He was always aroused when he arrived. She hoped he didn't ride his horse in that condition. It could be painful. "Not true."

It took a moment to notice that Constantine had not moved to embrace her. He watched her curiously, his green eyes serious. "So, is your name Miss Bower?"

Meredith released her grip on his waist and stretched to cup his rear. She squeezed and then kneaded the firm flesh. There was nothing quite like bedding a fit and heavenly scented man. Grayling was fast becoming a favorite. "Absolutely not. I cannot imagine where he heard such a falsehood. I merely chose not to correct him."

He caught her hands and lifted them high over her head before spinning her about and backing her against a wall. "Are you ever honest?"

"Frequently, my lord. But my identity is something I will never tell you or anyone that comes after you. That woman is dead."

Meredith saw the flinch of pain in his eyes at the mention of death. She rose up on her toes and kissed his jaw. "Can you not accept me as I am?"

He tightened his grip on her hand and stared down at her, the intensity of his gaze growing until she feared the answer would be no. She lowered her heels to the floor, but her arms remained trapped high above her head. When Grayling did not soften one inch, she dropped her eyes to his cravat. The mathematical knot was perfectly tied. Would she ever gain the satisfaction of untying it again?

Grayling lifted her face so he could look into her eyes. "Are you like this with every man who comes to your bed?"

Meredith rolled her eyes. Must every man demand to know he was the best when it came to pleasure? "No. You seem to bring out the worst in me. But that brings to mind a problem. I need to talk to you. Please, won't you release me so we might talk in a civilized fashion?"

He dropped her hand so abruptly that it wouldn't surprise her to discover he'd forgotten how he'd held her. Meredith rubbed her wrists and directed him to the couch by the window so she could see his expression clearly as they talked. "In my line of work, it is unusual for a woman to be bound to one patron every night for so long a stretch of time. In most cases, she would not spend the entire night with one man alone. She would service several. That is how such establishments—and myself, to a degree—make a living."

His face reddened. "I hadn't realized I'd become an inconvenience to your games."

Meredith pressed her slick palms together. "I didn't say I don't enjoy your company, but my exclusivity has become a sticking point with several patrons. As you just discovered, Lord Squires has an interest in my available time."

"Would you rather they fucked you instead?"

Meredith winced at the harshly worded question but did her best not to show her discomfort. "I never said that. What I'm trying to say, to warn you about, is that Mrs. Cohen may try to increase the fee she charges you and if you don't pay, I'll be forced to leave your bed before you might be ready for me to go. I cannot continue to sleep all night in your arms. It is impractical for a woman in my profession."

"A woman like you," he repeated. He crowded her, forcing her into the corner of the couch until she had nowhere else to go. His green eyes burned hot. "I've not imagined you lust for my touch."

Oh, how she wanted him. When he had her under his control, wringing pleasure from every nerve, she couldn't deny him. Even now, when he was so angry, his eyes had darkened to a shade she'd never seen and she still wanted him. "I've never denied it."

He blinked slowly. "So what do you want me to do? Offer you the position as my mistress? Bring you enough jewels and trinkets to slip on your arms that you could not lift them?"

Meredith grasped his shoulders. "I want nothing from you. Have I ever mentioned a hope of becoming your mistress?" She shook him. "No, I never intended to, but I do have a question to pose to you about your intentions. What on earth are you doing, coming here night after night? If you keep this up, you'll be nothing more than a penniless beggar. You have a wife. Go back to her."

"I can't go back. She left me."

Meredith caught her breath. Her pulse thundered in her ears. "When?"

"Two years ago now."

The woman was a fool to have walked away from such a man. Grayling had never struck her as a hard person to be around. Possessive, determined, and diabolically wicked with his need to have his way in bed, perhaps. She cupped his face with both hands and brushed her lips against his. "You've been lonely?"

"Never when I'm with you."

He stood and crossed the room to squat before the fire. He grabbed a poker and fussed with the embers, added more wood, and then dusted his hands off. When he faced her again, his expression was one of extreme sadness. He must have loved his wife very much. He must have been cruelly disappointed.

Determined to turn his mind from his troubles, Meredith rose and took his hand. She led him to bed, covered his glorious body with hers, and did her utmost to drive his loneliness from his mind. It was only later, when Meredith had exhausted every trick she knew to please him without intercourse and was on the brink of sleep, that she dared to ask why his wife had left him.

Grayling sighed heavily and tucked her against his chest, curling around her body to keep her warm through the night. His lips whispered over her shoulder in a gentle kiss. "You misunderstand. She didn't go voluntarily. I killed my wife."

Meredith held still until his breath evened out into the sleep of an exhausted man and then carefully slipped from his embrace. She huddled on the far side of the bed and tried to make sense of his words. Grayling couldn't possibly be a killer and admit it so freely. She didn't believe he was the least bit dangerous. Tomorrow, she would get the truth of it, but for now, just to be sure, she wouldn't sleep a wink.

Chapter Eight

The heavy weight lying in Constantine's pocket burned a hole through his coat. Calista had not been available when he'd arrived, and he'd been cooling his heels in the red-velvet bedchamber for at least half an hour. He supposed he deserved to wait after skulking like a thief from the bed where Calista slept in careless abandon this morning. He had a lot to make up for.

A woman moaned and he scowled at the wall dividing this room from the next. When the moans turned to full-throated cries of a passably believable orgasm, he shook his head. The question Calista had asked him yesterday came back to haunt him. *What was he doing here again?* The seventh day in a row. He'd spent a fortune to be with Calista. A fortune he'd spend a dozen times over to have more time with her. To have her all to himself.

He glanced at the clock again, wondering if she really was involved in the new prostitute's tutelage or writhing beneath a man like the woman next door. Calista had told him she couldn't be his alone. The madam expected her to service other men. But he didn't like it one bit. Calista was his. He couldn't imagine giving her up.

Jealousy was not a new sensation for him. He had always wanted what was his. The fact that he'd grown possessive over a woman so free with her favors, one he'd known less than a week, spoke volumes for his addled state of mind. He had meant his offer yesterday to make her his mistress. They could be very comfortable lovers.

But Calista didn't want to belong to him or any man.

He paced to the window and peered out at the gardens Calista could never bear to look at. The sun was setting over the distant valley, bathing the clipped rosemary hedges in fading light. A pretty scene. He couldn't understand why Calista disliked the view so much that she refused to look out the window. That same wild, earthy scent clung about her body and skin. A fragrance that drove him wild. Perhaps he'd lost his mind.

He turned as the door opened. Calista stopped in the doorway momentarily and surveyed him. He relaxed at the sight of her. She was wearing the blue velvet carriage dress he'd purchased to keep her warm. For one insane moment, he considered throwing her over his shoulder and stealing her away from this place, but then he noticed a footman lingered in the hallway beyond. He appeared idle, but perhaps he listened in.

From the wall beside them, a male voice shouted out and then the brothel's other occupants grew silent once more.

Calista, and the footman beyond, behaved as if they'd heard none of it. "Forgive me for keeping you waiting."

Wary, shadowed eyes met his. She moved away from the door and into the room but did not close the door behind her. The footman came closer and paused where he could see into the room. Constantine walked toward the footman. "Is there a message for me?"

"No, my lord."

"Good, then go away." He closed the door on the man and spun about. "What was that about?"

Calista clasped her hands before her. "A precaution."

That made no sense. "What for? Has a guest caused a difficulty for you?"

"No, of course not," she murmured softly. "Linnie is just being meddlesome. It doesn't matter."

"I'm glad you're here." He gestured to the couch where they began each day. The routine of simply talking over events in their lives soothed him in ways he hadn't anticipated. "Shall we sit?"

Calista nodded and glided toward him. As she drew level, Constantine reached for her hand, but she kept them before her.

He frowned at the absence of affection. He'd grown accustomed to her frequent caresses, and the lack troubled him. Something had changed.

He smiled to reassure her he would be the least of her problems. "Have you had a troubling day?"

"No, not really. It was an exceptionally pleasant one."

"Did you meet with someone?" The moment the question left his lips he knew he sounded like a jealous lover. He paid for her time, her body to be his alone. He didn't want to share her with other men. "Another man." The harsh edge to his voice made Calista jump where she sat. He swallowed nervously. He'd have to do better at keeping his possessive tendencies under wraps.

Calista shifted slightly, adding another degree of distance between them. "A dear friend returned to visit, Cook's son, and I spent the morning hearing Robbie's news."

White-hot jealousy burned the back of his throat over the question he wanted to demand answers to. He swallowed to avoid asking if she'd fucked him.

"And then we dined formally for luncheon to give Oralia more practice," she added in a clear voice. "I swear that girl's parents taught her nothing of deportment."

"And who taught you to choose the correct fork? Your mother?"

Calista didn't answer his question. She smoothed out imaginary creases in her carriage dress, and a frown appeared between her eyes. "You seem out of sorts today."

"I wonder why?" Constantine raked a hand through his hair and stood. "Yesterday I made you a perfectly respectable offer and you turned me down without apology or hesitation."

"I don't want to be your mistress, Grayling. Not every woman dreams of that life."

He would give his left arm to learn what she did dream of. If he asked, he doubted she'd honor him with a truthful answer. "So you prefer being whore to hundreds, thousands."

"Not quite that many. I made my choices long ago." She smoothed the folds in her dress again. "Regret is for the weak and sentimental. If I had either of those two character traits I would not have survived. T'is the reason I like to reinvent myself. I've had a dozen or more fresh starts."

Constantine considered her admission. A dozen or more names and no one knew her. That meant she'd been running from trouble for a long time. What if she was a wanted woman? She might need a man she could rely on one day. "Then start over again as my mistress."

"No. I couldn't do that to you. You barely wish to enter me as it is." She drew in a deep breath and stood. "Am I in danger with you? You've never struck me as a cruel or violent man, but after yesterday's admission I'm not sure I'm capable of judging your character. Did you kill your wife?"

He nodded slowly, remembering his joy at learning Augusta was with child again and then the crushing agony as he discovered her last breath had left her lips, her body bloody and limp across her bed. He clenched his jaw to hold back the grief that always came when he remembered. He did not want to burden Calista with such a scene. "I am responsible for her death."

She was silent for a long time. When he eventually looked at her, there was sadness in her eyes. "You still mourn her?"

He nodded and her hand rose toward him, then fell without connecting. He frowned at her continued distance.

Her head tipped to the side slightly. "How exactly did your wife die?"

"She died after my daughter was born."

"In childbirth?"

He nodded again, and instead of the sympathy he expected, Calista scowled at him. She strode to the door, spoke a few urgent words to the footman who had remained close to the door, and gestured toward the stairs. Eventually the footman nodded and hurried away.

Calista slammed the door shut. "For heaven's sake, never say you killed your wife again."

"Why not? If not for my need for an heir she would still be alive."

Calista crawled onto his lap. "T'is difficult to forget the ones you've loved and lost. There is no shame in mourning them."

Relieved to have her so close to him again, Constantine wrapped his arms about her waist. "You sound like Lady Farnsworth."

"A woman of sense." Calista pointed to the doorway. "Do you even realize why William was standing guard at the door?"

Constantine frowned at the door and then several things fell into place. Her distance, the wariness he'd sensed from his arrival. "I told you I killed my wife."

"And you made me doubt the wisdom of being alone with you." She shook him. "You wretched man. Don't ever do that to me again."

Calista pulled his head to hers and clung to him. Constantine gathered her into his arms and inhaled the tiny woman's distinctive scent. He'd never harm her. He'd taken every precaution he could to protect Calista from the same fate his wife had suffered. Although it wasn't proven, his good friend Rothwell claimed a condom could prevent the beginning of a new life in a woman's body. Since Rothwell had considerable experience in the area, and no offspring to date, Constantine had taken his advice and purchased one for himself.

"I'm sorry I worried you," he murmured against her ear.

"Fool. Women die in childbirth all the time. Her death can hardly be your fault."

It had been two years and the loss cut as deeply as the first day. "But it is."

Calista drew back and searched his face. "Did you beat her? Refuse her any comfort she needed? Deny her a midwife or physician's care? Let her wonder if you were thinking of her?"

He shook his head. "No. I did everything I could."

"Do you hear yourself, Gray? You did everything you could and it was not your fault."

He struggled with her denial of his guilt. He should have been able to do something to prevent her death. He'd never meant to risk her life. He bowed his head onto Calista's slender shoulder and held her tightly. Was she correct? Had he truly done all that he could?

"Men like to think they have the power to do anything they wish, but fighting against death is beyond even you. You must forgive yourself. Surely your wife wouldn't want you to suffer like this."

Constantine squeezed his eyes closed. Damn it all, he was on the verge of tears. He would not weep before Calista. How did she do this to him? Continue to turn his world upside down and side to side just with a few words from her clever mouth? The woman who had disrupted his life from the moment she'd walked into view. He couldn't give her up so easily. If she wouldn't be his mistress, perhaps there was another position he could offer her, a role that would not require her to be in his bed unless she wished to be there.

He caught her hand in his. "What if I offered you a different sort of employment? Could you be happy without earning your living on your back?"

Calista drew back, confusion filling her eyes "What are you suggesting? There is nothing else appropriate for me, my lord."

"I have three daughters." Constantine drew a deep breath and let it out slowly. "They are in need of a governess." A governess was always held in the highest regard.

Calista turned away, a laugh on her lips. "Of all the absurd things to suggest I might be suited for. I am a whore, my lord. There is no way to smooth away that blemish or make my past disappear. How could you even consider it?"

"From the moment we met, I've had the feeling that each meeting might be our last. I don't want to lose you, Calista. Not yet. Please."

Her mouth opened to protest, but a knock silenced her. She crawled off his lap and took care of setting out food. When she turned, he dug into his pocket and held out the jewelry box. Calista shook her head. "I'm not suited to the position of governess for an earl's daughters. Tutoring a young woman to be a whore is quite different. How old are they?"

"The eldest is not yet five."

"There, you see, what they need is a new mother, not me."

Constantine opened the box so she could see the rose-cut garnet rivière. "But I did not ask you to marry me, you will not be my mistress, so my only other option is to ask you to come and live with me and my daughters. I'd like to know where you are spending your nights."

Calista shifted closer to the necklace and shut the lid. After a moment, she began to laugh. "You, sir, are beyond amusing. You must think of your girls."

"I am." He scrubbed his hand over his jaw and scowled.

"When I am here, I'm thinking of them. And when I am there, I am wondering what mischief you're up to here. I don't like Squires or any other man sniffing round your skirts. But if you won't be mine exclusively, then consider this. My daughters don't need another mother. They need a friend. Someone who can make them laugh as they once did. You have far more intelligence than anyone I've interviewed for the position in the past. I choose you for them."

Constantine sucked in a sharp breath, determined to convince her his offer was worth considering. "If you remain here, I will waste my fortune to keep you to myself. The governess position is yours if you want it with no strings attached."

"Strings?"

"You would not be expected to share my bed."

"You've tired of me?" Her expression lost all animation.

"I never said I've tired of you." He held her hand to his chest. "I doubt I'll ever get enough, but I've come to believe you deserve better surroundings."

Her lips twisted and then she laughed. "How sweet. You mean to be a champion of old, a hero to take me safe into your realm and protect me from the harsh world. I am so very sorry for how your wife died and the suffering you and your daughters have gone through, but I could not inflict myself on them. I'm the least appropriate person to teach three young girls how to be ladies one day."

"You might surprise yourself with the depths of your knowledge, my dear." He shrugged out of his coat and tossed it aside. "You forget that we have spent as much time out of bed as in. You were born for more than this life."

"What I was born for is not relevant."

Constantine continued undressing. "That's what I like about you, Calista or whoever you really are. You never hesitate to challenge me. Another hint about your past left unanswered. Another glimpse of the woman you were supposed to be. You have had my complete attention from the moment our eyes met. Now I intend to convince you to run away with me."

He pulled his shirt over his head and stood naked before her. Her eyes drifted south over his skin, and the dark of her eyes widened. She licked her lips. Every emotion was there for him to see. His suggestion that she deserved more from life had terrified her, but she'd tried to hide it behind her laughter.

He scooped her up in his arms and tossed her on the bed with less care than usual. Her heavy gown had tangled between her legs, and she struggled to orient herself on the bed. Before she was ready, he pounced and caught her wrists. He lifted them over her head gently, and she bucked in mock protest.

"This is hardly fair," she complained.

He pinned her with the weight of his body. "The more you fight me, the more pleasure I'll lavish on you." He pressed his lips to the hint of cleavage the gown revealed. "Lie back and enjoy."

The carriage dress had buttons on the front and he slowly opened each, bestowing a kiss to each piece of new flesh revealed. Calista squirmed and he pressed his growing erection against her sex. Her thick gown created an impenetrable but necessary barrier between them.

Her nails sank into his back to hold him more closely against her. "We'll never see eye to eye except in this," she hissed. "I won't be your mistress and I can't be your governess, so if this is the last time you will visit me then we will do everything at least twice."

Constantine met her gaze. "Do your worst. I'm brave enough to take whatever you dish out."

Chapter Nine

———◆———

There were some advantages to being a dishonest woman in a responsible brothel. When her monthly courses came, Meredith was not wanted in the drawing room, so she'd learned early on to be indisposed for as long as possible. She curled up on her attic bed, huddled under the meager warmth of her blankets, wishing for the pains racking her body to ease and perversely hoping they would continue. The longer she stayed apart from the brothel's clients, the more time she had to think over her future.

Grayling had gone. After one last glorious night beneath his warm hands, he'd returned to his home a sexually satisfied man, and maybe he'd even forgiven himself for his innocent part in his wife's death. Women, no matter their station, risked much in childbirth. As Grayling had left, he'd asked her to reconsider becoming his children's governess and insisted she keep the necklace.

Meredith held the pretty stones up to the light, admiring the elegant design and foolishly wishing she could wear them every day. They looked very fetching beside the ring she'd won from Linnie for seducing Grayling. But only a lady wore such gems by daylight. Grayling's gift would be worn at night but he would not see them.

She'd reconsidered his offer. More than once. But Calista the whore did not belong in a grand house with innocent children. There was no way to move directly from a brothel to an earl's home without being noticed. He had to think of his reputation and that of his daughters. If the truth came out, there could be consequences.

Still, with ample time on her hands, his suggestion bore thinking about. Meredith was considering if she shouldn't change her name again and move on to a new life, a new career, somewhere where no one knew what she'd done. She was tired of smiling at leering men. She wanted no part in Lord Squire's plans to make her his mistress either. It was all Grayling's fault. He'd made her crave intimate relations with only him. Yet if she became his governess, he claimed she'd never need to make love to him again.

Was that a sign of his honor or an insult to her desirability? Meredith dropped the gems back into their box and hid them away.

When Gray had not come to the House again to claim her, she'd consoled herself that his absence was for the best. Yet if not for the convenient payment of her fee and the arrival of her courses, she would likely have returned to work, in bed with another man she didn't care a whit for. She'd heard more than once that Lord Squires was growing rather impatient to see her. She had no problem keeping him waiting. She didn't want his sweaty face looming over her.

Maybe it *was* time to go.

Footsteps thumped up the staircase toward her bedroom. Meredith placed her hands on her belly, fully prepared to convince the interloper that her pains were still as bad as the first day.

But it was only Cook who popped her head though the door. "There you are."

Meredith flailed around in a hopefully convincing display of surprise. "Agnes? I'm so sorry. I still don't feel well enough to come downstairs."

The cook harrumphed as she juggled a tray onto a nearby bed and then dug into her pocket. "You can quit your pretense. You've more than earned a rest of a few extra days. You'll be skin and bones if you're not careful."

Meredith inhaled the delicious scent wafting across the room. "With your superior cooking, I doubt that very much."

Cook shoved a letter across the bed. "Found this today."

Meredith peered at it curiously. Strong, bold penmanship graced the front and her heart leapt. Robbie. But why would he be writing?

Cook's son had been her first friend when she'd come to the area. Against his better judgment, he'd introduced her to his mother and then Cook had introduced her to Mrs. Cohen. She'd joined the brothel that same day with no regrets. It wasn't the first time she'd been the new girl.

Meredith quickly scanned the sheet of paper and by the end she was in shock. He'd left without saying goodbye. She swallowed past the lump in her throat. "He never said he was leaving."

Cook harrumphed again. "Why would he stay? You weren't exactly pining for him."

Meredith shook her head. "Robbie and I could never be. I've told him before he's far too good a man for the likes of me. I wish he could understand."

Cook heaved a weary sigh. "Sometimes there's no getting over your first love."

Guilt ate at her. Robbie was good. He deserved a woman who could love him completely. That wasn't Meredith. Love made one reckless.

Cook shoved the bowl of soup beneath Meredith's nose, driving thoughts of her failures from her mind. "Best eat now before you perish. You've a visitor to see."

Meredith's heart leapt. "Grayling?"

Cook appeared amused. "Only if he's taken to wearing expensive lace and an elegant wig. Your caller is a right proper lady. Her groom claimed she'd wait in her carriage until you deigned to step out. I'll let them know you'll come down soon, so don't make me a liar."

Meredith stretched to look out her small window. Standing some distance away from the house was a closed carriage drawn by two dark horses. Meredith couldn't imagine who the lady could be.

She set the bowl aside, threw her legs out from under the blanket, and smoothed her dark skirts into order. She glanced outside again. Storm clouds loomed on the horizon, making the coach appear menacing. Meredith hoped this visitor wasn't the spouse of one of her callers. She hated being brought to task by a possessive lady with no cause for her misplaced indignation.

She made her way down the servants' stairs, ducked past the dining hall, and before she stepped out into the cold afternoon, she drew her hood over her head. The groom lounging at the carriage snapped to attention when he saw her, whispered to the person inside, and then swung the door open before dropping the stairs into place. All Meredith had to do was step inside the dark interior.

She paused three steps away, keeping her gaze on those around her. "May I help you?"

A gloved hand appeared on the doorframe, the glove made of the palest and finest kid leather. A handsome lady stepped out, pulling her heavy, dark cloak tight around her chest. Tall, slender, and obviously well-to-do. Eyes of the brightest blue.

The lady smiled warmly and gestured they walk away from the carriage and the brothel. A groom trailed not far behind, only stopping when the lady waved him back. "Thank you for coming to meet me," she said after a long interval of silence. "I believe we have a mutual acquaintance."

A wife then. Damnation. She was too weary to explain that she wasn't responsible for a gentleman's amorous pursuits. She'd have to hear her out and then set her straight where they couldn't be overheard. She showed the woman into the private garden and faced her. "I cannot imagine who that might be."

"Can you not? I wonder if Grayling made so little impression on you."

Meredith closed her eyes briefly. Not a wife but a relation, come to straighten out Grayling's wayward life. Friends and family were often worse than a wife. "I suppose you are here to warn me off?"

"Quite the contrary." The lady smiled. "I'm here for the exact opposite reason."

A tight knot of apprehension twisted in her belly. "I don't understand."

"I am Lady Grayling's friend. We grew up together. In truth, we've had the devil of a time finding you."

Oh dear. This call wasn't at all good. Had Gray lied about his wife being dead? She eased back another step. "I was led to believe she passed away."

"Forgive me. That is true. She died two years ago, yet I find it hard to believe she is gone and I misspoke. The late Lady Grayling," she clarified. "It was my servant who acquired your location on my behalf. Quite the chore I must tell you, buried as we are in the country."

Her pulse raced that a lady's groom could find her so easily. She licked her lips and then cursed the obviously nervous gesture. "There is much to recommend in a country setting," she choked out.

"Grayling prefers the country for many reasons." The lady nodded. "He has always blamed himself for Augusta's death. Up until very recently, I despaired of him ever getting over her loss."

"Oh."

The other lady's eyes grew shrewd. "Did he mention how Augusta died? In childbirth. Augusta was determined to give him a son. She had a daughter instead but never recovered after the birth. Her death was a shock to all of us."

Meredith licked her lips. "I'm sorry for your loss, but I don't understand why you came to seek me."

"I came to ensure you continued your association with Gray. Aside from the past few days, he's been rather happy. Augusta would never have wanted him to mope endlessly."

Meredith rubbed her hands together to warm her chilled fingers. "Grayling has wisely, in my opinion, ended our association. He has a difficulty with my profession."

The beauty's eyes sparkled. "Most decent men would. Do you humor him with your passion? Do you lie to him when you are intimate?"

Meredith had lied to Grayling every moment they had been together, but not about the most important things. When they were intimate, he honestly aroused all her senses with his touch. She'd never lied about that. "No. He is a rather exceptional lover."

Color crept into her visitor's face. Cheeks pinked and her eyes grew round. "Then why did you not jump at the chance to become his mistress? He would have done everything in his power to give you a life of comfort."

Meredith gaped. If a proper lady failed to understand her reasons, then perhaps Meredith was more damaged than she'd suspected. There were very good reasons for keeping her independence and avoiding permanent ties. "Because he would have come to believe he owned me. Grayling is a man who believes he can have everything he wants."

"What is the difficulty in that? He wants you."

"Yes."

The lady strolled away a few steps and then turned back. "And no other since he met you, correct? And you've not been with another man, either, or so I'm led to believe."

Meredith nodded, rather puzzled at why such a lady had concerned herself with the intimate details of her exclusive arrangement with Grayling. Surely Grayling wouldn't confide in a woman of his own rank. The situation was hardly any of her business. "Not that I know of. Forgive me for demanding an introduction, but who are you?"

The lady rubbed her brow. "Pardon me for being dense this morning; my decision to come here has given me a sleepless night. My name is Lady Farnsworth, Arabella to my close friends."

"The paragon? Do you have no care for your reputation? Once lost, it is irretrievable, believe me. What on earth possessed you to come here?"

The lady made a face. "Struggling with two stubborn souls. Listen to me. If you are both so smitten with the other, why not indulge your senses in each other's arms? You make him happy. That is not a feat to belittle."

Arguing with Grayling's good friend was not something she'd ever dreamed she'd do. She'd never imagined meeting anyone from his life. "I do not wish to be a kept woman. I've always earned my way in the world."

"You would have that and more."

"But I would not be free. An arrangement such as he wants would have expectations placed upon me. If I wanted to end it quickly, there would be difficulties."

"He would argue."

So the lady did know Grayling. He could be very stubborn. "Undoubtedly."

The lady paced a few moments. "Are you very determined to remain here in this profession?"

Meredith shrugged. "It suits my experience."

"Have you no other skills to call upon? A talent for the pianoforte, a fine singing voice?"

Meredith grudgingly admired the woman's misplaced determination. "I can see why you and Grayling are friends. He, too, hoped to tempt me into another profession. I told him no. I've fallen much too far to be governess to his daughters."

The lady gaped. "He asked you that?"

Meredith nodded. "He seemed rather determined to make me leave with him but I've not seen or heard from him in the days since. I imagine he's come to his senses and regrets the impulsive offers he made. However, given other, completely unrelated circumstances here in the House, I'm considering whether a change of scenery might not be the best for me."

She shivered as she remembered their last night. Gray had done everything he'd wanted with her. At one point she'd even begged him not to stop. Meredith never begged. It was a warning sign of how deeply she'd fallen under the spell of Grayling's power.

"What if you did leave the brothel? What if you came to stay with me while you thought over where you will go? Our properties may share a boundary, but Grayling surely won't call for a few days. When he recovers and learns you've left the profession as he hoped, he would undoubtedly repeat his offers. You could take your pick and add as many conditions to the arrangement as you wanted."

"What do you mean when he recovers?"

"A trifling matter. Nothing to be alarmed over. I'm sure he'll be back to his old self in a day or so." The lady cast a quick glance at the brothel. She tugged her hood a little closer to her face. "If you are determined to turn away Grayling's attentions, I could employ you as a companion until you decide what to do. You could leave without notice if you find you don't like me very much."

Meredith stared at the hooded woman. "Why would you do such a thing for me?"

"Not for you. But for Gray I would do anything. He and the

children deserve to be happy once more. Their contentment means everything to me and I think you are just what they need."

Meredith couldn't help it. She laughed. "Did anyone ever tell you that you are inappropriately optimistic?"

"Yes." A flicker of a smile crossed her lips. "Augusta did once, just before she died. I promised to watch over her family and I meant that vow. Now, how easily can you leave the brothel to come with me? I fear you're in danger of taking a chill if we debate the matter any longer. You're shivering so hard I can see it."

The lady reached out to cover her hands and Meredith allowed it. But she wasn't shivering only from the cold. Hope, an altogether unfamiliar feeling, had crept over her while this stranger had talked. She could go if she wanted to. There was nothing holding her to this place save loyalty to a woman who'd given her a bed to rest her head. Perhaps if she returned the ring she'd won for seducing Grayling, Linnie's pride would be salvaged.

She glanced down at the ring on her finger. The pretty garnet stone shone dully in the sunlight. There could always be others. *Only if you are good, my girl. Only if you calm your temper and are civilized.* The voice in her head echoed down through the years as clear as if her mother was standing beside her.

While she debated her choice, a sleek carriage drew up before the house and deposited an elegant gentleman of imposing stature. A startled gasp left her companion's lips as the man hurried up to the front door and was whisked inside. Meredith swallowed her rising revulsion. If she were not already claimed and indisposed, she'd likely be entertaining that man. "Your timing is impeccable. I can leave today," she whispered.

The lady at her side tugged her cloak tighter about her. "Good. One of my grooms will come with you to collect your things. If you don't mind, I believe I should wait in the carriage."

Then she turned on her heel and practically ran for the safety of the distant carriage. Although puzzled by the speed of Lady Farnsworth's departure, Meredith headed for the brothel, pausing long enough for the groom to reach her side and follow. He appeared rather eager for the task of entering the establishment and craned his neck every which way as they entered the kitchens.

Linnie was waiting in the center of the room with only cook for company. "Leaving, are you?"

Meredith lifted her chin defiantly. "Yes."

"Good. Saves me from suggesting you move on. The gentlemen who come here require younger flesh."

The hurtful words cut Meredith to the core, but she didn't dare show how much. She'd thought Linnie had become a friend. Meredith had learned the hard way never to reveal the depths of her emotions. Instead of arguing, she twirled the ring on her finger, defiantly taunting the abbess—she might not be young but she knew how to win any bet that involved pleasuring a man.

Linnie turned to Cook. "See that she takes all her belongings. She has one quarter of an hour to go."

When Linnie's footsteps were a faraway echo, Cook gestured to the hallway. "Don't mind her. She'll have a drink to soothe her sadness once you've gone on your way. Come along then."

Collecting her things took little time. Stepping from the rear door took all her courage. Cook embraced her quickly. "Now." She sniffed. "I don't want to see your face again and I don't want you to write to say where you've gone. Best not to know."

Cook gave her a little push out the back door and when it closed, Meredith shivered. Alone again. Dependent on no one. Wanted by none. Well, that wasn't exactly true. The woman waiting in the carriage seemed sincere. Meredith strode from the brothel with her head held high and a saucy sway to her stride. A groom helped her step into the dim carriage and the lady held out a blanket for her knees. When the door shut, she glanced up at the house's façade. Linnie stood at the window to her office, one hand raised in silent goodbye, a tumbler in her other hand. Meredith blew a kiss in return and then faced forward for the next chapter in her life.

Chapter Ten

Calista had said no. Constantine cursed his poor judgment of timing, looking out at the bright day without enjoyment, wishing he was riding fast toward his lover.

She'd been adamant. She refused to consider that she might have sufficient skills to be a governess to his children simply because of her background.

She'd been angry. Despite his best efforts to convince her, she'd brushed his suggestions aside. When he'd promised that he would never lay a finger on an employee, she'd lost all interest in the topic and in him.

When he'd left, promising the offer was still open should she change her mind, she wouldn't look at him but reminded him that they'd never see eye to eye. That had been three days ago and he was miserable. Constantly picturing her in the arms of other men was driving him insane.

Constantine paced the room. The emptiness of his life, of Stanton Harold Hall, filled him and left him unable to concentrate. For a time, thanks to the lure of Calista's company, he'd thought he might have found his feet again. But his needs, his insatiable desire to know where the blasted woman was, who she was with, to protect her and keep her for himself, had driven a wedge between them.

It did no good to become attached to a whore, she'd told him. He knew that. Everyone knew that. Unfortunately, he'd been powerless to avoid falling under her spell. He'd never met another woman of her like and never would again. And the worst of it was that he didn't even know her real name.

"I've always preferred a man with a full head of hair. You'll have none left if you keep tugging at it like that."

A distraction, thank God. He turned to face the room again. "Your timing is impeccable, Lady Farnsworth."

"Hmm, I've heard that same expression twice this week. I do love coincidences." Arabella glided forward. "I have news and I need your help."

He stared at her. Given that she wasn't carrying Calista in her pocket, he doubted her news was all that good. However, he'd do her the favor of hearing her out. Maybe her news could provide enough diversion to save his hair. "Anything."

"My dear brother-in-law has ordered me to London to assist with his daughter's coming out months before the season starts." Her nose wrinkled with distaste. "Unfortunately, I am not in a position to take my companion with me. Farnsworth would grumble incessantly about the expense, but I have a feeling the lady might be better suited as a governess if you like her."

"You're not going to Mercy's wedding?"

"No. Farnsworth's note did not allow for any delay. I am disappointed beyond all reason."

Since when had Arabella gained a companion? Had he been so wrapped up in his own concerns that he'd failed to remember her telling him when she'd been here yesterday? He must have been. "Surely Farnsworth would not be so cruel as to deprive you of company."

"As Farnsworth has told me before, he may do as he wishes and I must comply." Her eyes dimmed. "But enough of me. I'm sure you've forgotten the details already, but you might recall I chanced upon a young lady a few days ago in need of honest employment."

Grayling couldn't remember her saying a word about it and he wasn't keen on the idea of letting a stranger near his daughters. To consider it, the woman would have to be extraordinary. "Surely there are other ladies of your acquaintance who might take her in?"

"Not when she was dismissed for failing to perform her

duties."

"That is not altogether comforting." Constantine raised a hand to his head, but at the last second refrained from tugging his hair out. "I need someone who will not run away when the children are difficult and who will obey my instructions. I've the devil's luck at keeping governesses."

"If you allow her some independence then you should have no problem. I interviewed the lady at length these past few days while she stayed with me and I understand the difficulties she had when faced with a task that had grown distasteful. I can tell you anything you need to know without adding to her embarrassment. Nothing you ask would be too much, I'm sure, but a little latitude would be advisable. She dislikes being taken for granted or taken advantage of."

He understood the feeling. No one liked being taken advantage of. Constantine skirted his desk and sat behind it. If Arabella had undertaken the interviewing, then he would trust her knowledge and acquire the information he needed directly from her. When they met, he could decide very quickly if he wanted her or not. He pulled out a notebook and pen, poised to take notes. "Her age?"

He needed someone young enough not to complain about the number of stairs and to play with the children. They were fond of hide-and-seek.

"She didn't say, but what woman likes to admit to that?" Arabella shrugged. "Her age is a little beneath mine, I imagine. She's quite small and that does tend to skew one's estimation of her years."

Calista had not wanted to reveal her age either. Was that common among all women or just the ones he met with? A woman slightly younger than Arabella would be good. His own wife was of a similar age when she'd passed. The children would benefit from someone with more energy than the frail nurse currently supervising their care. "Who has she worked for in the past? Anyone I know?"

Arabella made an odd sound and he looked up. Her face had twisted in distaste. "That question does pose a problem unfortunately. You, see she was dismissed without a reference after a year of exemplary service. She's guided many a young lady to come out, as it were. There is really no one to speak up for her experience, but she has all the poise and grace of a lady. She has impressed me beyond measure these past days. The girls would thrive under her influence."

Constantine carefully placed his pen on the table and then closed the book. "How can you expect me to go along with this? You don't know the first thing about her, do you? She could be anyone, masquerading under a false name, for all you know." Calista had opened his eyes to that. A lesson he'd not soon forget. "You trust far too easily."

Arabella drew in a deep breath. "I am an excellent judge of character. I took one look at her defiant eyes and knew that here was a woman with fortitude. She's more than a match for the rigors of any position in this house."

"I'll be the judge of that."

"Oh, good. That was remarkably easy to convince you to see her. I'll just pop out and fetch her from the carriage. Miss Clark seemed rather reluctant to step inside before I spoke to you first. I find it hard to believe she was shy of meeting you."

Before he could stop her, Arabella swept from the room, only to return a short time later with a darkly clad figure at her back. "Lord Grayling, may I present Miss Meredith Clark."

Gray's eyes narrowed on the tiny woman at Arabella's side and then his pulse leapt. He fell into the familiar world-weary gaze, now hidden behind wire-rimmed spectacles, and he stiffened. Everywhere. Calista. But looking nothing like he'd ever encountered before. Her beautiful hair was cropped short and sleeked against her skull. Her drab clothes covered so much of her that she appeared perfectly spinsterish. She did not look anything like the ravenous creature who had crawled all over his senses for hours on end. But he could not dismiss the resemblance.

She'd come to him.

And yet again, she was pretending to be someone else.

Calista dipped a curtsy, eyes downcast and demure. When she rose, she did not meet his gaze.

Then he remembered what Arabella said about distasteful requests. He met his friend's gaze and saw her happy smile dim and fade away into seriousness. She must know where Calista had been formerly employed. But how could the two of them be together? He thought back over all that Arabella had said. Had Calista been thrown out of the House when he'd not returned, even if he'd paid to keep her nights free? He swallowed past the lump forming in his throat as he imagined the worst. Anything could have happened to Calista. Arabella had rescued his lover from the worst straits a woman could be in.

He rocked on his heels, trying to find the right words to convey his gratitude, his panic, his hope. He'd been worried. He should have gone back of his own accord, if only to ensure her nights were free from others. He should never have let her dismiss him so easily.

Arabella smiled again, nodding as if approving of his line of thought.

He glanced at Calista. He had to talk to her about their last morning together and he would rather do so alone. "Arabella, would you be so kind as to…"

"Fetch the children? Yes, I really do think a meeting today would be a perfectly acceptable beginning. Excuse me."

When Arabella swept out, Constantine surged around the table and caught Calista's hands in his. They were so cold he immediately began to chafe them with his own to warm her up. "I never thought to see you here."

The mask of indifference fell from her eyes, and she wrenched her hands from his and set them on her hips. "You have terrible friends."

"Excuse me?"

Calista waved toward the door. "That woman convinced me that she had a place for me, then today informed me she no longer did, and all the while hinting that you were sickening slowly. Despicable woman. She's a far better liar than I am."

So her spirit had not been crushed by recent events. She was still as feisty as ever. "Do not be angry with Arabella. She has a difficult time of it. Her brother-in-law treats her as a marionette since he gained her late husband's title. She has no love for his brat of a daughter, either. But Arabella is completely dependent on him, so when he says come to London, she must."

An indelicate snort left Calista and the sound made him smile. She was here. He had another chance to keep her safe, comfortable, and warm. He wrapped her small hands in his. "So, tell me truthfully. Is Calista or Meredith Clark your real name? When will you tell me your secrets?"

"It is Meredith Clark for now. Next week, I could change my mind and be someone else entirely." Her brow rose haughtily. "But my secrets are mine to keep. Coming here was a mistake. Goodbye, Grayling."

When she spun on her heel, headed toward the door, Constantine quickly blocked her path. "Wait. Please. I only need to know what you want to tell me. Please don't go yet. I have worried for you."

"There was no cause for alarm. I'm quite capable of taking care of myself." She glanced toward the door. "What on earth possessed you to mention my existence and our association to a countess? Have you lost your mind?"

Bravely, Constantine took her hand in his and kissed it. "I told her nothing, but she doesn't miss a trick. She saw an improvement in my temper and divined the reason for it on her own. It was never my intention for you to meet, but I am not sorry that you have, for you are here now."

He guided Calista, Meredith, away from the door. "How did you come to be acquainted? I cannot imagine she would come to the bawdy house where you lived."

Calista's brow rose. "And that, my lord, is where your reasoning is in error."

Constantine gaped. He dropped into a nearby chair, taking Calista with him so she sat at his side. "She didn't."

"She did. Though I must admit I am grateful. The lady has impeccable timing. I was on the point of resuming my duties."

Constantine brushed his fingers along the length of her sleeve. A question burned his tongue. Had she lain with another? Had she enjoyed another man as much as she appeared to enjoy what they had done together? He wanted to ask, but he didn't know how to phrase the question without sounding as jealous as he was. Calista did not like expectations. She didn't want his affection.

Calista heaved a heavy sigh. "I've slept with none but you. My courses arrived and prevented my return to entertaining any other guests in the interim."

Constantine closed his eyes. That last night together had preyed on his mind. Once he'd almost been too late and had come close to spending inside her. At least now he knew she didn't carry his child.

Calista relaxed eventually while Constantine rubbed his fingers over her palm. "However it came to be, I'm glad you're here."

"I'm not. I swore I would never do this."

"Do what?"

"Depend on a gentleman for my welfare. I've always preferred my independence, but I've nowhere else to go given the speed of Lady Farnsworth's departure."

"Were you not beholden to the bawd for your living?"

"The House was not the first brothel I've lived in, nor should I think it the last."

The idea of her walking from his door and into another similar situation appalled him. "Stay with me instead," he blurted quickly.

She shook her head. "I cannot promise that."

"For as long as you can bear it then. Stay and be governess to my daughters. But if you wanted it, you could have my protection for the rest of your life."

She rubbed her brow. "You're just keen to have your wicked way with me again."

Why deny it? He'd give his fortune to keep the little minx in his bed. But he'd made a promise and, difficult or not, when she entered his service he intended to keep it. "While the idea definitely appeals, I gave you my word. Sharing my bed would never be part of our new arrangement. As much as I would enjoy it, and I hope you would too, I'd much rather keep you safe and warm."

"Such a gentleman."

"I try to be." He kissed her hand again. "I'm not saying it will be easy. I've no doubt it shall be hard to forget sharing your bed. But I'm willing to ignore your allure if you can do the same for mine."

Her hand wrenched free from his as she faced him. "Why do you want me here if not to take me to bed?"

Constantine leaned back against the chair. "I can't be certain but I think I may like your company. You're a bright spark of light I run to catch. Arabella sees the good in you, too. She would never have brought you here to meet my children if she thought you in any way inappropriate. She was my wife's best friend."

"You don't like to speak of her."

He smiled. "It's hard to admit I've not set aside the memory of my first love when I have a woman writhing naked on my lap. When would have been the right time to mention I had trouble sleeping at night for missing her?"

An unladylike grunt left Calista's mouth and then she scowled. "You sleep soundly enough most nights."

He couldn't help but smile. "You may take credit for all of that if it pleases you. If it eases your pride somewhat, my spirits have been quite low since we parted company."

She could take credit for the immediate improvement and a whole lot more but he wouldn't mention the changes she'd brought to his life already. Just seeing her again was enough.

Calista scowled. "You look terribly healthy to me."

He caught her hands again. "I'm not. I truly am miserable. It's just the unexpected surprise of seeing you again and here that has improved my spirits. If it helps, I can pretend to be unwell. Would you be my nursemaid and visit my sickbed?"

"I see that you lie very well, too. You told me you did not opportune the women in your employ. I was wrong about you."

"Ah, but you haven't said yes yet, and I've fallen into our old habit of teasing each other. I've always enjoyed our little battles of words and you are a hard woman to deny. Almost irresistible." He had meant that he would keep her at a distance, but he was simply too overwhelmed with relief at seeing her again to behave appropriately. "I would keep my word if you were to stay. I promise."

Although her gaze was skeptical, the arrival of his children halted their conversation. Arabella carried Poppy toward Calista and stopped before her. "This is Grayling's youngest, Lady Poppy Hunt." She gestured to each of the girls. "Lady Willow and Lady Maisy Hunt. The sweetest girls you could ever hope to meet."

To Constantine's surprise, Poppy leaned toward Calista and attempted to catch her glasses in her chubby little fists. Surprisingly, Calista merely moved her head back, slipped her glasses off and into her reticule, and took the child. She turned Poppy to face the room. An effective way to avoid similar incidents, one that had taken some time for him to discover and implement.

Calista brushed her chin against the baby's hair. "They have such lovely names."

Seeing Calista with his youngest daughter in her arms settled his anxiety. She appeared confident enough to hold a young child. How she would handle the other two remained to be seen. "My wife chose their names. She was very fond of flowers and shrubs."

Calista smiled ruefully, her eyes growing distant. "I know what that can be like. At least she didn't name your girls after vegetables. Wouldn't it be terrible to be named Lady Spinach Hunt?"

An involuntary giggle left Willow's mouth, but before he caught a glimpse of her face, all amusement vanished.

Arabella smiled serenely. "So that settles it then. I must take my leave to pack for my sojourn in London. Miss Clark will return tomorrow to begin her duties?"

Calista quickly handed the baby to him while he gaped. He wasn't ready to let Calista go yet. She'd only just arrived. "She's not staying?"

Arabella's smile grew rather devious. "Oh, no. Miss Clark has promised to dine with me this evening. There is so much information I must share with her about you before we part company. You may expect your new governess at nine o'clock tomorrow."

Chapter Eleven

— ◆ —

"**W**ell, I must say that all went remarkably well," Lady Farnsworth confided as the carriage rattled along the road to her neat little manor house, if a thirty-six room country home could be considered small.

Meredith was not inclined to speak to her just yet. She felt rather foolish for how she had reacted to Grayling and the sparkle lighting up the lady's eyes hinted she was well aware of her lack of indifference to the man. The fact that Meredith had been eager to see Grayling again was not in dispute. What troubled her most was the way she had lapped up his gorgeous warmth like an eager puppy.

If they had been alone much longer she might have climbed onto his lap and curled contentedly into his strong arms. Leaving quickly had been imperative if she wished to avoid appearing foolishly sentimental. Tomorrow she would be the invisible governess and not needed for anything else. Meredith folded her arms over her chest. Grayling would regret that decision.

"There is so much yet to do," Lady Farnsworth said. "I wish Farnsworth hadn't written. I hate London in the winter. Constantine is stubborn. Augusta often complained that he'd cut off his own arm rather than ask for help. He will take time to understand what you want. I expect him to make many mistakes. I'm just sorry I won't be here to smooth things over should you quarrel again."

"We did no such thing." Meredith glanced sideways at Lady

Farnsworth. "But with friends like you to do his bidding, I'm sure he doesn't need to learn the skills necessary for greater understanding."

Instead of taking offense, Lady Farnsworth merely laughed. "Nonsense. All men should learn how to better appease the women in their life. It's their duty, in my humble opinion, to see we are happy. So many gentlemen fail."

At that, Meredith's curiosity was stirred. "Lord Grayling's children are rather quiet."

Their silence had been rather concerning. Children so young had no cause to be so restrained in the presence of a parent.

"They miss their mother terribly." Lady Farnsworth sighed. "She was their whole world. Gray wasn't always so good with them and the eldest remembers. I've done all I can, but a succession of governesses coming and going hasn't helped ease their grief. The girls need stability. So does Gray."

"They have you."

"Not really." Lady Farnsworth frowned and looked out the window. "Everyone expected us to wed when he came out of mourning. I'm sure my brother-in-law did, or hoped to be rid of me. Yet while I'm fond of the children, Gray is more like a brother. I could never marry him."

With her stunning good looks, Lady Farnsworth could marry anyone she chose or none at all. It was a pity she didn't have an easier time of it with her family. But wasn't that the way of the world? Friends were often more reliable. "Grayling explained some of the difficulties you have with Farnsworth. Is there any way to be free? Or is there someone you want to marry so you may escape him?"

A sad smile crossed her face. "No one comes to mind."

They were silent as the carriage drew to a halt before the large manor house. Meredith stepped out onto the front steps and looked around curiously. Lady Farnsworth's estate, or rather her brother-in-law's, was rather too neat for her taste. Not a leaf out of place and no color due to the time of year. Since Meredith had come to stay there had been few visitors for the lady. She must get lonely. "So you live here alone most of the year?"

"At the moment I'm alone. Francesca, a lady whose husband deserved a sound whipping, has recently returned to her family in York. She stayed with me a few months while waiting for word from her brother that he would take her in. Farnsworth doesn't much care for strangers living in his house, but what he doesn't know doesn't hurt him."

The butler, in the act of allowing them to pass inside, grinned widely. "Will you be needing the carriage again today, my lady?"

It was clear the servant approved of their lady's decisions to keep Farnsworth in the dark, too. How interesting.

"Not until tomorrow for the journey to London," she said. "We'll dine informally tonight and then tomorrow you may close the house at your leisure. I won't return for some time."

The butler nodded. "You'll be very much missed, my lady."

Lady Farnsworth glanced left and right into the empty lower rooms, her expression pensive. Meredith never liked to stay in one place for long. She liked to have options. However, even she could imagine being summoned to London must seem like exile to a lady who liked her home.

Meredith caught the lady's eye. "Do you do that often? Take in strays like myself?"

Lady Farnsworth linked arms with her and led her up the stairs, deeper into the house. "I'd hardly call you a stray, Meredith Clark. I was rather impressed with how you conducted yourself when we met. I wish I had your courage."

Meredith followed Lady Farnsworth into her dressing room and assisted in removing her pelisse to begin packing for the trip to London. "I'd say you already had enough courage of your own. Proper ladies do not visit bawdy houses to steal away a woman with my background, Lady Farnsworth."

"Oh please, it's Arabella." She returned her bonnet to a shelf. "And what exactly is your background? Your diction and grace belie the life you were living." She wagged a finger. "There is something about you that tugs at the mind. I feel we have met before, a long time ago, but that cannot be, can it?"

Assured no one would ever make the connection to her past, Meredith shrugged aside the question. She had covered her trail rather well. "You, my lady, have an overactive imagination. Why did you really bring me back here for another night? A servant could have fetched my meager possessions and brought them to Stanton Harold Hall."

"Ah." Arabella sighed as she glanced over her shoulder, checked for servants, and then closed the door. "I'd like to take advantage of your unique expertise."

For a moment, Meredith couldn't imagine what expertise she had of value until she realized that a lady, a widow, might have a keen interest in broadening her knowledge of the intimate arts. "With men?"

Arabella nodded slowly, a flush of color sweeping up her cheeks.

"But you're a widow. Surely..." Meredith left the rest unsaid as she divined the nature of Lady Farnsworth's marriage and her current level of discomfort with the subject. The frequent blushes and oddly stilted phrases about intimate relations had not been what she was used to hearing, but she'd failed to detect the correct level of Arabella's experience. She might not be a bride anymore, but she was no experienced widow either. Meredith would bet her prettiest bauble on it. "You're a virgin."

The lady glanced away, her cheeks turning a fiery red. "My husband already had two healthy sons from his first marriage and lacked only funds to keep him in life's little luxuries. He wanted my dowry but not me. I'm eight and twenty and haven't the faintest idea of what to do to correct the oversight."

To tutor a virgin, a proper lady, in the intimate arts would be the challenge of her life. She would have to only convey the most useful information and give her confidence enough to carry it out later. She had less than a day to do all that, yet there was nothing she liked more than to teach what she knew. Meredith caught Arabella's hand in hers and squeezed. Men would crumble under such a delicate touch. "What is learned, discovered, cannot be unlearned. You may never look at a gentleman the same way again. Are you sure you are prepared for that?"

"No. But I must." Arabella shook her head. "I refuse to die a virgin. I saw how keenly Grayling regarded you. He did not want you to leave his home today. If I had not come back when I did I am sure he would have been rather more flustered. No gentleman has ever looked at me in such a fashion. I should like that at least once before I die. Can you teach me to be more like you, to capture a man's interest?"

Meredith felt the stirrings of sympathy. A life without intimate relations was a barren life. Meredith tried not to remember that she had agreed to such a thing, even for a little while longer in Grayling's company. She paced the room, stopping to occasionally admire the extensive wardrobe of fine dresses around them while she considered the chances of success. Too many of them were too prim for her taste, but the colors were lovely. "Does this fellow have a name? The one you hope to seduce."

"He does, but I cannot speak it. In truth we've never spoken more than a few words, but I fear he will not be interested in a woman like me." She scrunched her nose. "A bookish virgin. Never. He prefers women who frequent establishments such as the type you were living in recently and other women who have few morals."

Meredith turned that over in her mind. "He wouldn't happen to be the gentleman entering the House when you came to visit me a few days ago?"

Arabella nodded shyly.

"Lord Parker." Meredith sighed. There were days when she knew far more than was good for her. Parker disliked inexperienced talkative women, but he *did* like to spank his bed partners until they couldn't sit easily. He would not be the best choice for a virgin.

Meredith turned Arabella toward a mirror and began to unbutton her gown while she wondered how to warn her off that particular man. Given the lady's willingness to court scandal for a friend, Meredith had to protect her from making a grave mistake. "Consider someone else. Please. He's much more dangerous than he appears to be. Choose someone who will talk to you, too, and yet has the experience to make the tryst enjoyable. Surely there is another you know to be in London for the winter, or even the coming season. Even the most scandalous rake should have the skills to hold a conversation first. An unfeeling and selfish scoundrel is not for you. Parker thinks only of himself. You want… a man who can look at you and turn your legs to jelly. Do you know someone who fits that description?"

Arabella nodded so fast her ringlets jiggled. "But he's considered rather a rake."

Meredith laid the prim, expensive gown over a chair and worked on loosening the lady's corset. "Is he intelligent?"

"Yes, he's rather eloquent on the topics discussed in parliament. When he speaks, he draws a crowd and not just ladies come to listen."

Meredith tossed the corset aside to cover her urge to laugh. Arabella sounded as smitten as any debutante. She hoped this fellow was as good as he sounded. "Is he handsome? Clean in his habits?"

"He's rather devastating when he smiles. Many a lady has ruined their reputations to be with him. Sadly, he rarely smiles in my direction."

Arabella could be describing Grayling's unsmiling twin. Meredith shook herself. She'd done enough fantasizing about Grayling's many charms to last a lifetime. "And you'd like this intelligent rake to look again?"

A dreamy smile flittered over Arabella's face, but then she glanced down at her hands. She twisted a ring on her third finger. "I would, but I doubt my chances. Perhaps I should forget about it after all. What would such a man want with me?"

Meredith slipped her finger beneath Arabella's chin and lifted her face to her reflection. "When I'm done, he won't just be looking and smiling. With luck, you'll have him eating from the palm of your hand and whimpering like a puppy for more of your attention."

She caught Meredith's hand and peered at the ring. A wedding ring. That had to go first. "There is nothing more off-putting to a man than a reminder of the one who came before. Trust me on this. Leave the ring behind when you go to London."

"Are you sure?" Arabella worried at her lip as she tugged the simple gold band from her finger. She stared at it for a long time and then met Meredith's gaze in the mirror. "I don't want to give anyone the impression that I'm in search of a husband."

"They say rakes make the best husbands."

"Oh, I don't want to be a wife again." Arabella shook her head violently. "I'd just like to discover what every other bride knows."

The ringlets had to go, too. Too much like a debutante and too difficult for a man to take down in the heat of passion without ripping half her hair from her head. The one thing Meredith had discovered in her line of work was that the faster a woman could be divested of her embellishments, the better.

"And I don't want to be a mistress. What a pair we make." Meredith slid the fine chemise from the countess's body and stood back. Not an ounce of undesirable flesh anywhere. Arabella had a body any woman would covet and any man would crave for his own. Whoever the gentleman was that Arabella had set her sights on would be a lucky man. When the countess moved to cover her breasts, Meredith stopped her. "You must grow accustomed to nudity before others. If you're not, it will give away your inexperience. I assume you don't plan to tell your intelligent rake of your untested state until after the deed is done?"

"I can hardly tell you, let alone consider telling him or any other man."

Meredith nodded and circled the woman. "Probably for the best, but I should warn you that he might have enough experience to guess. Now, I don't mean to embarrass you, but what exactly do you know of a man's intimate proportions?"

A fiery wash of color swept over Arabella's cheeks and Meredith chuckled softly at her obvious distress. "That little?"

"I've never even seen."

Meredith smoothed her hands down Arabella's arms and rubbed away the woman's gooseflesh. "There is no need to be embarrassed. I'm sure I can impart enough information that when the time comes you don't squawk like a scared infant and run away. All right, let's start with the easy part, your wardrobe for the season, and go from there. If you are going to catch a rake's eye, you need to be properly dressed for battle."

Arabella frowned. "I didn't think it would be so complicated."

Meredith rolled her eyes. "Men make everything complicated. Even the simplest seductions can be derailed by a man's sense of honor. Grayling is proof of that."

"Did he seduce you?"

"You know, I'm still not exactly sure which one of us seduced the other." She grinned at Arabella. "It wasn't anything like I planned, but the end result is all that matters."

Arabella glanced at her slyly, amusement hovering behind her green eyes, but wisely kept her mouth shut. It wasn't Meredith's fault she'd fallen victim to a dangerously wicked earl. Arabella would find out just how hard they were to master in due time.

Chapter Twelve

———◆———

The steady knock on Constantine's study door sent his pulse skyrocketing. He glanced toward the trembling wood and swallowed nervously. He couldn't believe the promises he'd made yesterday to Miss Clark and the hours since had made him question his decision. Could he really keep his hands to himself and what the devil could Arabella know that was worth imparting to his new governess?

Constantine stood, tugged his waistcoat down, smoothed his hair, and then cursed himself. What did it matter what he looked like for Miss Clark? She was here for his children not for his pleasure. He sat back down again. "Come," he called.

Cunningham widened the door and a small, dainty body followed, clutching a bag and a lace-trimmed bonnet. Prim, respectable. She was everything a governess should appear to be. Yet Miss Clark, like Calista before her, set fire to a gloomy day. Her gaze flickered to his from behind a pair of ridiculous spectacles—only worn as part of her latest disguise, he suspected—before her lids fell demurely over her expressive eyes. The dull brown dress covered every inch of her delectable skin. Outwardly, she looked nothing like the lover he couldn't get out of his mind. If he didn't know better, he'd think her a virginal spinster. Yet his body's stirrings proved he wanted her no matter how she looked to others.

"Miss Clark, my lord." Cunningham's thoughtful glance in

her direction told him full well that the butler suspected her character to be somewhat in question already. If the stodgy fool scared the woman away in the first week, he'd get his marching orders.

Constantine got to his feet and bowed. "Miss Clark, so good to see you again. I am very grateful you were available for the position on such short notice."

Let the old stick-in-the-mud stew on that. It was about time Stanton Harold Hall employed someone with younger blood and shimmering vitality than the relics Cunningham had thrust before him for the governess position.

Calista, Miss Clark, dipped a graceful curtsy. "Good morning, my lord. It's a pleasure to be here."

He struggled to hide a smile. It was a relief that she'd finally arrived. He'd spent the morning debating what to do if she never appeared. "Did Lady Farnsworth get underway without incident this morning?"

"Yes, her carriage departed at the same time I did. She looked to be in excellent spirits and health for the journey."

Constantine flicked his head, dismissing Cunningham. When the door closed, Constantine gestured to a chair set before his desk. "Won't you sit?"

Her lips quirked up at the corners and he remembered he'd said that very same thing on the last night they were together. However, in this instance he wasn't inviting her to mount him. The condom was returned to a drawer in his bedchamber and there it would remain.

When she passed him to sit where he indicated, Constantine inhaled sharply. Damn, she smelled good. He quickly sat behind his desk before he forgot his own rules. He would treat her as any other servant applying to enter his employ. They would talk, discuss her past and any references, and determine her wage. He would ignore the thickening length in his trousers and hope the desk hid his reaction to her presence. "Was your journey pleasant?"

"Yes, my lord. The light rain last night didn't make the travel so bad as to be impossible." She dug into her bag and thrust a wad of papers at him. "Lady Farnsworth asked me to pass along her best wishes and these letters. She apologizes for not delivering them in person, but she thought you might like to have a letter of reference from her. It's the uppermost one. I'm not sure what the others might be."

In all honesty, Constantine couldn't care less about references, but their existence would lend credence to her claim of experience in educating young girls. He peeled open the missive she mentioned and read the short message it contained.

Don't let her push you away. She needs you as much as you need her. She'd make you an excellent wife.
Bella

Constantine shuffled in his chair. "Did Arabella mention what she relates in this letter?"

"No."

Constantine grunted and folded the letter. So Arabella thought she could manage him from London, did she? Admittedly, she'd done a spectacular job of reuniting him with his lover, albeit in a respectable guise this time. But a marriage between them was hardly likely.

A man with three daughters had to consider their futures and happiness, too. Calista, or Miss Clark, was a liar and the ultimate dissembler. Constantine had no idea who she really was beneath the superficial identity she showed the world, and that changed almost daily. It was true that one day he would have to bury his fear of putting a woman in peril and marry again. He needed a son to carry on after him. Yet he couldn't consider any woman for a wife unless they were completely honest with him. That certainly wasn't part of Miss Clark's nature today.

He pushed the notion aside to contemplate on another day. He wouldn't consider a second marriage for a long time, not until he had his daughter's happiness in hand. Miss Clark had met the girls briefly, but she had a long way to go in gaining their trust. He would wait until he was sure of their contentment and they were showing signs of improvement with their new governess's help before he turned his mind to his own needs. Their happiness was his first consideration.

His gaze fell to where Miss Clark twisted her gloved hands in her lap. Was she cold? He glanced toward the fire and considered adding more fuel to heat the room, but that was what he'd have done with Calista. With Miss Clark he shouldn't be so obviously solicitous of her comfort. He clenched his hands before him on the desk and tried not to think of dragging her into his lap and wrapping her tight in his arms to warm her up personally.

Miss Clark cleared her throat. "Perhaps you might share with me your requirements regarding my duties here."

An image of Miss Clark spread over his desk, legs wide as he tasted her, filled his mind. He shook his head to clear the image away. Miss Clark was only for his daughters now. He shouldn't think of her any other way, but curse it, he was going to struggle not to. "My children require a firm but gentle hand. They are not unruly but are prone to tears. They have a nurse on hand at all times, as well as a maid, but they miss their mother. She had a way of bringing out the best in them and making them laugh. Their best hasn't been seen in a very long time and your predecessors failed to make a lasting impression. You face a difficult challenge."

"They are just children and seemed very shy. May I ask their exact ages?"

"Willow is five, Maisy four, and Poppy is nearing two years of age. Far too young to be motherless."

Miss Clark smiled, a hint of dimple appearing on one cheek. How had he never noticed a dimple before? Yet when Miss Clark pursed her lips tightly, the dimple disappeared as if it had never been. "Well, I'll leave it to you to procure a mother for them in due time, but for the present, can you tell me of any important events that should be celebrated?"

"I hardly think a party should be planned for. The girls need routine and order and stability. Their environment has been a disruptive two years."

"That's to be expected. The loss of a girl's mother is a pain that never goes away." Her eyes grew unfocused. "But a forgotten birthday, an event that should be at least marked by those closest to her, is never truly forgotten, no matter how many years have passed."

Constantine leaned forward eagerly. Was that a chink in her armor, or was he simply hoping to finally see one? "I take it you've missed a few birthdays with your family?"

"Enough to regret each and every one." She shook her head. "Whose birthday is next?"

"Poppy's, but we don't celebrate it." Gray glanced at the tabletop, guilt and grief filling him. Eventually, he glanced up. "It is the day my wife died."

"Of course." Miss Clark glanced over her shoulder toward the door. "Would you excuse me a moment? There is something I must attend to."

She got up quietly, removing her scarf as she walked to the door and then tied it about the handle. Puzzled, he studied her handiwork, not understanding until she stood at his side that she'd blocked the view from the keyhole. "I hope you don't mind, but I've never enjoyed the sensation of grown men spying through keyholes at me," she murmured softly.

"Clever girl," he whispered back. "You might just be a match for Cunningham one day."

"I should think I already am," she whispered back with a cheeky grin. Her smile broadened and then she did the unthinkable. She cupped his face between her hands and stared deeply into his eyes. "You mustn't punish the child. It's not her fault."

Constantine closed his eyes as the touch and scent of Calista filled his senses and ran amok with his resolve. "I know."

When her fingers tangled in his hair, he opened his eyes. The same mesmerizing stare that he'd grown to admire peered from behind the spectacles. A warm, urgent longing to hold her and touch her everywhere surged within him. If she remained close, he would break his word.

He didn't want to behave dishonorably while she was under his roof. He couldn't ask her to on her first day of employment. He'd made a promise not to expect her presence in his bed, or on any other piece of furniture, but he had the feeling he'd be hard pressed to keep his hands from wandering over her delectable body if she touched him like this again.

"I'm not sure how to do this," he whispered.

Her gloved fingers caressed his face and then she drew back. "You're making excellent progress, my lord. But rather than subject you to further temptation, perhaps I should begin my duties with the children. The rest of the details can be discussed later. The children are the reason I'm here, after all."

Her brow rose, challenging him to deny he hadn't brought her here for his pleasure. He'd brought her here to keep her away from Lord Squires and other gentlemen callers visiting the brothel. Purely selfish reasons, of course, yet he harbored no regrets whatsoever.

He did need help with the children, especially as the anniversary of his wife's death drew closer. He hoped Miss Clark might have the power to distract them all from their maudlin thoughts. She backed away slowly with an amused glance for the state of his bulging trousers, then retrieved her scarf from the door handle. While she slipped it around her neck again, he soaked in her every move. She collected hat and bag and offered a sunny smile when she faced him. "Ready."

Constantine willed his desire to ebb quickly. He stood and walked to the door slowly with his hands clenched behind his back. This was it. Time to act like the gentleman he aspired to be. He did not molest the help, no matter the sorry aroused state they left him in. He would do nothing to lure the pretty, wickedly talented, and energetic governess into his bed. He would behave.

He grabbed her hand and dragged her away from the door, hopefully out of sight of the keyhole. "What did Arabella tell you yesterday?"

Miss Clark grinned. "Worried for your reputation?" she whispered.

"Terrified." He released her and folded his arms across his chest. "Now, out with it."

"I have to give the lady credit, she has completely bamboozled you, and it only took a moment of conversation." Her hand rose to squeeze his arm. "I never divulge a secret, but in all honesty, we spoke a great deal but of you only a very little."

Constantine was actually disappointed. Given the contents of the note, he'd assumed Arabella had regaled Miss Clark with a list of his better qualities and faults. "What could Arabella need to talk to you about in private? You barely know each other. I'm her friend. She could have confided in me."

Miss Clark's lips pressed together as if holding back laughter. She took a moment to collect her thoughts. "It wasn't so much confiding as asking a woman's point of view on a delicate subject."

The world wobbled again. Miss Clark's skills in the bedroom were exceptional. If she'd shared even a tenth of her experience in the bedroom, Arabella was bound for trouble. He glanced toward the door nervously. "About what?"

"To tell you would be betraying her trust." She wrinkled her nose. "I cannot do that, even for you."

Constantine rubbed a hand over his face. Hell and damnation. He couldn't write to ask Arabella what the conversation had been about. Farnsworth might open her letter. Constantine would have to go to London before the season started to warn her off acting on Miss Clark's advice.

Miss Clark rubbed his arm again. "You really are the worrying sort, aren't you? Trust me. Lady Farnsworth knows exactly what she's doing. I would never provide answers to questions that were not in her best interests to know."

"What the devil do you mean by that?"

"Gray, there are some matters that only a woman can give an opinion on. If your wife had lived, I'm sure Arabella would have posed her questions to her instead of me."

"Then I would have learned them," he grumbled. "Augusta did not keep secrets from me."

She reached up to brush her gloved fingers over his cheek. "Arabella is counting on my silence, so it is just as well that I'm not bound to you."

He set his hands on his hips rather than crushing the woman in his arms and never letting her go. "You really are the most confounding woman I've ever met."

"And you have a singularly rare gift for compliments," she murmured. "As much as I'm sure you'd like to argue the matter all day, we had better end this discussion before your butler finds a reason to burst through the door."

She walked away quickly and regained her possessions.

After a moment's consideration, Constantine trailed after and when he joined her, he smiled down on her unguardedly one last time. "Cunningham will show you up to the nursery and acquaint you with the house and its schedule. I'd like to see you at the end of each day, after the children are asleep, for a report of your progress with them. We can discuss your wage and employment terms and other matters then."

He would find out what she'd spoken to Arabella about whether she liked it or not. Eventually, he'd have all her secrets.

She dipped a curtsy. "As you wish, my lord."

When she rose, her remarkable whiskey-brown gaze was fixed somewhat lower than his, most likely on the red-stoned pin holding his cravat in place. He grinned. He'd picked ruby especially to mark the beginning of her employment and his sad return to celibacy.

Constantine wrenched the door opened and glanced out. Cunningham, the wily devil, was exactly where Constantine expected him to be—three feet away and wearing an expression of complete innocence. He'd likely heard and seen everything until the keyhole had been covered and they'd begun to whisper.

Grayling struck out his hand to Miss Clark. "Welcome to Stanton Harold Hall. I hope you'll be with us for many years to come."

The hand in his was tiny, but he remembered all too well the strength of her grip about his privates. A flame of heat swept his body, and he retreated to his study quickly before he did something stupid like kiss her. He already missed her taste.

Chapter Thirteen

———◆———

Heavens above, that man could make her head spin. Meredith forced her feet to move her away from the study as she struggled to suppress the confusion she experienced at being so near Grayling but not permitted to touch. Of course, she'd failed to keep her hands to herself for even five minutes.

When they'd first met, Meredith hadn't imagined he was nursing such a wounded heart. Their attraction had been immediate, his interest obvious. But the mere mention of the late Lady Grayling was enough to bring his melancholy to life again. She hadn't been able to maintain a distance.

Behaving properly when alone with him was going to be a struggle. A governess was thought of rather poorly if she flirted with her employer. Grayling had hinted her good standing was important to her position. She would have to find other ways to help him set aside his regrets for his wife.

She glanced around the hallway, wondering at the faces staring from the frames. Was one of them the late Lady Grayling, who had left such loneliness in her wake? Meredith was keen to find her portrait and learn more about her.

"Don't think the children will be as easy to win over as His Lordship," Cunningham grumbled before they had gone many steps away from Grayling's study. "They are not concerned in the least about their governess's pretty looks, unlike their father."

Meredith regarded the butler's frosty visage. She was used to people expecting the worst of her. A whore had no status to speak of. But to act so rudely to a stranger from second meeting without knowing anything of her past showed an overpowering lack of manners. She shrugged away her irritation. She had come for Grayling's daughters and nothing else. What the butler thought of her was inconsequential. "I have no notion of what you refer to, Mr. Cunningham, but rest assured my sole concern is for the young girls I've been asked to care for."

Cunningham stopped in the middle of the hall. "They've done all right without your sort."

"My sort?" Really, this was too rude to ignore. She didn't have a brand burned into her skin to say she'd been a whore. Given the time she'd spent perfecting this prim identity, Cunningham shouldn't see anything untoward. "What exactly is my sort?"

He looked her up and down. "A class above the rest of us. A meddler like Lady Farnsworth. You're only pretending to be a governess until you can snare His Lordship."

Meredith almost choked on her surprise. A woman with her past was far beneath a butler in status. Clearly her disguise and acting talents were even better than she dreamed. She stepped around Cunningham and hitched her skirts to start up the stairs. "I would be careful how you speak of Lady Farnsworth. Your employer might not like his friends slighted in such a manner. She was his late wife's good friend, too, wasn't she? Now, if you're finished gossiping, would you be so kind as to show me the way to the nursery? I would like to begin."

Cunningham scowled but grudgingly hurried to lead the way up the stairs. He directed her all the way to a stout oak door without another word, but as he set his hand to the handle, he looked over his shoulder. "I'll be watching you closely. Any sign of mischief and I'll see you dismissed."

Meredith smiled brightly. "The only mischief I see is a butler standing between me and my charges."

Cunningham tapped on the wood and then opened the door slowly. Meredith peered into the gloom and spotted shapes huddled around the fire on the far side of the room. She took a pace in and then Cunningham slammed the door behind her back. She cursed him, out loud too, as she struggled to acquaint herself with the room. And then cursed herself under her breath for forgetting to behave properly around the children. She was no longer in a bawdy house where such language could be used without raising a fuss.

First impressions were important. That moment could never be recovered.

She waited while her eyes adjusted to the darkness and she could see the occupants of the room better. An old woman sat in a far corner with a young nursery maid, darning by the insufficient candlelight at her elbow. Across the space, three sad little faces watched her. The eldest held the infant close to her chest.

Meredith's temper rose that the children were smothered in darkness. It was little wonder they were not happy. This had to stop. Hoping there was nothing blocking her path in the shadows, Meredith walked across the room. The little girls drew closer to each other, their ease of yesterday long gone.

Meredith paused to look about and give them time to grow used to her presence. "Oh, what I wouldn't give for a firecracker right now so that I might see how pretty you all are. How do you do? My name is Miss Clark. Do you remember me from yesterday? Lady Farnsworth sent me to be your new governess."

The little girls stared and clutched their cloth dolls, saying nothing. Meredith turned to the older woman and held out her hand. "Hello. I'm Meredith Clark, and you are?"

The old woman didn't move a muscle. "Ridgeway," she mumbled slowly in a voice so thick Meredith almost couldn't understand her. "I'm the nurse. Been with our lady since she was small. This is Miss Cunningham, the butler's niece."

"How wonderful." Meredith withheld a groan. A servant with ties to the past lady of the house and a relation of the butler. They'd likely be against her, and the girl was sure to tell the butler everything she did in the day. "A pleasure to meet you both."

She glanced about curiously and noted the table was bare of food and teacups. She'd thought she'd timed her arrival to coincide with breakfast or perhaps even morning tea, but that did not seem to be the case. She set her bag at her feet and worked her gloves from her hands. At least the nursery was warm enough for her taste. She flexed her chilled fingers. "If you could point me in the direction of my room, I should like to lay my things aside and commence my duties."

The old woman's right arm lifted awkwardly to touch Miss Cunningham. "Show her the room and fetch tea," she mumbled again.

The girl stood quickly and rushed for a far door. Meredith followed, casting a discreet glance at Ridgeway's right arm again. Was she injured?

The gloom was as thick inside as the previous room and Meredith stumbled to the window to draw back the drapes so she could see. Bright light flooded a cheerful, papered room, and feeling better, she smiled at the girl. "Thank you."

The girl yanked the drapes closed, hiding the pretty wallpaper in darkness again. "They're to be kept closed out of respect for the mistress."

The mistress had died two years ago. Good heavens. Was the staff expected to mourn her still? The study and the lower rooms hadn't contained the least look of mourning. If Grayling could move on with his life, surely the staff could, too. "But I cannot see anything with them closed."

She shrugged. "Butler's orders."

Ah, perhaps that was the real reason. Was Cunningham a fanatic about the proprieties? Extending full mourning to the whole of the house might not be within his reach, but he could impose it upon the servants under his control and Grayling might never suspect. He did not wear mourning dress and by his own admission had begun to return to society. Did the butler still mourn the lady of the house? Was that the reason for Cunningham's frosty greeting to a newcomer, a potential temptation?

Meredith sighed heavily.

At Ridgeway's call for Miss Cunningham, the girl bustled out quickly, leaving Meredith alone in the dark. Meredith did not like the dark except when it was supposed to be. At night. She yanked open the drapes again, tied them back out of the way. The view from the room was lovely. She could see the gardens, the distant woods, and the spire of a far structure. A folly, perhaps. If she was still here when warm weather came, she might even enjoy exploring the estate in her free time.

She turned about to inspect her bedchamber. A narrow bed was crammed against the far wall, and a chair, a cupboard, a tall mirror, and a washbasin on a stand completed the furnishings. An adequate carpet covered a good portion of the hardwood floor to keep her feet warm when she rose from bed. Perfectly enough for a governess and exactly what she'd expected to find. There would never be indecent objects of pleasure in the drawers of the cupboard; there would never be another body to share the bed. Given the proximity to the nursery, Grayling would never visit her.

Fighting off her disappointment, Meredith hung her bonnet on the point of the mirror and tucked her bag beneath the bed. There. She had moved in. There wasn't much else to do but return to the children and see what she could make of them. Despite the strangeness of the situation, Meredith was looking forward to the challenge. At the House and other places she'd plied her trade, she'd always offered advice to the new girls, molding their habits to be pleasing, teaching them to dress and present themselves as a lady should, even if they were so new from the farm that they still had manure under the soles of their slippers.

More than a few had gone on to permanent situations as mistresses. One had even become a wife. Meredith was rather proud of the fact that every one of them was better off with her help and had made something of themselves. They'd found their place.

What could she do to shape three sad little girls into happy creatures? Only time would tell. When she returned to them, the girls were just as quiet. Their silence bothered Meredith, as most children she'd encountered in her life were chatterers, every last one. She'd spend no time shushing these little mouths. Getting them to talk would be her challenge.

Determined to draw them out, she carefully parted the drapes, aware that if they were always drawn shut then the brighter light might hurt their little eyes. As she'd feared, when she turned, the children and the old woman were blinking their eyes rapidly.

With the new light, she studied the old woman quickly, noting an odd slant to her features. Her arm lay unmoving in her lap, her legs were tightly bound in a woolen rug. She *was* injured.

Did Grayling realize he'd left an old woman, who possibly did not have free movement, in charge of his children?

Fearing it likely, she turned away to hide her rising annoyance. Grayling should have taken better care of such precious treasures. The children needed more than to sit about and do nothing. Resolved to lure the girls away to something pretty, she eyed the rest of the room. Unfortunately, she could see nothing with which to amuse them.

"No use getting your hopes up," Ridgeway warned. "Cunningham packed it all away into those far cupboards after the mistress passed."

"That's terrible," Meredith replied, noticing the little girls had leaned forward at the mention of their mother. She moved back to the warmth of the fire to watch them. When Ridgeway said nothing more of the late Lady Grayling, their little faces dropped back to their dolls.

They were so sweet and so sad. Meredith was determined to see them smile at least once before the day was through, but she didn't expect much assistance from the other servants.

Ridgeway sat stiffly, right arm on her lap, odd smile twisting her lips into a frown. Except she wasn't frowning. Her eyes were sharp dots of blackness as she cleared her throat. Swallowing seemed to be an effort. "They only have those dolls to play with. Can never get them out of their hands unless they're asleep," she offered.

While Meredith would love to get to the bottom of the puzzle of Ridgeway's illness, her priority was getting to know the children. Meredith crossed to them and sank to her knees on the worn rug. They each held those little dolls tight against their chests, as if they expected her to snatch them away. "Do they have names?"

Silence greeted her question.

Meredith swiveled to look at the old woman. "Do they not speak?"

"They only speak when their father comes and then very little. The eldest hasn't said a word to anyone else in close to two years. If not for hearing her with the master, I'd swear she was mute."

Meredith turned back to little Lady Willow Hunt. A pretty face peeked out from beneath poorly arranged dark locks. The child's large eyes were fathomless pools of sadness. Poor angel. "That's all right. You don't have to talk to me if you don't want to, but should you ever, I would love to hear your voice. I'm positive I can talk enough for everybody in the room."

Meredith leaned forward and kissed the top of the child's head. She winked at the middle child and brushed her fingers over the youngest's cheeks. Such pretty children needed to be loved in the light, not neglected. She left them and opened all the drapes in the room and one window. It was time to end the mourning before these children were irreparably damaged. Grayling couldn't possibly want his children to live in the dark.

Dust motes swirled in the air and she regarded the cupboards Ridgeway had spoken of. She tested the door handles, but they merely rattled. Locked. How cruel to store precious things but keep them in plain sight. Meredith raised her hands to her hair in search of a pin but remembered at the last second that she'd cut off her hair. Drat. How was she supposed to pick a lock without one?

As luck would have it, Lady Willow's hair provided the needed pin. Meredith inserted it carefully into the lock and concentrated on the task at hand. It proved only the work of a moment before the lock clicked and the doors swung open freely.

Inside lay a treasure trove of childhood toys. She swiftly took inventory. Dolls, puzzles, pigskin balls to toss about. A closed box caught her eye. When she opened it, Meredith found it contained only brightly painted blocks of wood. Perfect for young Poppy to stack and knock down.

Meredith carried it across the room and then sat on the rug before the fire. She relished the heat permeating her gown before she upended her treasure and began to play. It took only a minute for the children to slide onto the floor and investigate what she was doing. She made a tall stack with the colored blocks and held her breath as Poppy reached for them.

When they crashed to the floor, she laughed and restacked the pile. As she did, she caught the swift exchange of glances between Willow and Maisy before they inched closer. Had they expected Meredith to scold a baby? Meredith gritted her teeth and considered how willing Grayling might be to providing her with a list of his former governesses. They deserved to be hunted down and expelled from their current positions.

When Poppy again destroyed her tower, the other two joined in and made their own. Meredith eased back a bit to give them room to play. Poppy chortled and stood. The next tower was felled by a wild swing of her foot. Meredith reached for her. "Be careful of your sisters, Poppy, love. Don't hurt them."

Meredith released the child and she squatted down to better view her sister's work. This time, she used her hand and both Maisy and Willow complained. "We weren't done yet, Poppy."

Willow held Poppy back with one hand. "Wait."

"No, not yet."

"Now."

Meredith smiled as the girls worked together to build a tower as tall as they could make it and then leaned back so Poppy could destroy it. Blocks scattered far and wide and the girls scurried to retrieve them to build again.

Meredith glanced at the nurse who was staring at her with openmouthed surprise.

"I think we're going to need more blocks," Meredith suggested.

"That and an increase in your wages," Ridgeway said. "That was remarkable. How did you know Her Ladyship used to play on the floor with them?"

"I didn't, but it seemed the sensible thing to do." Meredith shrugged. "Wait till you see what else I'm capable of."

Chapter Fourteen

---◆---

Silence could only be good, surely. That's what Constantine kept telling himself as the second day of the new governess's employment progressed. So far, he had managed not to wander upstairs and see for himself how Calista, Meredith (God, he wished he knew what to call her) and his daughters were getting along. Maybe he could continue to call her Calista, but only in his innermost thoughts or when they were alone and no one could hear them. Especially in his fantasies.

No, he had to get used to the change.

Meredith Clark—another name that didn't suit the woman. The name sparked images of a cold bookish spinster. There may be little gentle sweetness in the woman, but steel, nerve and cunning she had in spades. She *was* kind. He'd never thought her heartless, which was why he had no concerns about her influence over his daughters. Under her guidance they might grow to be strong young women, not one of those listless beauties waiting for a man to sweep them off her feet and propose before their first season had even begun.

He shook his head and cursed under his breath. What was he doing planning so far ahead? He knew, and Arabella had warned him, that Miss Clark might not stay in his employment for very long. She had a past that would scandalize many if the truth came out. Yet the thought of her leaving wasn't a pleasant sensation. Not now he had her under his roof where no man would dare touch her.

By sheer force of will, Constantine had not grumbled about her missing their arranged meeting last night when Cunningham had subtly asked if she should be summoned. As the woman had reminded him yesterday, she was here for his daughters and not him. Her time wasn't wasted if she was with his girls.

Yet he had not laid eyes on her all day and curiosity was driving him mad. He'd remained in his study, tending his correspondence in frustrated solitude. But as he'd paused for luncheon, Cunningham had relayed the particulars of what the governess was doing with the children. The butler had sounded aghast that she was seated upon the floor to play with them. Constantine was rather pleased by that news.

But Miss Clark was causing additional work for the staff with her demands, Cunningham had confided. After breakfast she had demanded tea and sweet cakes to be immediately sent up to the nursery. Warm baths had followed and she had spent an hour dressing hair. She had not even begun conducting lessons. The young maid, Cunningham's niece, had been assisting nurse but had been excused for other duties for the rest of the day, and the man was afraid of what else Miss Clark might be doing.

A smile tugged at his lips. Amongst his set lingered the idea that ladies should have little part in the raising of their offspring. Augusta had defied them all and taken an active part in raising their daughters with little assistance from the servants. The girls must miss that. Miss Clark's behavior, rather relaxed for a servant, would feel familiar for them.

Many things about Meredith Clark felt familiar. She was easy to be with.

He picked up the most recent copy of the *Times* and scanned the pages, looking for a distraction from the direction of his thoughts. He'd spent too long wallowing in the past or contemplating his former lover today. It was time to move ahead with life before he became obsessed with what he didn't have.

An entry low down on the page caught his eye. As he read it, his eyes widened. Mr. Leopold Randall was appealing to his sister to come home, and to Romsey Abbey no less. The woman would be welcomed with open arms. Constantine gritted his teeth. The nerve of the man to behave as if the abbey was his. He might be the heir, but he was not the duke. When they finally met, he would lay down the law about Randall's attitude regarding things that didn't belong to him. Constantine did not support this marriage. When his children were settled and smiling, he would make the trip to Romsey and tell his sister so.

Unfortunately, the trip would most likely be after the wedding.

A nervous giggle caught his attention and he peered past the paper to the doorway. A dark head, Maisy, pretty ringlets bobbing on each side of her head, was peeking at him from the door, waiting to see if he would invite her in. He dropped the paper to the desk and crooked his finger. The little scamp rushed right to him. She was in his arms before his surprise sank in. For the first time in a very long time, his middle daughter wanted him.

He held her against him as tight as he dared. He'd missed the impulsive hugs more than he'd thought possible. When he raised his head and glanced toward the doorway, he saw Miss Clark had brought Willow too; she held Poppy in her arms. But they, too, were waiting at the doorway for an invitation to enter.

"Come in. Please, come in," he urged. He couldn't remember the last time a governess had brought them to him during the day. "It's nice to see you all."

Willow drew closer, stopping to stare at him and Maisy cuddling behind his desk. Constantine opened his arms and his eldest daughter leapt into them, burrowing against him and her sister. "Hello, Papa," she whispered softly.

He eased back to look at her closely. Today she resembled her mother very much. Her hair was brushed till it shone a bright blond; two plaits were looped about her head to keep the long strands neat. A lump formed in his throat. "Hello, Angel. You look very pretty today."

His gaze shifted to where Miss Clark stood, arms filled with a wriggling, squirming child.

"You had better hand Poppy over, too," he warned, "or you'll be in danger of dropping her. Never one to be left out is this little lady. We'll have our hands full when she's older."

Miss Clark said nothing as she placed the child on the center of his chest, between her two sisters. She brushed her fingers over the short curls on Poppy's head before she turned away.

Poppy caught his face in her chubby little hands and rubbed their noses together.

He sighed. "You are lovely too, little one. Is that a new dress you're wearing, Maisy?"

Maisy plucked at it. "It's my new pretty one," she said proudly.

"It was mine, but Maisy needs it now," Willow said quietly. "Miss Clark said she never had a sister to give her prettiest gowns to, but I can show Maisy how to be all grown up."

He smiled at his daughter, but his heartbeat sped up. Willow was talking a lot more than she normally would. He swallowed past the lump in his throat. "That is very sweet of you."

When Maisy wriggled free of his grip, grabbed a heavy glass paperweight from the desk, and scurried into the desk well at his feet, he let her go without a word of protest. It had been an age since they had all come and he was pleased to see it did not take long for old habits to resurrect themselves. He hadn't realized they'd stopped coming, and all it had taken was one day and a very crafty woman to tumble his world again.

He glanced at Miss Clark, surprised to see her frowning at the newssheet spread across his desk. She had even removed her spectacles, proving she did not need them to read. Maybe one day she would stop tormenting him.

He laughed at the idea and tickled his eldest beneath her chin. "There is no need to grow up too fast. You're all the perfect size for sitting on my lap." Including Meredith Clark.

He hugged Willow again and rejoiced when her arms tightened about his neck. She held him a long time, only releasing him because Poppy was selfishly pushing her away.

He reached into his desk drawer and withdrew a scrap of paper and stick of lead. "Willow used to draw for me," he told Miss Clark, who had replaced her spectacles and was standing at the window, looking out at the grounds. "I wonder if she would like to today?"

Miss Clark did not respond, but his daughter's eyes lit up with interest. She nodded enthusiastically, hurried around the desk, and climbed onto a chair placed across from him. It wasn't close enough, but Miss Clark was quick in offering assistance. She drew the chair closer and lingered until Willow was settled. That left him with only Poppy to entertain. The little scamp touched his face, his cravat, and the bright, shining ruby pin holding it in place. Without further ado, she embraced him, a little whimper of sound leaving her lips.

He glanced up at Miss Clark and noticed the frown had been replaced by amusement. He winked at her. "I thought we were to meet last night."

"Forgive me," she murmured, lowering her eyes. "I hoped you wouldn't mind the delay too much if you received a visit from your daughters along with conducting our meeting. I became caught up in a story last night and lost track of the time."

He juggled Poppy so she could see her sisters. "What was the story about?"

"Their mother," Miss Clark told him, her eyes softening when she looked down upon him. "Nurse was kind enough to recall some events in Lady Grayling's childhood for us. Your daughters were enthralled and took a little longer than normal to fall asleep afterward."

"Ah," he murmured, but he was rather surprised that his former lover, now his children's governess, had encouraged talk of his late wife. But then, Miss Clark was not particularly sentimental about certain things. She undoubtedly didn't find mention of Augusta's life the least bit troubling. "What did nurse have to recount?"

"Oh, lots of things. She mentioned the horse Lady Grayling loved to ride when she was just Willow's age, the friends she had, and the mischief they occasionally got into when no one was looking. The way she loved her daughters and how she sees so much of Lady Grayling in them."

Constantine glanced at his daughters and saw that their lips had lifted into smiles, eyes sparkling at the mention of the resemblance. He saw it every day but rarely mentioned it to them. How clever of Miss Clark. She'd discovered in a day how to make his children smile again.

He'd never meant them to forget Augusta. He would try harder to keep her memory alive.

When Poppy began to grizzle, Miss Clark moved to take her. "I believe the young lady requires a rest. She's had an eventful morning knocking over wooden block towers. If it's not too much trouble, might we have more? There are not enough for all three to play with at once. And this little miss does enjoy causing havoc."

"Of course. You may have whatever you require."

"Thank you."

Poppy went to Miss Clark easily, Maisy obediently crawled out from beneath the desk, but Willow lingered over her drawing.

His eldest wasn't at all ready to end her visit. The thought pleased him immensely. "I can bring her up in a little while," he murmured softly. "Let her finish."

"Very well, my lord." Juggling her bundle, Miss Clark held her hand out to Maisy and guided her from the room. He watched them go, doing his best not to stare at the gentle sway of Miss Clark's body, and then turned his attention to his daughter.

Constantine craned his neck to get a better view of Willow's efforts. The rough pencil strokes he remembered from previous visits had smoothed. It almost looked like a dog instead of a lump with sticks. "That's coming along nicely."

Willow held the picture out in front of her and eventually nodded. "It's Mama's horse. She had a black pony."

"I'm sure she would have loved your picture," he assured her.

Willow smiled and then she carefully slid the pencil across the desk toward him before looking toward the door, lower lip between her teeth.

He touched her hands and she jumped. "Shall we rejoin your sisters?"

As Willow nodded and clutched her drawing to her chest, it occurred to him that the girls had rarely been apart for any length of time. By necessity they were always together, but the surprising thing was he wouldn't mind spending more time with them. He'd speak with Miss Clark before he went to bed and arrange another, longer, visit. Perhaps they could visit him while Poppy napped.

When they reached the nursery, Miss Clark was bent over the cot, singing softly to Poppy in an effort to lull her to sleep. Maisy watched from another bed, her dolly clutched tight in her arms. Miss Clark's head lifted and she smiled at Willow's picture before resuming her lullaby and patting Poppy's back. Willow scrambled up beside Maisy on her bed and then she too only had eyes for their governess. Constantine could understand the fascination.

No matter how many times he found himself in Miss Clark's presence, he always detected yet another feature, flaw, or behavior that contradicted what he thought he knew. If she had turned her talents to the stage, she'd have made an excellent actress. As it was, she merely performed for him. Constantine was utterly smitten despite the layers of misdirection.

He backed out the door as quietly as he could, amused by how easily Miss Clark had adjusted to his children's life. There were few overt signs of the woman he'd first met. Anyone else looking at her now would never suspect her of being new at this career. She handled his children's care as if she had spent her whole life around the young. It gave him hope that she would stay with them for a long time to come.

Perhaps forever.

Buoyed by an optimism he hadn't experienced in quite some time, Constantine headed for his bedchamber. He'd go for a long ride while the weather held because very soon he might be housebound with a woman he wanted more and more each day. The long cold days of deepest winter had been more enjoyable when he'd had Augusta to share them with, and he wasn't looking forward to spending another winter alone with his own company.

As he finished changing for the ride, he glanced at the connecting doorway. His wife's room was exactly how she'd left it. He hadn't had the heart to pack away her possessions after her death. Up until now, he'd shied from the idea. Yet as he walked to the door and stepped quickly inside before he lost his nerve, he didn't have the same hesitation.

The room had a chilly, unlived-in air, yet he remembered how it had been when his wife had lived. He'd spent many an enjoyable hour on that bed, and only the bedding had been changed from the day of Poppy's birth. A maid still tended the surfaces to free them of dust. Augusta could sweep in from her dressing room at any moment and not find anything amiss.

But she had died and he had to accept it. Let her go and look to the future. One day he had to marry. He still needed an heir. But that need was exactly the event that had led to Augusta's death.

He breathed out slowly, letting his mind turn over those last terrible days. The pregnancy had not gone well from the beginning and Augusta had gone into labor in the dead of night. By late afternoon, the physician had suggested he pray. He'd done that, but it hadn't been enough. As Poppy had opened her eyes upon the world, Augusta had slipped away, so quietly that he hadn't realized she was gone until the doctor broke the news to him.

He should have been with her. He could have proved to her one last time that he'd loved her above all others. He'd been faithful from the day they'd met until recently and regretted nothing of their life together save that it had ended all too soon. Only with Calista had he found an echo of that same contentment, but now even that was denied him.

He thumped the post of the bed he'd loved and lost in. A ride was just what he needed. The cold air might blast his regrets into dust.

Chapter Fifteen

Meredith let the nursery curtain fall back into place just as the sun set on a fulfilling day and Grayling's horse thundered toward the Hall. She was rather impressed by how easily she'd made the transition from whore to governess. Each job held its own set of challenges, but she had to admit caring for three small girls far exceeded her expectations. She'd actually enjoyed an entire day for a change. That had rarely happened in her former career.

She smiled as she recounted the time when a day at the House had been pleasant. Grayling had been there, half-naked and smiling cheekily because he was planning something wicked to fill up the time they had together. If only she could have that too, then Meredith would have no cause to be unhappy. Yet Meredith had not had intimate relations in more days than she cared to think about. Celibacy, of any kind, was rather a foreign state for her to be in.

When she had taken Grayling's daughters to see him, it had been as much for their benefit as her own. With careful questioning, she had discovered from the other servants that daily visits between father and daughters had ceased some time ago. It seemed Grayling could go for days without remembering to come see them, so she'd made the decision to take them to him. She wouldn't allow him to forget the three little girls needed him, too. With their mother gone, he was the only one who mattered.

Yet when she'd met him, looking so lost and lonely in his

book-lined room, she'd forgiven his preoccupation with estate affairs, but only just. Men were not always ideally suited to raising young girls. They needed a push in the right direction to share their lives. The visit from his children had considerably altered his mood toward the one she knew best. She'd never seen him without the abundant confidence and vigor with which he had boldly introduced himself at the bawdy house. The change was rather marked and she'd missed the teasing light in his eyes when he'd spoken to her, his prim governess.

It was very easy to see Lady Grayling was sorely missed, not only by her husband and children but also by the entire staff of Stanton Harold Hall. She didn't envy Grayling's second wife, whoever she ended up being. Encouraging the staff to speak of the late countess with the children at her side had been remarkably easy. The servants' obvious devotion to a woman dead these past two years would make any newcomer feel inferior without much effort. A timid soul would find it painful to be compared to a first wife, especially if she hoped to lay claim to Grayling's heart.

Meredith quietly paced the room. Restlessness had settled into her bones in the past hour and she hoped additional exercise would exhaust her body before she attempted to sleep tonight. The sounds of Stanton Harold Hall at night were so different from what she was used to. Her bed was lumpy, the sheets scratched, and the snoring servant in the next chamber kept interrupting her rest several times a night. She even missed the sounds of ardent lovemaking, although she'd never consciously noticed them before.

It was probably because she slept alone. She hadn't always wanted the touch of a man every moment of the night, but she had missed Grayling. In the dead of last night, she'd considered creeping from the nursery to find where he slept.

Meredith raised her face to the ceiling and silently cursed her impossible fantasy. That part of her life was over. She couldn't go to Grayling to have sex with him just because she wanted to. He wasn't hers. He never had been. He'd paid to inhabit her bed and nothing more. Even now, he paid her to make his life easier. Grayling was a man clinging to the past with a woman universally admired. The more Meredith learned, the more certain she became that she had imagined any deepening of affection on his part. His wife had been a saint and Meredith was so far from that it was laughable.

She took another silent turn about the room while she suppressed her growing sense of inadequacy. She hadn't enquired after Lady Grayling's character to be nosy. She'd asked because Grayling's daughters were clearly so very lonely without their mother. She knew what it was like to lose a parent. Little things were forgotten so easily, and with them being so young, the only way to keep their mother's memory alive was to have everyone begin to speak candidly of her again. It just didn't help Meredith remain in a good mood.

"Ooh, Cook is in such a mood today," Miss Cunningham exclaimed as she burst into the nursery without thought for the sleeping children. "Someone stole her best laying chickens right from under our noses and there's not enough eggs for breakfast in the morning."

Meredith quickly shushed the girl and took the tea tray from her hands. "Then we won't all get eggs for breakfast. Now go back the way you've come and quietly. The ladies are still sleeping."

Miss Cunningham had no sense to be around the young. She was as scatterbrained as any debutante before her first ball. Meredith wasn't about to have her hard work foiled. The children needed a routine and she intended to establish one immediately. Luckily, she and the late Lady Grayling shared a trait for organization that the senior servants approved of. Without that similarity to back up her intentions, Meredith would have undoubtedly had more trouble setting her plans in motion.

She set the tray on a side table and placed her hand on Nurse's good arm. When the older woman slowly woke from her doze, Meredith asked, "Tea?"

"That would be lovely. I shouldn't sleep the day away but it's ever so calm in here." Nurse glanced across the room to where the children still rested. "Never known them all to go down so easily since Lady Poppy came along. You have a gift."

"Children are easy to manage." Just like men, Meredith thought with amusement as she set the cup and saucer down beside the nurse, within easy reach of her good hand. "They only want every moment of your attention until they don't need it anymore."

Nurse reached for her cup and sipped the hot beverage. "They've had lots of servants fussing over them. You somehow do a better job of it than anyone since their mother died."

Meredith knew high praise when she heard it. She dipped a quick curtsy, balancing her teacup between her fingers, and then took a place opposite the old woman. "They are lovely girls. They would make anyone proud."

The older woman snorted. "I suppose you've got more questions. What else do you want to know?"

"Everything, but not so much for me as for them. They enjoyed your stories last night very much. Do you feel up to sharing more of their mother's antics tonight?"

The nurse's eyes narrowed. "Shouldn't you begin their studies soon? Your predecessors liked them to walk in circles with a book balanced on their heads."

"What a ridiculous thing to do with a child so young. There is plenty of time for lessons in deportment yet." She shook her head. No wonder the girls had been so unhappy when she'd arrived. A five-year-old had no need to be proper so young. A little laxity in the social graces would be excused and taught by example later. "I think having Lady Willow speak to me and laugh along with her sisters is the first step on the long road ahead. Needlework, languages, and the perfect curtsy can wait. I've heard the lass speak so infrequently. She's much too quiet."

The nurse's expression grew dark. "She saw too much. Heard too much of her mother's last day. God forgive me for not protecting her better, but everything was in chaos. Grayling was inconsolable and we had a wee motherless babe in arms to find a wet nurse for."

God had other business than the needs of women. The only person she could rely upon was herself. She patted the older woman's lax hand gently, noting the chill of her skin and the lack of reaction. "Then let's fill Willow's mind with better memories, enough to make her smile and play again. It is my hope the other servants will help her along the path to happiness."

Nurse's face grew serious as she considered. "I'll speak to Cook and the housekeeper. They knew our lady the longest of everyone. Mrs. Smith met with Lady Grayling daily. She should have many stories to relate. They'll support your plan and will stand up to Cunningham if needed. He thinks we shouldn't mention our lady near the girls. He's afraid of upsetting them."

Meredith shook her said. "But that's why they are so miserable. Having your mother wrenched from your life leaves a yearning that cannot ever be filled completely. As they age, they forget so much. It's up to us to prevent that."

"You've very strong opinions for a governess." Nurse's eyes narrowed. "Where did you say His Lordship found you?"

Although Nurse was a rather inquisitive creature, Meredith gave the same answer she gave to everyone who'd asked so far. "Lady Farnsworth recommended me for the post."

"And where the countess found you don't bear mentioning?" Ridgeway snorted when Meredith remained silent. "The less said the better, I suspect. Well, if you'll excuse me, I best head below."

When Ridgeway stood, the older woman tottered a bit and then slowly left the room. Meredith noticed she dragged her right foot immediately and was reminded that she'd seen this sort of ailment before in a place she'd never mention being and bearing a name that wouldn't ever be repeated. Another part of her past she'd locked away and hidden. There was no cure for Ridgeway. She would always suffer the weakness in her limbs.

"Thank you," she called softly, both for Ridgeway's support and for dropping her inquisition into Meredith's past. However, nurse was too focused on getting her limb to cooperate to notice she'd been spoken to. Poor woman. A house of this size must present such difficulties in getting around in her condition. It was perhaps good that she only went belowstairs but once a day. She wouldn't return for an hour yet.

When Meredith could no longer hear nurse's heavy tread in the hall, she stood to check on the children. All three were sound asleep, limbs sprawled on the bedding in the way that only young children could consider comfortable. They were sweet little things. Adorable together and close. When one stubbed her toe, the others came to soothe her.

A wave of longing swept over her. If she ever had a family of her own, she hoped her children would always be there for each other. She hoped they would never drift apart and always be supportive of each other's lives rather than cause each other pain. She clenched her fists. There was nothing worse than knowing your family had betrayed you.

When she turned away from her contemplation of the sleeping angels and faced the door, she startled. Grayling stood there, still dressed for riding and looking every inch the lord she'd first met. She took in his windblown hair and high color to his cheeks and concluded the ride had driven his doubts from his mind.

She smiled and drew closer to greet him. "Do you need anything, my lord?" She glanced over her shoulder and peered into the adjoining room. "The children may not wake for some time if you were after them."

Grayling said nothing, but his fingers rose to touch her short-cropped hair. The decision to clip it had not been taken lightly, but it was infinitely more practical than keeping it long. She no longer needed to fuss with it for hours on end before facing each new day. A servant had little leisure for personal grooming.

"Then I should leave them in your capable hands." His fingers brushed forward to caress her jaw.

Meredith clenched it, fighting the impulse to turn her face into his palm for the warmth she craved. Grayling had promised to stay away, but soft touches were fire to her senses. Even though he'd been out of doors, heat blazed from his fingertips. She shivered as a sudden chill raced over her skin, and she drew her shawl closer about her shoulders.

He stepped even closer so that the heat of him was mere inches away. He smelled of horses, leather, and gorgeous, vibrant man. If she were to lean forward a touch she could be cuddled against that warmth. She'd envied his daughters today. They could climb on his lap, tangle their arms about his neck, and keep him for themselves. But by becoming the governess, Meredith had put such indulgent luxuries aside.

She met his gaze and saw his green eyes had brightened with merriment. Damn him. He knew she enjoyed his warmth. He began to smile but then with one stroke of his fingers over her skin he broke away, leaving her yearning for what she couldn't have.

Puzzled by his antics, Meredith stepped out into the hallway and was rewarded with the view of his large body striding up the hall purposefully. He really was remarkably well built, and since she'd explored what was under his clothing in detail she knew exactly what she missed.

Before he rounded the corner for the staircase, Meredith spun about and returned to the nursery. She couldn't think of Grayling as a lover anymore. She had a job to do and the children needed her. Meredith had a chance to be something other than a disposable woman, used for a while and discarded without being thought of again. She wasn't going to let anything get in the way of mending three broken hearts, least of all a man who was desperately in love with his dead wife.

The battle wasn't worth it. Not even for the best sex she'd ever had.

Chapter Sixteen

———◆———

Constantine stepped from the main doors of Stanton Harold Hall and pulled his coat tighter about him as a sudden blast of icy cold wind hit his body full force. It had been a miserable few days and he'd come outside to see what fool dared to travel in such ghastly weather. He gaped at the crest gleaming through the mud-splattered carriage sides. "What the devil brings you to Wiltshire on such a dreadful day, Rothwell?"

His oldest friend emerged from his vehicle and grimaced up at the sky. "I'm here to see if you still live. Why the devil were you not at the wedding? I would not care to be in your shoes. Your sisters are rather put out with you."

He grinned and strode down the steps quickly. "As am I with them for marrying so far beneath them."

They shook hands amiably, but Rothwell's eyes narrowed. "You've never even met their new husbands. Everyone knows you disapprove. But given one is the boy's heir, and wealthy, their marriage will be accepted in due time. Too late now they've tied the knot. It's official and been witnessed by quite a few of our mutual friends so all of London will know the details of the matches already."

"Well, if that's the case, I'll meet the upstarts at my leisure."

Rothwell appeared ready to argue, but Constantine held up his hands to hold him off. "Come inside where it's warm and have a drink. You'll stay, of course?"

He gestured to the front door and was very quick to lead Rothwell into the warmth of his study. The room was comfortable and he had a good supply of brandy on hand.

"Unfortunately, I cannot. I'm needed back in London tomorrow for a meeting but I could not pass through without checking on your welfare." Rothwell's gaze grew sharp. "How have you all been? Well, I trust?"

"We are all very well." Constantine grinned. The past weeks had done much to mend three very small hearts. Employing Miss Clark had been the best decision he'd ever made. "You'll find the girls much the same as before."

"Still too quiet?" Rothwell asked.

"Actually, no. I have had the good fortune of securing a new governess, and she has worked miracles in lightening the girl's spirits. It's a rare day now that I do not hear them laugh as they used to. They are almost as they were before Augusta passed."

Rothwell squinted at him. "Seems you've had a change of heart too. You've not spoken of your wife so easily since her death."

"I've had a lot of time to think about what I lost, but it is time to move ahead."

In the weeks since Miss Clark had come, he had taken stock of his situation. He was still young. Everyone had told him that Augusta would not want him to mourn her forever. He should not feel guilty for laughing or enjoying life without her. He should remember the past was not all there was to life. There were endless possibilities for happiness, yet each included Meredith Clark.

Rothwell clapped him on the shoulder. "Excellent. I shall expect you in London for the season. It'll be like old times. We'll drink, dance, and do the pretty for the ladies. Who knows, perhaps you can find another diamond among the lumps of coal crowding the ballrooms."

Constantine laughed along with Rothwell at the picture he painted, but his heart did not leap with excitement. Sifting through the *ton* in search of a wife or even a lover held little appeal. The woman he wanted was already under his roof. "I don't intend to rush toward matrimony."

Rothwell grinned. "Who said anything about marriage? Many

diamonds have a chance to shine by moonlight without a ring upon her finger."

Unfortunately, Constantine was rather taken by a garnet-loving minx in spinster's clothing. The last weeks had been a struggle, but he'd managed to keep his word. He'd barely touched Miss Clark, just the occasional fleeting caress to her jaw when no one was looking. What surprised him was how that small caress was almost enough to satisfy him. He could look whenever he wanted. He could touch, although fleetingly.

He poured Rothwell a drink and they toasted. "To the future."

"And the past." Rothwell settled himself in a chair. "I had a chance to speak with your new brothers-in-law. The elder is quite a serious man, rather well traveled too. The younger is a far different kettle of fish. I have a feeling Blythe keeps him on a tight leash. They were rarely apart during the party."

Constantine snorted. "I knew she'd made a mistake."

Rothwell leaned forward. "Not a mistake. I've never seen Blythe smile so much and I've known her since she first learned how to turn up her nose at me. This man could be the best thing for her if he can make her happy. However, when she's not around he curses like a Barbary pirate."

"I imagine that is because he was as close to one as it is possible to be. I've been supplied with all the disreputable facts of his past, so I will not be surprised by any gossip. But I must say he is exactly the opposite sort of what I'd hoped for her second husband."

"Sometimes we do not get what we want. Only what we need."

Constantine studied his friend. "Since when have you been a philosopher?"

Rothwell laughed. "I had the opportunity to spend some time with the middle brother, Oliver Randall. He thrust a book at me rather than continue our conversation. Some of what I read must have rubbed off."

"Well, Blythe must live with her choices, as must Mercy. I give them a year before they regret their decisions."

Rothwell dropped his drink to the table. "So you've become an opponent of the married state. I'm surprised Lady Farnsworth would allow it."

"Arabella's not around to meddle in my affairs right now." Constantine swallowed a mouthful of his drink. "She's gone to London. Farnsworth summoned her for his daughters coming out a few weeks ago now, denying her the chance to attend the wedding too, by the way. Callous bastard. The season could be a disaster socially for her, though. Bella's let slip a thing or two of the niece's nature that is not promising of an easy or scandal-free first season. Farnsworth will likely blame Bella for any lapse."

Rothwell shuffled in his chair again, his expression changing to curiosity. "If you'd married the lady, she wouldn't have to put up with Farnsworth carping like an old woman. Your daughters love her. Why haven't you married her yet?"

"I've told you before that Bella and I are simply friends. She's very fond of my daughters and likes to visit with them whenever she can. You know as well as I do that I am very fortunate to have her friendship. Before she left she was good enough to send me an excellent governess. As I've already mentioned, the improvement in my daughter's tempers has been remarkable."

Rothwell chewed on his lower lip. When he released it, his brow had creased in a frown. "Forgive me for being blunt, but why wouldn't you want to marry Lady Farnsworth? She's lovely and in possession of a fine mind."

"Perhaps because she's never encouraged me to consider more and even told me we would not suit. She was my wife's friend. Perhaps she sees me as a brother."

Rothwell shifted in his seat. "So when are you bound for London?"

"I've no firm plans as yet, but I must call on Arabella before the season starts."

"Oh. For what purpose? I'll likely see her first about Town. Can I pass along any message?"

Constantine still had to find out what Miss Clark had told Arabella before she left for London. The longer he wondered what it might be, the more he worried. Someone had to watch out for the woman. "Ah. That's very decent of you, but no. It is a delicate matter that unfortunately requires a private word. Don't trouble yourself about it. I'll speak to her soon enough, I hope."

A timid tap on the door sounded and Cunningham entered. "Sorry for the disturbance, my lord, but could I have a moment of your time? It's rather urgent."

Puzzled, Constantine excused himself and approached the door. Cunningham held it open for Constantine to step through and he raised a brow when he closed the door behind them. "It's about the governess."

The weight of disapproval on the word *governess* raised the hair on the back of Constantine's neck. Despite having won over the sum total of his household and outdoors staff, Cunningham still held firm to his disapproval. For the life of him, Constantine could not work out why. Miss Clark had been exemplary in her attention to her duties. She spoke kindly to everyone and appeared rather fond of his daughters, even allowing them into her own bed to play on a particularly chilly day. "Oh."

"Miss Clark has been precipitous and brought the children down to be presented to Lord Rothwell without waiting for a summons. They are waiting in the morning room, but I can send her away until you want them."

Constantine grinned. "That's an excellent idea. Send for them at once. Rothwell is not staying long and will want to see his goddaughters before he goes to London."

Cunningham's indignation deflated like a hot-air balloon. His face grew pinched. "As you wish."

When he turned to go, Constantine called him back. "Cunningham, might I give you a word of advice? In matters that relate to my daughters, I'm prepared to give Miss Clark considerable leeway. She chose correctly to prepare my daughters to greet our visitor, and as you would well remember, my late wife would have done exactly the same."

Cunningham appeared a little easier at last. "Of course, my lord."

Constantine watched him go, wondering what it would take to have Cunningham's disapproval vanish. There was no reason to fight every decision Miss Clark tried to make. Some of them were imminently practical. Augusta had always claimed that their daughters should not be shut away, that they should know their elders. Since Rothwell would be their guardian should anything happen to him, it was prudent and advisable that the girls were comfortable with him.

"The governess will bring the girls in a moment," he told

Rothwell as he rejoined him.

Rothwell grinned. "Couldn't help but overhear that Cunningham does not care for the new governess. Is she pretty?"

Constantine shrugged, wondering how Cunningham was treating Miss Clark when he wasn't looking and whether pretty was a strong enough word to describe Meredith Clark. "Everything will work out in the end, I'm sure."

Cunningham tapped on the open door and his daughters filed past, heads high, appearance flawless. Miss Clark carried Poppy past the stiff-limbed butler and then lowered her onto her feet. At two, Poppy tottered toward Constantine. Miss Clark followed until he caught the little minx up into his arms. He smiled at Miss Clark. "I'd like you to remain, please."

"Yes, my lord," she agreed quickly.

Rothwell strolled to his side. "And who is this lovely creature?"

When he glanced around, Rothwell stared only at Miss Clark, his gaze bold and full of speculation. Constantine ground his teeth. "*My* governess."

The *my* might have sounded a touch possessive, because Rothwell's brows rose. Miss Clark was his, no matter that she did not share his bed now. He wouldn't allow his friend to get ideas into his head, no matter how short the visit. Miss Clark was off-limits to all others. If he had to be celibate, then so did she.

"Miss Clark, my lord." After a quick curtsy, Miss Clark retreated to a far chair, as far away from Rothwell's roving eye as she could get.

Constantine breathed a sigh of relief. Rothwell had a large appetite for pretty women and was considered handsome. Constantine didn't think he could stomach Miss Clark revealing a mutual attraction to Rothwell. The idea of it ruined his good mood.

Although she did nothing to be noticed, Rothwell couldn't take his eyes from her. To distract him, Constantine all but threw Poppy into his arms. "Say hello to Rothwell, sweetheart."

His friend appeared startled by the child in his arms but made a passable attempt to speak with her before quickly handing her back. He cast one last look at Miss Clark before bowing to Willow. "Lady Willow, a pleasure to see you again. Do you remember me?"

Willow dipped a much-improved curtsy and smiled up at Rothwell. "Yes, sir. You used to spin me around till I was dizzy. Will you do it again?"

"Anything for you, Lady Willow."

Willow hadn't spoken to Rothwell very much on his last visit, yet now she was confidently conversing and even making demands. Constantine threw a quick, grateful smile at Miss Clark as Rothwell clasped Willow's hands to spin her around. Miss Clark had exceeded his expectations and he intended to show his appreciation later. There was a garnet bracelet burning a hole in his coat pocket.

Greeting Maisy took a little more effort. She'd retreated beneath the well of his desk, ensuring that Rothwell had to bend upside down to see her, looking quite ridiculous in the process. "Lady Maisy," Rothwell said from the same position, "so good to see you."

When he was upright again, a giggle sounded behind him. Miss Clark, and then Willow, began to laugh at Rothwell. Neither of them could stop even when Rothwell glared at the noise.

Constantine probably should stop them, but he rather enjoyed their antics. "Laughing at Rothwell's expense is rather unbecoming for ladies."

Miss Clark struggled valiantly to keep a straight face but failed terribly. "Forgive me, my lord, but I was not laughing at His Lordship." She glanced at Willow as his daughter drew close against her side. "I was simply amazed at what Lady Maisy can accomplish at the tender age of four. Her coming out should prove to be remarkably memorable."

A warm thrill filled him that Miss Clark was imagining the future too. At least he wasn't the only one considering possibilities. "If you were to write down her antics, I doubt anyone would believe you."

Miss Clark's eyes glowed when she looked upon him. "We would know the truth."

Constantine's heart skipped a beat and he took a pace toward her. But then Maisy latched on to his leg, halting his plans to touch his governess. Thank God she had. Rothwell was already looking between them, suspicion clear in his eyes.

The smile on Miss Clark's face dimmed and she glanced down. Was she embarrassed that he was attracted to her still?

He glanced at his children. "Thank you for bringing them."

"Of course, my lord. Ladies, let us leave the gentlemen to their pursuits." Miss Clark gathered up the girls and quickly departed.

"Governess, my arse," Rothwell muttered. "At least you are no longer moping."

Constantine poured another drink. "Don't be simple."

Miss Clark was exactly that. A governess. But the lover was always there behind the wire-rimmed spectacles when she looked upon him.

Rothwell leaned against his desk. "It's about time you found a distraction. She's a fine-looking woman."

Constantine tossed back his drink and refilled it. "It's not like that."

"But was it ever? You've a proprietary eye when you look at her. Same expression you used to cast upon your wife when any scoundrel got too close."

There wasn't much to dispute in Rothwell's statement, so he remained silent. It seemed the best way to avoid admitting he lusted after a servant.

Rothwell only laughed. "I'm sure you can lure the woman back into your bed. You just have to find the right incentive. Jewels usually work."

That might be so, but Constantine wasn't sure he wanted her there under those terms anymore. He liked to think their attraction was mutual. He'd give her jewels if they pleased her, but that wasn't all he wanted.

Seeing her with his daughters, how she encouraged them to laugh, to be close sisters, and how she cared for them made one thing very clear. He wanted Miss Clark to stay for as long as she would for their sake. He didn't want to risk driving her away just because he couldn't keep his hands to himself. Meredith Clark deserved better. She deserved to be respected.

Chapter Seventeen

Meredith glanced out the window at the fine white powder falling from the sky and gnawed at her lower lip. Very soon she would be trapped inside Stanton Harold Hall with three very energetic children and one sinfully handsome widower. The girls had blossomed in the past few weeks with the servants' help. Mealtimes and bedtimes were full of chatter, stories, and contented smiles; the days were full of energetic games. It was a pity the activities did not meet all of Meredith's needs, especially the ones filling her mind at night.

She missed Grayling. She missed being held in his arms. After his friend Rothwell's visit, he'd become even more withdrawn. That brief moment of possessiveness he'd shown after Rothwell had inspected her from head to toe had brought back the reminders of how pleasant, exciting, his company could be. Perhaps their bargain had been a mistake. Meredith had never been celibate, either by choice or by need.

A male throat cleared nearby, and when she glanced up, she noticed the butler had come to spy on her work again. She groaned under her breath but managed to smile. "Mr. Cunningham. What a pleasure."

"Miss Clark," he said rather severely. He stood aside for a footman to pass him, the man's arms full of treasures to amuse the children. "Mrs. Smith sent these down from the attic."

Meredith was almost as excited to see what new

entertainments had been found as she was by the man carrying them. "Kindly place them by the window." Meredith followed, letting her eyes rove over the footman's physique. Not as fine and large as Gray, but not running to fat either. As far as she was concerned, no one could be as well put together as her employer. But as far as views went, the sandy-haired footman was rather easy on the eye.

She shook herself from her daze. There was no use letting her imagination run away with itself over a pretty body. That part of her life was over. She leaned over the pile and found a ball-and-cup game to show Lady Willow. Meredith turned the ball over in her hand and let the cup dangle from the string. "I had one as a child."

Cunningham's voice cut through the distant memory. "That belonged to the countess when she was a girl. I should not like anything to damage it."

"Games are for playing, Cunningham. But I am sure the ladies will cause no lasting harm."

Cunningham's face grew pinched and then he withdrew, leaving the footman standing beside her. "I'd play any game you wanted. Just say the word and I'd find you."

Meredith blinked, realizing at the last second that, now Cunningham had gone, the footman was interested in her. She hadn't seen it. She hadn't detected any interest in her person from any servant since she'd arrived. Meredith eased back a touch and did her best to ignore his comment. Unfortunately, he followed, cutting her off from reaching Willow and Maisy where they played farther along the gallery.

"Let me pass," she said firmly.

"Not yet." His hand stretched toward her waist. Time slowed. Meredith dragged in a sharp breath and caught his hand before he made contact with her body. The fool smiled as she turned his hand so her thumb rested in his palm. When he tried to pull her into a tight embrace, she pressed her thumb hard into his hand. His nostrils flared as she increased the pressure. If he did not relent and move away, she would injure him.

"Release me now." He had to be in pain from the pressure of her thumb.

Meredith smiled sweetly at him. "Yield, or I will break your hand."

The fool had assumed that with Cunningham gone, she would not protest. She might miss intimacies with Gray, but Meredith was not a weak woman to give herself to just any man. Calista was the aberration.

He yanked his hand back immediately as he realized she made no idle boast and rubbed it. His glance told her he was furious. Meredith took a pace toward him. "Let me give you a piece of advice, sir. Gentlemen who force themselves on women, especially ones in service, are nothing better than rutting pigs. If you want one of your own, you'd better learn to listen, because if I ever hear of you forcing a woman against her will, I won't speak to His Lordship about you. I'll creep into your bedchamber one night and geld you. Do we understand each other?"

His face grew ashen. "Yes, Miss Clark."

Meredith skirted around the oaf and took the ball and cup to Willow and showed her how to do it. While her back was turned, Cunningham swept into the room and berated the footman for lingering. Meredith turned to see the effect of the butler's admonishments, but that was exactly when Willow made a wild swing and the ball connected soundly with Meredith's head.

Dazed, she fell, crashing to the ground in a sprawled heap, her head hurting like the very devil. Her eyeglasses spun away as she clutched her head, and the sharp crack of glass breaking told her they were ruined.

Cunningham ran the length of the room and knelt at her side. "Heaven help us."

She pressed her hand against the injury, hoping touch would ease the pain. As she did, she grew aware that Willow had begun to cry. Meredith stretched for the child, caught her hand and drew her close. "No harm done, my lady. No need for tears. I'll be all better in a moment."

But Willow was not calmed by her words. She wrenched free of her grip and bolted for the door. "Willow," she called. Although she called out as loud as she could stand, the girl did not return. Maisy came closer, crouched down at her feet, watching with no idea of what had happened. Meredith was relieved she was not the least bit upset. She wasn't up to cheering anyone just yet.

Cunningham caught her elbow and eased her to her feet carefully. "Are you truly unhurt?"

The room spun slowly and she grabbed Cunningham's arms desperately to keep her balance. "Oh, dear. I see a bump the size of an apple in my future. Please, can you find Willow and make sure she understands she didn't really hurt me? I don't want her to be anxious. She's come so far these past few weeks."

He improved his grip about her body. "I'll take you to her instead."

With Cunningham's help, Meredith struggled to the doorway and into the hall. She glanced up the stairs and winced as her head throbbed. Footsteps pounded in her direction and she was caught by stronger arms than Cunningham's. Warmth, security. Gray. Meredith clung to him.

"Willow said you'd been injured," he whispered.

She winced at the worry on his face. "It's not serious. An accident. Where is she?"

"I didn't mean to," the little girl sobbed. "And I broke her glasses, too."

Meredith reached blindly for the girl, relieved when her cold clammy hand clenched hers. "I must remember to pay more attention. I'll be fine, really. The glasses can easily be replaced. I just need to sit for a few moments."

"You'll rest for the remainder of the day," Gray corrected. He swept her up into his arms and began to move. "Cunningham, fetch the housekeeper at once. This bump will need a poultice."

"Don't. It's nothing really," Meredith protested feebly.

"Sweetheart, there is a large bump forming on your head. Mrs. Smith will know how to deal with it, I assure you."

Meredith's eyes grew heavy. "Don't call me that."

"Well, what should I call you instead? None of the names you've offered up suit you in the least," he grumbled and then pressed his nose to her head. "God, you smell good."

As he carried her upstairs, Grayling issued a stream of orders to every servant he encountered. Most often his command was to see what was taking the housekeeper so long. "Willow, could you open the door like a good girl? I'd like to get your governess into bed."

Meredith's eyes flew open and she stared up at Gray, noting

his smirk was back in place. "That woke you up," he whispered. "Don't tell me you don't miss being in my arms."

Meredith closed her eyes again. "Conceited."

"But I'm correct."

He eased her down gently and bundled pillows behind her head. When Grayling sat at her side, her head really began to throb in earnest. His fingers brushed her face. "Stay awake. Talk to me."

She scowled. "Terrible question to ask an injured woman. What would you like to talk about?"

A wet cloth pressed at her temple. "Cunningham appeared rather too free with your person."

Meredith pressed the heel of her hand to her head. "Oh for heaven's sake. Now is not the time to gripe about overfamiliarity between servants. He was there when the accident occurred and helped me to my feet. When the world wobbled, he supported me. If he'd not done so, would you still be complaining?"

"Damn right I would." The cloth was removed and returned colder than before. "He should have called for help before making you walk the length of the Hall."

"A dozen or so paces," Meredith murmured. "I was worried about Willow."

The bed dipped again and a small shape brushed her limbs. When Meredith peeked, Willow had climbed up on her bed, but her eyes were filled with tears again. Meredith opened her arms to the terrified girl and let her sob against her chest.

When the tears eased, Meredith rubbed her back. "It will take more than a child's toy to hurt me seriously. Why, I once escaped bandits and lived in the woods for a whole month on morning dew and green pickles. A little ball is nothing compared to that."

As hoped, Willow ceased crying and simply snuggled against her. The feeling was rather nice. Gray's children were very cuddly creatures. They were forever sitting on her lap or sneaking into her bedchamber in the morning when they woke before her. Her narrow bed got rather crowded at times.

Gray, however, wasn't in a similar mood. His eyes narrowed to slits, gaze growing hard as ice chips. "Is any part of that true?"

Meredith shivered. "You never know."

"No,' he said angrily. "I never do, and I think you enjoy

keeping me in perpetual confusion."

"You sent for me, my lord?" the housekeeper asked from the doorway.

Grayling quickly spun off the bed to make room. "A blow to the head."

The housekeeper's glance was shrewd. "Let's have a look at her."

The housekeeper had a light touch and soft voice. Meredith appreciated both. Now she had time to consider the matter, she felt rather foolish for being felled by a child's toy and by Grayling's panic. He shouldn't behave in such a way where other servants could hear. She hoped he would not take long to get command of himself again.

When Mrs. Smith drew back, she smiled kindly at her master. "No need for a poultice, but best keep her awake with chatter, my lord. I'll send Miss Cunningham up to assist."

Meredith groaned. She could never be comfortable with Miss Cunningham in her bedchamber. But she wasn't really in a position to argue. She was a servant and had to do as she was told. She closed her eyes, very ready to feign sleep to avoid looking at the girl.

"Excuse us," Grayling said and left her alone once more. Meredith watched him follow the housekeeper out with a heavy heart and then closed her eyes as the pain throbbed. For a moment, it had been lovely to be so cared for.

Willow shuffled about, the bed depressed as another bundle fell across her skirts. When she cracked her lids open, Maisy had arrived to share the vigil. She smiled at the little girl and brushed her finger over the tip of her nose. The little ball of mischief grinned and then quickly wriggled off the bed, disappearing beneath. "Maisy come out of there," she whispered softly and then regretted speaking in the first place. The thumping in her head increased. "Please."

"I'll keep an eye on her," Gray informed her as he drew a spindly chair close to the bed. Dear God, he didn't mean to have Miss Cunningham sit that close, did he? She'd never have a moment's peace.

Meredith licked her lips. "Where's Poppy?"

"Nurse is with her for now."

Meredith struggled to rise. Nurse would not be able to cope with the little one on her own.

However, Gray placed his hand on her thigh and held her still. "Rest is what the housekeeper ordered for you, my dear. Miss Cunningham will do the heavy lifting for Nurse, should it be required."

Meredith glanced toward the doorway. "So you know about your nurses difficulties?"

He gave her leg one last pat and sat back. "Of course. Why do you think I was so eager to have you here? Nurse has a lifetime of experience to offer but lacks the strength in her limbs."

Meredith digested that. "What will you do with her?"

"Exactly what I am doing now." He smiled. "Nurse has no family of her own. She will remain here where we can keep an eye on her."

"You are very kind for a lord."

"Handsome too." He checked over his shoulder. "But I'm sure you noticed my appeal the first night we met."

"Vain," Meredith murmured softly, but there was no strength to her complaint. He was good to look at and rather nice to talk to. If he were an ordinary man, she might have entertained thoughts of a future that featured him. But she couldn't. She was utterly ruined. The only future they had was an illicit one should either of them break their agreement. And her resolve on that issue was already wavering, had in fact been wavering since the first day of her employment. It was rather hard to turn away from a situation that had been so very agreeable on so many levels. This was just another challenge to face, and Meredith had to forget what had come before.

An hour later, when only Gray was still at her side and they had covered topics ranging from farming to her opinion on the perfect gemstone—type, size, and shape, including the many applications for jewelry—she scowled at him. "The servants will talk about this for months."

He glanced over the paper, from where she believed he was gaining his many and varied topics of conversation, and winked. "I'm unconcerned about my servants' possible disapproval. They've already been informed I could be found here until Mrs. Smith declared you out of danger."

Meredith snatched the paper from his hands and peered at the page he was on. "And when do you imagine that might be?"

"Oh, at least morning. Maybe late afternoon."

Grayling had turned to the section containing announcements of births, deaths, and marriages. She read a notice and her mouth dropped open. She shut it quickly and read the short notice again. It was not possible. Her brother had married her best friend from childhood. She swallowed and closed the paper quickly. "You're being ridiculous. The blow was mild."

Grayling snatched the paper back and found his place again. "To what do you compare it to? A proper beating?"

Meredith scowled again. "No one has harmed me in a very long time."

"Once was too often," he said, although it appeared he had clenched his jaw tightly.

She shrugged, determined to make light of a bad memory. "In the beginning, I had some lingering ambitions to make my mother proud, so I hesitated to enforce my will. Circumstances proved that such reservation was not in my best interests."

He leaned close and stared into her eyes. "Who are you really? Where did you come from, and why won't you tell me what happened to you?"

Poor man. He truly disliked being thwarted. "There's nothing you need to know. I am the woman you met. Nothing has changed."

He wagged his finger at her as footsteps sounded in the room beyond, coming closer. "I will convince you to trust me one day. I insist."

"Now you sound like lord of the manor. All who depend on you must obey or else suffer for disobedience."

When Gray's face darkened and he stood, Meredith knew she'd gone too far. He was angry. He'd never behaved callously to anyone she'd met.

"Excuse me for a moment," he said before storming out. He barked at Cunningham to sit with her and then there was only silence. Meredith closed her eyes as the pain in her head returned threefold. Of all the stupid things to do. Now she had to sit and listen to Miss Cunningham's opinions on ruffles and lace and such. The chair creaked but she kept her eyes closed.

After what must have been half an hour or so of near silence save for Miss Cunningham's surprisingly heavy breathing, Gray's heavy tread returned. Meredith gingerly opened her eyes and saw his jaw was still set angrily. He stopped at the foot of the bed, holding a large wooden box. "I trust you have played chess before."

"Yes."

Gray moved to place the box, really a low table similar to a breakfast tray, over her lap. The surface was checkered parquetry. A drawer had been fashioned with little handles on each side to hold the pieces.

"Good. That will give you something to do other than think ill of me. A game to while away the hours. Cunningham, I'll take dinner here at eight."

The chair creaked and Meredith was startled that it hadn't been Miss Cunningham keeping her company, but the butler. He even appeared amused. "Of course, my lord. I'll see to it personally. Enjoy the game."

Meredith couldn't be certain, but she had an idea that Cunningham was smirking. He must expect her to lose. Foolish man. When Meredith could no longer hear Cunningham, she turned on Gray. "Why did you not stay away? Do you want me to leave because the gossip is so thick that I lose everyone's respect?"

Grayling struggled out of his boots and then, to her surprise, sat cross-legged at the foot of the bed so the chessboard sat between them. "Do you know what I discovered just now?"

Meredith crossed her arms over her chest. "I cannot imagine."

"I'd much rather fight with you than anyone else." His expression turned teasing. "I'd much rather do a great many things with you than with anyone else. But sadly, this bed is too small."

He glanced at each side of the narrow bed and then around the room.

"I thought you were here because of the blow to my head."

Gray, finished with his inspection, set the carved chess pieces in place. "There is that, but there are days when a man desires a woman's company, no matter the cost."

Meredith's heart skipped a beat. She placed a hand on her stomach to steady herself. "Please remember that when I'm dismissed for misconduct. I'd like an excellent letter of recommendation for my next position."

"Oh, I doubt I'll ever dismiss you." His smile returned, but he kept his gaze on the board. "Let me ask you a question. How does the very proper, very lovely Meredith Clark feel about spending even more time with her employer? Because I have to tell you, seeing you in bed, seeing you anywhere about the hall, in fact, brings to mind that we made a very poor bargain. We are very similar creatures, you and I. We are both used to acquiring our heart's desire."

"We're nothing alike."

"Oh, I beg to differ." He offered a dazzling smile. "And I aim to convince you to give me, us, another chance." He swung a garnet bracelet before her face. The gemstones winked prettily in the afternoon light and Meredith almost reached to catch them. She held back but the cost was high. She was well aware that a man gave gems to his mistress or his wife. Never to a governess. He was cruel to tease her like this. "To what end?"

"You'll see." He tucked the trinket back into his coat pocket and then tipped his head at the board. His brows rose, mocking her chances of winning. "Let's see just how far you will go to get what you want and what else might be claimed in the process. It's your move, sweetheart."

"I'm not your sweetheart," she grumbled.

Grayling shook his head. "You see, even that name doesn't suit you. I'm definitely going to need the real one. No matter how long it takes."

Chapter Eighteen

———◆———

Snow crunched beneath thick boots as Constantine trudged across the grounds of Stanton Harold Hall in search of forgiveness. He had not enjoyed or looked forward to Christmas since the day his wife had died and he wanted this year to be different. Augusta had died today, exactly two years ago, and the cheer the season had once evoked had fled with her.

Yet this morning, Christmas Eve, had dawned clear and bright and full of hope. He glanced up at the crystal-blue sky and smiled. The world outside his windows, his domain, had beckoned him to explore during the brief lull between snowstorms to clear his conscience, to make peace with his past and prepare for the future.

A future he wanted very much, no matter the cost to his social standing.

The snow was thickly piled on the earthen path, but he knew where he was going and trudged the short distance with sure steps. He'd walked this path countless times in the past, more so in the past two years. The Lynch Gate stood open and he passed beneath the snow-covered structure, pausing momentarily to glance around the shrouded cemetery. It was as if he'd stepped into another world. A world where hopes and dreams must end.

He walked past the grave markers of his ancestors, some grand, others tilting beneath the weight of age and snow. His parents' graves were side by side and he passed them by with a momentary pang. They'd had years together, not always civil, but together, none the less, passing away within months of the other. He'd always thought he'd have the same life.

The one he wanted was farther back, a few more steps to the right.

He paused when he reached his destination and glanced down at the snow-covered plot.

Here lies Augusta Regina Hunt. Beloved wife and mother. Forever young.

Constantine stepped around the grave and brushed snow from the headstone. "The weather has cleared, my love. Just in time for Christmas."

He clutched the headstone briefly and then stepped back, pulling his greatcoat closer about him as a light wind stirred the cold air. He removed his hat. "The new governess has done what she can to mend their broken hearts, but our daughters still miss you. They always will. You should see Willow now. You always said she'd be a beauty, and I see more of you in her eyes every day. She will cause me no end of trouble with the fellows when she's grown enough to have her coming out."

Lord help him. If Willow grew to be as beautiful as her mother, then he would have to always keep his dueling pistols primed and ready once she came of age. Constantine stared at the distant snow-dusted woods. "Maisy is completely unlike her elder sister. You picked her nature to perfection when she was little. Miss Mischief. She's still hiding under tables despite the governess's best efforts to keep her on her feet. I may have to pry her out into the light when it's her time to be a debutante. I wonder what she'll make of society's strictures. I don't know how she'll survive all those rules."

He laughed as he imagined the trouble coming his way. "I always wondered how you would cope with them, but it seemed God had other plans for us both. I'm sorry, love. I never should have got another child on you. I put your life in danger. But as you pointed out, I needed an heir. I still do."

Constantine glanced down at the gravestone again. "Poppy is so beautiful. The gift you left to me fills the space in my heart I never knew existed. I've struggled with my joy and sadness so often when I hold her. You never got a chance. She's the sweetest of all our children and she needs more love than I can give. I'm not enough for her. Not enough for all of them."

He curled his hands into fists. "I've missed you so badly these past years. Do you remember how we were together? Snugly curled about each other in your bed every night, sneaking away from our guests to kiss or make love. We had a good marriage. You were the mother of my children, but you also became a good friend. No one could ever know how much your absence has cut into my soul. Marrying you was the best thing that ever happened to me. I treasured our life together."

He took a deep breath, ready to say what he'd been struggling not to admit these past weeks. "But that life is gone. I have to accept it and move on."

Across the way, a few adventurous souls were trudging their way through the snow-covered fields, people who relied on him for the livelihood of this generation and the ones to follow. He owed it to them and to himself to safeguard the legacy of the Grayling estates. But that was not the whole reason for this visit today. He still had another confession to make.

"I've met someone, Augusta. Someone I'd very much like to spend every part of the day and night with." He shook his head. "She's not at all like you, but I think you would like her. In all honestly, I don't know who she is or what her connections might be. She could be a flower seller's daughter for all I know, but I very much doubt such a creature could intrigue me as she does."

Constantine rubbed his jaw. "She's wounded, I think. She keeps secrets but reveals so much by the hundred kindnesses she shows others. She's strong and independent. If I can convince her to stay, she'll be a good influence on our daughters. She's done so much to keep your memory alive already and I can see how Willow has responded to her. She's talking again, laughing as she plays. The woman would never take your place in their hearts, but they need her. And so do I."

"Can you forgive me, Augusta? For falling in love again? I didn't mean to. Never intended to give my heart to another soul, but she snuck beneath my defenses and burrowed into my life before I realized I liked her there. What started out as lust has grown into something so strong that I cannot deny my feelings. I haven't told her that I'd like to marry her. One day, when she trusts me enough to share her true identity I will see what she has to say to that. She makes me happy, Augusta. Just as you did. But it's different. Does that make sense?"

He faced the distant house, the manor where he was born, had loved and been loved in. The sight of it was no longer so bleak and cheerless, even with the absence of Augusta. Meredith was inside, the blinding presence that had turned his world upside down and brightened every dark corner. His heart beat for her. "I will never forget what we had. Please forgive me. Can you?"

He faced the gravestone again and memorized the lines carved into the cold stone. He would never allow Augusta to be forgotten. He bowed his head, praying he was making the right decision for them all. That he wasn't rushing the situation. He would convince Calista, Meredith, or whoever she might be to be his wife one day, no matter how long it took her see the sense of it. He would take care of her without smothering her independence. He would make her laugh, and even convince Cunningham to accept that her place was here.

An icy blast blew his hat from his hands and he glanced around him. A light snow fell from the bright clear sky, growing thicker by the moment. The snowflakes swirled around the gravestones and him and then died as swiftly as they had come. The day brightened again, warming him with hope and a sense of purpose. Augusta had always enjoyed Christmas and this year he would too. She would want him to be happy. Constantine collected his hat from where it had fallen to rest against Augusta's headstone and set it on his head. He brushed his fingers over the cold stone one last time. "Farewell, my love. I will never forget you."

He strode back to the Hall, eagerness almost making him rush. He and Meredith needed to talk about the past and the future, but first, he had something vital to do. Today was the birth of a new life. One filled with the wild passion of one tempting wench—a near stranger without a name.

The return trip to the manor proved much faster and happier for him. He stepped onto the rear terrace to find Cunningham lying in wait for him just inside the doors. As soon as he was inside, he shrugged out of his greatcoat and hat. "Cunningham, would you by any chance know the location of Miss Clark?"

"She's in the nursery with the children, my lord."

"Hmm, very good." He'd forgotten the time. Poppy and Maisy often rested at this time of day and Willow, too, occasionally would lay down for a quarter hour or more. He probably shouldn't go up and interfere with Miss Clark's routine. She might become testy and that would ruin the evening he had planned. Now that he had decided on a course of action, he wanted no setbacks.

Cunningham raised a brow. "Should I have her fetched, my lord?"

Constantine could imagine how little Miss Clark would appreciate such a summons. She'd been in an odd mood since Willow had smacked that ball into her head. Sitting with her for so many hours had stirred up talk among the servants. His actions, although perfectly restrained and chaste, had set her apart from them.

Aside from her injury, he'd never enjoyed a day more. Yet Miss Clark had grown suspicious when he lingered in the nursery for any length of time. She much preferred to meet him on her terms, but that would change tonight. He grinned. "I think not, but could you send Mrs. Smith to my wife's bedchamber and join us there? There is much to do."

Cunningham frowned but was quick to arrive upstairs with the housekeeper in tow. Mrs. Smith smiled hesitantly. "You sent for me, my lord."

"Yes, I'd like you to pack."

Her face filled with confusion. "Wouldn't your valet be better suited for the task?"

Constantine glanced around the bedchamber. "I would appreciate your help to pack the contents of this room. I don't want anything thrown out or passed on to the other servants. I hope there will be no hard feelings among the staff about that, but I want everything left for my daughters for when they are old enough to choose."

Mrs. Smith took a moment to wipe a tear from her eye and then nodded. "That is a reasonable decision, my lord."

Cunningham, however, looked anything but happy. He'd been devoted to his late wife and had taken her death harder than any other member of staff. Loyalty to the family was important, but the family had to continue. Constantine had the perfect explanation that would make his butler bury his reservations. "I am in need of an heir, Cunningham, and I cannot contemplate another marriage without attending to this room first."

The struggle was clear on Cunningham's face, but eventually he nodded. "Very well, my lord."

"Thank you, Cunningham. I trust I can depend on you to make any transition as smooth as possible."

The servants both blinked at him. But it was Mrs. Smith who asked the question. "Did you already have a lady in mind, my lord?"

"Actually, I do. She just doesn't know it yet."

Chapter Nineteen

---◆---

Meredith tucked the covers tightly about Poppy and brushed the soft curls back from her forehead. The little girl grumbled a bit but then stilled as sleep pulled her into its grip. Meredith watched her for a space of time and then drew back. She'd grown to love the little imp. "Happy birthday, sweetheart," she whispered softly.

Today had been rather draining. The anniversary of the last Lady Grayling's death had begun with long faces and ended just as quietly. There had been no festivities for the holiday, none at all to mark Poppy's second birthday. Meredith had not wanted to let the occasion pass without marking it somehow. She had carried Poppy away to a quiet room and given her something she'd made with her own hands, a small cloth doll with lopsided braids and button eyes. Poppy hadn't let it go for one moment since it had fallen into her hands.

Meredith straightened and surveyed the nursery. The room was now an overflowing haven of entertainments and daily laughter. Nurse still came to sit with them each day and tell stories of their mother, yet Meredith was sure the woman loved them in her own way. She always had a kind word or soft touch to offer them. After weeks of soft rebukes and dismissals, Miss Cunningham had finally learned that she could not romp into the nursery at will simply because she was the butler's niece.

Everything had turned out how Meredith hoped. And that was the whole problem.

She had made sure the girls were happiest here, yet she herself wasn't entirely so. Meredith loved nothing more than to be woken by the sleep-tousled girls and did not even mind their cold feet in her bed. She loved them all, truth to tell, even if she found Maisy's habit of hiding beneath tables, chairs, and beds somewhat exasperating.

She turned to where Maisy should be, in the bed she shared with her sister, rather relieved that the little scamp was actually still in her bed and hadn't disappeared beneath it tonight. Timid eyes stared up at her and she tweaked the girl's nose, earning a giggle and contented sigh for her efforts. Maisy closed her eyes and hugged her pillow tightly. Meredith pulled the curtains closed around her side of the bed and walked around to the other side quietly.

Gray's eldest was still sitting up in bed, wrapping her dolly in a baby blanket so she'd stay warm for the night. Meredith sat beside the girl and brushed her hair behind her ear. "Time for bed, sweetheart."

Candid green eyes met hers. "Can we have sweet cakes again tomorrow?"

The girl had a remarkable appetite for sweets. Another reason Meredith was so fond of her. "Of course, but I should think the Christmas Day feasts would have many more treats in store for you than just sweet cakes. Lie down now so you'll be as warm as dolly."

Willow wriggled beneath her blankets, her eyes growing round. "Will you be at the feast tomorrow?"

"Of course. All the servants will be, but there is nowhere else I want to be more than with you and your sisters."

That seemed to appease her. Meredith straightened her braids on the pillow. Occasionally, Willow asked if Meredith would be there when she woke up and she guessed the girl was occasionally beset by memories of her mother's sudden death. Poor child. Meredith tucked her in snugly, brushed a kiss across her brow, and remained on the edge of the bed. Her heart, however, had clenched with anxiety.

They needed her. They needed her to stay, and she didn't like to consider what harm her eventual departure might cause. She'd never meant to become so attached to Gray's girls, but their sadness had touched a part of herself she'd thought long buried. She missed having a family and this time with Gray was as close as she'd ever come to that perfect situation.

If only perfection were possible.

When Willow's breathing evened out and Maisy stilled, she pulled the bed curtains tight to keep out the drafts and considered what she was going to do when the time came to leave. It had been almost two month since she'd come to Stanton Harold Hall for a temporary stay. And even longer since she'd lain sated in Gray's arms. She missed his warmth more and more each day. And Gray had made the yearning hard to ignore by constantly being underfoot.

According to nurse, he'd never spent so much time in the nursery. The children had thrived with his constant presence. Yet there were times when even she forgot he was her employer.

As if summoned by her thoughts, Grayling appeared at the door. "Am I too late?"

Meredith couldn't fight the smile that spread over her face. "I'm sorry, but I believe you are out of luck."

Gray squeezed her shoulder as he snuck past and she noticed he walked softly. She glanced down and saw he'd removed his footwear and was padding through the Hall barefoot. The sight of his bare skin, close on the heels of her wayward thoughts, made her breath catch in her throat. She hadn't seen him improperly dressed since she'd come here. The memory of his taut flesh brushing against her own had her pulse skipping a beat.

He threw cheeky grins in her direction as he went from daughter to daughter. The girls didn't make a sound, so she assumed they had fallen deeply asleep very quickly. A pity. They did enjoy his nighttime visits and it had been an up-and-down day for them. The servants' long faces they likely didn't understand, and the mood in the Hall was palpable with grief.

When Grayling had trudged out into the snow to visit his wife's grave, every servant had pressed their nose to the glass to watch him go.

Meredith moved to the lamp and as Gray approached, she extinguished it, plunging them and the room into darkness. After a moment, her eyes adjusted and she made her way to the door. Grayling could find his own way out.

Yet when his fingers tangled with hers, Meredith did not pull away immediately. His grip firmed as he tugged her closer, and together they moved into the playroom. He pulled the bedroom door closed, and when Meredith attempted to withdraw her hand from his, although she wanted nothing more than to keep his warmth for herself, he held on. "I'd like a private word if I may?"

"Of course, my lord. Is it about tomorrow?"

He shook his head. "Tomorrow, and the day after, and the day after that."

Meredith frowned. "I'm not sure I understand you."

He glanced around. "This isn't private enough for our conversation. Come with me. Please."

———◆———

Gray tightened his grip on his future and hurried her down the hall. He didn't want them seen. He didn't want her embarrassed, but he was taking her to his bedchamber where she could be warm and all his for a few hours. She could speak her mind without fear of being overheard. When he reached his bedchamber door, he saw indecision in her eyes. But when he held it open there was only a moment of hesitation before she glided in ahead of him.

She stopped when she saw the room. He'd already stoked the fire so it burned hot. He'd lit candles everywhere so there were no shadows to hide within. It was important to him that there were no misunderstandings between them tonight or any night. It was time to lay his cards on the table and see what his chances were. He locked the door behind them and drew her to the fire.

Meredith's whiskey-colored eyes glowed as she looked up at him, firelight reflected in their depths. "Hardly proper," she admonished.

"You've had over a month of proper. Do you want to continue with that nonsense?" He brushed his fingers against her nape, brushing the short-cropped hair aside gently. He didn't mind it so much anymore. The unique look suited her character very much. Prim or not, she tempted him a thousand times a day. Keeping his passions hidden had been a strain, but he hoped after tonight he wouldn't need to anymore.

"No," she whispered.

With that one word, she flung herself into his arms, burrowing against his chest as if she craved him. Constantine held her close, caressing her and remembering he'd wanted her from the moment they'd met. Had he fallen for her from that very first glimpse? He thought it might have been the case.

Meredith rose up on her toes, her mouth seeking his. Happy to oblige, Constantine kissed her as he'd wanted to all these weeks. Everything he'd wanted was still there. Meredith tasted the same as Calista. Her passions were just as alluring. The trick would be getting her to agree to a permanent arrangement between them.

He eased away slowly, reluctant but sure. Talking first, pleasure later. "I was hoping you'd missed me," he told her. "Missed kissing and touching like this."

She fiddled with his cravat. "Grayling, has anyone ever told you that there are times when actions speak louder than words? You could have had me any number of times, but you didn't. What stopped you speaking up before tonight?"

"Our bargain." He pressed a kiss to her hair. "I told you I would honor it and leave you in peace. I thought I could be satisfied to see you and not touch."

Her brow rose. "Difficult?"

"As you would not believe. Or maybe you would, as you're here in my bedchamber now."

She stroked his chest and then peered at him from beneath her lashes. "It has proven rather arduous to be virtuous. Perhaps harder than anything I've ever done."

"Then we are in agreement. We belong together."

Meredith eased back. "I never said that. What I did say was that attraction does not go away simply because one wills it. I don't belong to you."

"But I belong to you," he said quietly. "Quite frankly, I think you ruined me for anyone else."

"Don't say that. You don't know me."

"I know enough. For now."

She broke away. "You only know what I've told you."

Constantine watched her steadily. "Have you lied to me about more than your name?"

He saw her throat move as she swallowed. "No. But I've withheld the truth."

"Why can you not trust me? I would never harm you. I would take care of you if I could."

"I've always taken care of myself. Living on my own terms has served me well."

Unable to remain apart, Constantine crossed the room to stand before her. Her jaw was set defiantly, her eyes narrowed. He slipped his finger beneath her chin and lifted her face to his. "I don't want to change you. You've no idea how much I admire you, wretched lies and all." He smiled when he said the last. Her lack of name was the least of his concerns. "But I would like to take care of you. To keep you with me always so I know how you fare."

"I thought you brought me here for your daughters."

"And I did." He caressed her cheek. "They have blossomed in your care."

She squinted up at him. "Why do you want me around? I'll bring nothing but trouble."

"On the contrary, you bring excitement, and passion, and uncertainty, and contentment. You are a thousand contradictions all at once. No day is ever the same."

She swallowed again. The pause unnerved him, but then her hands rose to her neckline and she unbuttoned the front of her gown, revealing the top of her unmentionables beneath. "Is this the excitement you crave?"

"Yes, and more."

When the gown was loose enough, she peeled off the bodice and slid the material over her hips. She toyed with the string of her corset while observing him. "What about this, Gray? Is it in the way?"

"Constantine," he corrected. "Use my name, and yes you damn well know I prefer you naked."

A teasing smile flittered across her face. "So impatient."

"You're a fine one to talk. I wanted a conversation before we ended up in bed together."

She smiled again as the corset fell. "Talk is overrated, Constantine. Are you going to simply stand there and deprive me of my view? I haven't seen a naked man in two months. If you're not careful I'll go in search of someone else."

Her taunt was made to infuriate him, but Constantine didn't care, he hauled her against his chest and lifted her from the floor. "Do it and he's a dead man. You're mine, whether you like it or not. The sooner you become accustomed to the feeling, the better it will go. Or would you rather I found another woman to make love to? I could bring her home to the Hall and make love to her right in front of you while you're supposed to be tending the children."

Her legs locked tight around his waist. "Don't you dare."

He waited, hoping to hear her utter the words that *he* belonged to her as well, but she wouldn't. However, she did wrap her arms around his neck and tangle her fingers in his hair rather possessively.

Constantine skimmed his lips across hers softly. "I'm yours. I've always been yours."

A soft smile played around her mouth and she leaned close. He waited for her to kiss him, but her lips stopped a whisper from his. Her breath danced across his skin and then her tongue darted out to lick his upper lip. He withheld a groan as she did it again, the effect on his body immediate. When she brushed her lips softly against his, he closed his eyes and let her have her way.

Meredith teased him with her tongue and her kisses burned his skin. She slithered down to her feet, got her hands beneath his waistcoat, and unfastened his trousers. Constantine opened his eyes. Celibacy had clearly not agreed with Meredith any more than it had with him. He removed his waistcoat and shirt and shoved his trousers down to his ankles. "Is this what you want?"

She offered a saucy wink and fell back onto the bed, kicking her slim legs up into the air, teasing him with a glimpse of heaven. Constantine pushed his trousers away and covered her with his body, letting the weight of his erection lay against her skin.

Her breath hissed from her lips. "I missed you."

Constantine's heart began to pound. "And I've missed you. My best fantasies cannot compare with having you in my bed."

She smiled and rubbed her lithe body against him, ran her hands over his flanks, and then looped her arms about his neck.

She met his gaze. Her whiskey-brown eyes were alight with desire. "Where is it?"

Constantine frowned, not understanding her question. "I'm sorry?"

"Your little velvet pouch. Hurry, Constantine. I need you inside me."

Lust battled with his conscience. If he did not use it and got a child on her, he would worry. But he wanted her in his life, to be his wife, to bear his sons. But he was utterly afraid she would run if he told her that so soon. He drew back and cupped her cheek.

"What's wrong? Have you misplaced it?"

"No. I'm just not sure I should use it." He pressed his head to hers. "Damn, you decide."

Her fingers played over a spot on his upper arm. "If you fear I'm diseased, then you should wear it. Many gentlemen prefer it with women in my profession."

Constantine's stomach lurched. He caught her face between his hands. She hadn't understood. "That's not why I wear it," he whispered.

Her brow creased. "Then why?"

What had he done? Had he made her feel cheap and dirty? He kissed her passionately and blurted out, "Rothwell claims they can prevent a woman from conceiving a child. That's the only reason I have one. I didn't want to ruin another woman's life."

Her eyes widened and then she hugged him tightly. "I told you I was quite capable of looking after myself. Especially in those matters. Do you see that I don't have any children of my own?"

Constantine felt a little foolish. He buried his face in her neck and inhaled.

Meredith held his head in place. "I knew what to do even before my fall. My mother was a very practical-minded woman. There was no chance I would conceive unless I wanted to."

If he'd known, considered the matter properly, he might never have tortured himself and denied them both greater pleasures. Before he reconsidered, Constantine positioned himself and entered her in a single, slow thrust. The difference took his breath away and Meredith's too, for her nails dug into his back and she moaned. He began to move, slowly at first and then with gathering force. He levered up onto his arms to watch the play of emotions on her face.

God, she was beautiful, and wicked. He groaned as she tweaked his nipple. "Don't do that, sweetheart," he complained.

The minx battered her eyelashes at him. "But Constantine, you said you were mine, so that means I can do anything I like with you."

He grinned. "Are you claiming me, then?"

"Oh yes." She ran her hands over his chest possessively. "There's so much more we can do together if we cease being proper."

Constantine lowered himself, keeping his weight on his forearms as Meredith undulated beneath him.

"Don't stop," she warned. "I've only a few hours before the children might need me back in the nursery and I want you at least several times more."

"I may be incapable of letting you go." He kissed her again. "Have been since the day we met."

He rolled onto his back, taking Meredith with him so she was on top. She shifted position till she was comfortable and then smiled down gleefully. "Now you cannot say no to me."

"Believe me sweetheart, I've no intention of ever doing that."

Chapter Twenty

Christmas Day left no time for contemplation of the events of last night. Meredith might have been a fool to lapse back into old habits, but being alone with Constantine had proved too great a temptation. The things that man could do with his mouth and his hands were beyond description. She'd succumbed to his warmth without a second thought. Only now was she wondering how great a mistake she'd made.

The other things he wanted from her were not so easy to give or agree to. She coveted nothing and offered nothing but her passion. Wouldn't that be enough? Couldn't that endless well of desire satisfy his hungers if she could meet with him from time to time? But Constantine wanted more. A great deal more than she could give. He was clear that he wanted her in his bed every night, but that would lead to problems. The other servants were already suspicious. Her time here was limited.

Meredith circled the room restlessly. Not bored, but not knowing where to stand. The children were playing with their new dolls and did not require her attention for the moment. She was free to drink punch and eat minced tarts and mingle with the other servants. Yet the other servants had grown distant in the weeks since she had injured her head while playing with Willow. Conversations had come to an abrupt halt when she entered the servants' hall more times than she could count. On most days, the excuse of the children needing her provided the perfect alibi to stay away from everyone. Only Mrs. Smith, Nurse, and Cunningham seemed inclined to draw her out for conversation. If they discovered she'd spent half the night in Constantine's bedchamber, she would be further ostracized and left out.

The housekeeper smiled invitingly when their eyes met and Meredith forced herself to join them. Mrs. Smith leaned close to whisper, "So, how long do you think before he goes for the marriage mart?"

Meredith blinked. "Excuse me?"

Mrs. Smith looked about them. "His Lordship's cleared out his lady's old bedchamber yesterday. I expect he'll go up to London for the coming season for a wife."

Meredith forced her hands not to clench. "Is that so? I never heard mention of it till now."

"Hmm, not surprising being as you are so diligent with your duties to the wee poppets. Just yesterday His Lordship sent for Cunningham and myself and requested we store his late wife's possessions away till the girls have grown old enough to choose their favorites. I hope His Lordship picks someone worthy of him. He's much too handsome to be alone so young."

Meredith's pulse raced. She studied Constantine. He'd never said a word about making such a drastic change to his life. Or had he tried last night and Meredith had misunderstood his intent? She'd thought his mention of bringing a wife home to Stanton Harold Hall was to tease her into revealing how much she wouldn't like that. Why resume their affair if he planned to take a wife soon? Although her mouth tasted of ashes, she forced herself to speak. "I imagine he would choose wisely."

"Oh, the debate that went into his choice of his first wife, you would not believe. I remember his mama worrying that he'd never choose a woman on his own. With her gone, he'll have to make the decisions himself, or maybe Lady Farnsworth would steer him in the right direction. I wonder if he'll marry for love this time instead of for duty? He told us yesterday he needs a son, but he married for duty last time and didn't get one."

A lump formed in her throat. His reliance on the condom to avoid getting her with child sprang to mind. Of course he wouldn't want a bastard to spoil his plans for the future. He must have been relieved that she could take care of any indiscretion herself. "I thought," she swallowed. "I thought His Lordship loved his wife."

Mrs. Smith patted her hand. "Oh, he did love her, but as is often the case, not at first. Arranged marriages are rarely a love match, but I'm sentimental. I like the idea of two people meeting and marrying despite their connections and fortune. As long as their heart is in the right place, I'd not care one whit for their background. It's not that he needs the funds a dowry would bring. All he needs is someone young enough to bear him a son, and maybe a spare into the bargain." Mrs. Smith bit into her minced tart and moaned. "Cook really has outdone herself this year."

Meredith's stomach tumbled over and over. She and Mrs. Smith held the same idea of the reasons to marry, except Meredith had never imagined those reasons ever applied to herself. The most she had considered was the idea of being Constantine's mistress. "That she has. Would you excuse me?" Meredith thought she might be sick.

If Constantine intended to marry, then why hadn't he said so? If she'd known, she'd never have spent last night in his arms because now she had lapsed once she feared she'd never be able to stop. Could she bear to look on as his properly connected wife brought his heir and a spare into the world? She'd have to leave. She couldn't face that prospect. Yet it would break her heart to leave him and his daughters.

The time spent in Constantine's arms had filled a void, and throughout the day she'd been anticipating his being inappropriate with her person many times. Except he hadn't come close again. He'd been near but kept a respectable distance. There were servants about in almost every room. She'd not caught a moment alone with him since she'd left his bed. Had he only wanted her closer at night when he could touch her intimately? Had he only wanted someone to fill the void until he could survey the latest crop of debutantes this season?

But that wasn't good enough for Meredith anymore. She wanted more of his touch to go along with his laughter. She wanted what they had during the day as well as the contentment of last night. She was tired of being second best. She wanted...

Willow tugged her sleeve. "Are they going to play?"

Several servants had converged in one corner, their hands

holding instruments, including fiddles and lutes. Despite the rare treat, Meredith's mood did not improve. She would not leave Willow, Maisy, and Poppy to be neglected by Grayling's next wife when a son came along. "It appears so."

Willow clapped her hands together and then tugged Meredith until they had a clear view of the musicians. When they sat on a lounge placed close to the fire, Maisy rushed over to climb into her lap. Meredith cuddled the girl fiercely. She would never allow anyone to neglect them again. They were too important to her to see them hurt.

Across the room, Poppy noticed her sisters had gone and began to cry. Before Meredith could fetch her, Constantine scooped his weeping daughter into his arms and they took up the remaining two places on the lounge. Meredith glanced sideways and he grinned at her. Blasted man. How dare he look so happy when he planned to get married?

His grin faded. "Is something wrong?"

"Everything." The rate he was going, grinning at her like that, the servants would guess there was so much more between them. Once the new wife came and the gossips shared their suspicions, she'd be sent away from the girls.

She kept her eyes steadily forward on the players and fought her temper back into submission. She almost had it under control until Poppy stood on the lounge and latched on to her hair with her little fists. She winced and jerked back. "Don't do that."

Constantine shuffled closer and carefully loosened Poppy's grip. "I swear she only hurts the ones she loves." He sat the child on his lap and clapped Poppy's hands in time with the music when it began. "You wouldn't happen to play the pianoforte, would you?" he asked, leaning against her shoulder.

Meredith stiffened her spine. She had dispensed with most of the arts necessary for a lady of good breeding. "Not for a long time. I'm sure I'm out of practice."

Constantine grinned. "Then you should practice. There is a pianoforte in the drawing room. I'll ask Cunningham to have it tuned soon."

"No, thank you. I'm sure I'll be too busy."

He bounced his daughter on his knee in time with the music. "Did you play for many years before you became out of practice?"

Meredith slanted her gaze in Constantine's direction. Why bother getting to know her if he planned to marry someone else? "Fishing again?"

"I like fishing," he told her. "It requires patience and trickery."

If he would just go away, she'd have a hope of controlling her temper. But the man was blind. Every time he looked at her, he smiled. How could he when she was so angry with him? Did he think he had the right to toy with her affections like this? "I played poorly till I was sixteen."

"What happened after sixteen?"

"I never played again." Meredith rested her cheek on Maisy's head and listened to the rest of the tune in fuming silence. When the next one called for dancing, she immediately declined Constantine's invitation to dance with him. He studied her a while before he passed Poppy to Miss Cunningham to entertain and then requested a dance with the housekeeper, then Cook, before he finally collected Willow for a dance.

Meredith watched the laughing pair as Constantine struggled to juggle his smaller dance partner while holding on to his dignity. It appeared to be quite a stretch and in the end he lifted his daughter into his arms and waltzed her about the room.

That seemed the sign for the remaining servants to partner together. Sets were formed as the tune changed. Mrs. Smith and Cunningham made a regal pair while the younger ones moved a little awkwardly. Willow pulled Maisy away to dance together, turning in circles without any real idea of what they were doing. They were beautiful. The lost, sad children she had first met had fled.

When another dance concluded, Constantine approached. "May I have the pleasure of this dance, Miss Clark?"

How could any woman deny such a gallant invitation? Even when she was in a temper and there were servants all around. Meredith reluctantly placed her hand in his. "Of course, my lord."

He called out to the players. "A waltz, if you please."

The other servants drew back to give them space and to stare. Meredith was not sure she wanted to be center of attention, but Constantine did not give her a choice or a chance to back out. He pulled her into his arms and smiled. "What didn't I do?"

"I've no idea what you mean," Meredith muttered as the music started. When the dance ended, she intended to leave the party.

From the first step, Meredith knew she was in the hands of an accomplished dancer. His sure grip and measured tread proved him a master at the art. She succumbed to instinct, remembering the discipline a former dancing master had drummed into her head with such condescension. A lady must follow a man's lead. How those words had made her angry when she was young. At least in Constantine arms, there was no danger of having her toes mashed as her brother had used to do. Constantine was born for the best life had to offer, which made Meredith even more bad tempered.

A chill raced over her and she quickly brought her mind back to the here and now. It was best to never think on what she'd run away from. Regrets were for the foolish and weak.

Constantine spun her to the sidelines and stopped in front of the fire before the tune ended. The room broke out in applause. She glanced around with an embarrassed smile and was relieved when another set formed and the dancing resumed.

Constantine's hand fluttered over her back. "Cold again, or was that an unpleasant memory?"

Meredith increased the space between them and regarded him warily. "Whyever would you think such a thing, my lord?"

A frown tugged at his lips and he glanced around them. No one was near enough to hear. "Your mood has changed considerably as the day has worn on. I much preferred the way you looked when you snuck from my bed this morning. I hope you found no fault with my dancing."

"None, my lord." Meredith drew a deep breath. "You dance so well I forgot I was out of practice. I merely remembered that my toes were once squashed by a terrible dance partner."

"A former suitor?"

"No." She smiled sadly. "A brother."

His brows rose at her admission. On a normal day Meredith did not like to think of the past. She'd not lose any more peace than she had previously with thinking of them. It was only at Christmastime that she couldn't bury her memories completely. At Christmas she missed her family so much she ached, but finding out Constantine planned to marry had added far more pain to the season.

Instead of pressing for more information, Constantine smiled and gestured across the room. "Well, I for one am pleased to spare your feet from mischance. You dance very well. Would you like to sit again?"

For the number of hours Meredith had spent in lessons when she'd rather have run free, it was not surprising that some part of her former life had remained. "Thank you."

That twinkling light returned to his eyes. As they made their way back to the couch, he took Poppy from Miss Cunningham and set her between them. "Now, while we are alone, I wanted to tell you we're leaving the Hall for a short holiday after the new year begins."

A ripple of anger filled her. Her breath grew difficult to catch. "Oh?"

Constantine's eyes softened. "Nothing too arduous. But we will need to pack for a weeklong sojourn, maybe two. I'll leave my daughter's preparations in your capable hands, if I may. Be sure to pack warmly."

Meredith swallowed. She wasn't prepared to lose him so soon. Not yet. She needed more time. "You're going to take them in the middle of winter?"

Constantine looked out over the gathering, a regretful expression on his face. "While this is pleasant, I've put off visiting my family for some time and I'm regretting that today. It has been a long time since I've seen them, and I'd like to begin the new year with a visit. There have been many changes in their lives that I've missed by being wrapped up in my own affairs."

The relief that coursed through her was immediate. She took a moment to get her thoughts in order. She didn't want him to know how happy the news made her. "You were grieving."

"So were they. But I intend to mend the breach, do the pretty, and accept responsibility for my mistakes. I want you there with me. The girls would not like to leave you behind. Please say you'll come with us."

Meredith glanced about to make sure they were not being watched. She was very sure they could not be overheard, so she did not have to moderate her voice. "I'm a servant, my lord. Of course I would travel with the children."

"You are much more to us than that. I'd prefer you to come of your own free will. Perhaps I was not clear last night about my intentions."

"Your intentions?"

He eased back in the chair, looking to everyone else a man completely at ease. Meredith knew better. "I don't dabble with my servants."

"So what does that make me?"

"A woman I want to know in every way imaginable. A woman I want to wake up beside no matter how long it takes her to accept that." He glanced at her briefly, his smile warm, his expressive eyes lust filled. "You know me. You know my nature and temperament. I want you, but I don't want to force you to anything. I admire you. From what I've learned from the tidbits you've let slip, you have survived whatever it was that befell you with remarkable courage. I would like to make you forget that if I can."

Meredith stared across the room without really seeing it. "There is no escaping the past."

"Forgive me if I disagree. I was once a married man. I loved my wife, but she is gone and I have put her memory where it belongs. Behind me. Life is for the living and I want to live it boldly. With you."

If Meredith hadn't been sitting, she would have fallen. "Are you proposing to marry me? You cannot be serious."

His glance grew sly. "I never said a word about marriage, but I could be tempted if the right woman, with an honest name, presented herself for consideration. Now, if you will excuse me, I must hand out gifts. Think on it, Meredith. There is nothing I wouldn't face with a woman who placed her trust in me absolutely. And remember, pack your warmest gowns."

"Wait." Meredith grasped at the most immediate concern. "Where exactly are we going?"

"That I cannot tell you. It's a secret." His smile was serene. "I hope you like surprises."

Chapter Twenty-One

———•◆•———

Constantine strode through the Hall and rushed up the stairs, impatient for them to be on their way. The New Year had come and gone and the weather had finally cleared enough to make travel possible. He'd woken alone again and was rather put out. He'd wanted to begin today with a kiss or maybe even a little more than that. The gleaming black traveling carriage was almost ready to spirit them away. All he needed was Meredith's presence and his children's cooperation to make the journey pleasant.

Meredith had not been quite so easily led away from the children these last few evenings as she had been at Christmas. Since the feast, her mood had swung from happiness to wary watchfulness. He'd had to work hard to convince her that his daughters would be fine if they woke to find her absent. He couldn't go every night without having the woman in his arms.

He eased the door to the nursery open, catching Meredith and Poppy cuddling beside her cot. The sweet bond that had formed pleased him. He'd wanted Meredith to love her future stepdaughters as much as she would their children. "Happy New Year."

Willow ran to him, bouncing on her toes. "Please, Papa. Where are we going?"

"Not yet, my sweet." He kissed the top of her head. "You know I like to surprise you."

She set her hands to her hips. "Can you not whisper?"

He leaned down close to her and grinned. "No, because Miss Clark has devilishly good hearing and I want her to be surprised, too."

He'd told no one of his destination just to be sure it remained a mystery. The only one who might guess was his coachman. He alone knew how far the beasts pulling the carriage would have to travel.

"Oh," Willow said and nodded. She looked past him to Meredith. "Papa's surprises are the best, but he never likes to tell."

Meredith snorted as if she did not believe a word of it.

Constantine saw Willow's warmest coat laid out on the bed and helped her into it. "Where's your scarf and gloves, sweetheart?"

Willow gestured under the bed. "Maisy keeps sneaking them. Tell her to stop, Papa. She'll make them dirty."

When Constantine glanced under the bed Willow shared with her sister, he found Maisy lying with her head pillowed on the scarf and gloves. "Come out, little one," he whispered. "Time to go. You don't want to be left behind without Miss Clark to tuck you in at night, do you?"

Her little mouth fell open as if that thought had never occurred to her. Maisy scurried from her hiding place and threw the scarf and gloves at her sister. Meredith sent him a look that said thank you and hurried to dress the wriggling child in her warmest and best clothes while he finished with Willow.

When Meredith was done, Constantine scooped up Poppy, and since Maisy was dressed, he caught his middle child's hands. "I'll deliver these two downstairs. Do you have everything you need?"

Meredith's expression turned glacial. "Given I've no idea what to pack for, I suppose I must be ready."

"Patience," he said with a laugh. "You'll learn to like my surprises."

He hurried out, more pleased with himself than he had been in years. He could not wait to see how Meredith took to his sisters. He was sure, given her love of his daughters, that they could find common ground with which to build a friendship.

He delivered Maisy into a footman's hands at the main door.

"Make sure she's tucked under a warm blanket and stays there."

Maisy was hurried out. She always liked to be first into the carriage.

"Excuse me, my lord," Cunningham said as Constantine returned inside from the carriage to wait on Meredith and Willow. "But might I have a moment of your time before you depart? There is an urgent matter I wish to bring to your attention."

Mrs. Smith stepped close to take Poppy from his arms, and the disapproving expression she cast at Cunningham told Constantine she knew all about the matter. He groaned, wishing that any unpleasantness might wait till he returned. Reluctantly, he waved an arm toward the drawing room, ushering the man before him so he might say his piece. "What seems to be the problem?"

Cunningham appeared to have swallowed a raw fish. "It has come to my attention that a person in your employ has been sneaking from their bed at night."

He almost groaned aloud but held it in. Cunningham was the biggest prude. Constantine cared little for becoming involved in affairs between servants. "Are you certain?"

"Yes, my lord. I'm afraid I am, and the timing couldn't be worse." His mouth pinched as if he'd tasted something tart. "It's Miss Clark, my lord," Cunningham confessed at last. "She has abandoned her post for the past two nights and I've not been able to determine with whom she might be meeting or where she has gone. A woman like that..." Cunningham left the rest unsaid.

Constantine pinched the bridge of his nose. He had hoped Meredith's absence from the nursery might have gone unnoticed, but it seemed that she was right and he was wrong about being found out. He might have to set the record straight, at least as far as Cunningham went, before Meredith lost the staff's good opinion. "Miss Clark did not abandon her post. If the children were sound asleep, then they needed nothing from her."

Cunningham frowned. "Nevertheless, her place is with the children."

"Her place is where I say it is." He drew in a deep breath. "With the children, and with me. Miss Clark will be allowed considerable latitude for the foreseeable future, Cunningham.

The reasons will become apparent in good time."

"I…" Cunningham's frown turned into shock.

"Try not to worry. When we return, I hope to have good news. Do you have any further questions about the matter?"

Cunningham's skin turned pasty white. "No, my lord."

"Excellent." Constantine left the butler grappling with the idea and returned to the main door just in time to intercept his governess and eldest daughter.

"Mama never liked Papa's surprises very much," Willow told Meredith as she skipped to the door and into the waiting care of a footman who urged her to walk down the stairs instead of skipping and helped her into the carriage.

Meredith took Poppy back from the housekeeper. "Now then, Miss Poppy, shall we humor your father and join your sisters?"

"I'll take her," Constantine told her. Yet Poppy was none too happy to lose her grip on her governess and grumbled, straining toward Meredith. Constantine understood her feeling exactly. He felt the same way every time Meredith left his side.

He gestured to the door. "Come along, Miss Clark, we've many miles to travel today."

Her eyes rolled as she passed him. Constantine laughed, catching the startled expression on Cunningham's face as he walked to the door. He hoped by the time they returned, Meredith would have agreed with his hopes for the future and Cunningham might have reconciled himself to his new mistress's identity. In fact, if he showed Meredith the least sign of disrespect the man would be out on his ear before he finished protesting.

Constantine followed Meredith to the carriage and waited until she was settled before passing Poppy in. When he joined her, he was seated beside the governess. His youngest had claimed the window, forcing Meredith to the center. He didn't mind that arrangement at all.

When the door shut, he made sure everyone was snugly tucked beneath thick quilts. When the carriage lurched off, he waved and then faced forward. No more looking back. He pulled the blankets tighter around Meredith. "Let me know if you grow chilled."

Meredith faced him. "Tell me where we are going?"

"Oh, no.' He grinned at her persistence. "Not until we stop for the night. It would spoil the surprise."

Her lips pressed together, her gaze narrowed. "So the journey will take two days?"

"At least," he confessed. "But it depends on the roads, the weather, and the tempers of three little misses and one fetching governess. I hope there will be few long faces during the miles ahead."

Her face grew pinched. "You're asking for trouble, you know."

He shuffled a little closer. "I'm looking forward to it."

Her glance skittered toward his daughters and she sighed. "What did Cunningham want with you this morning?"

"A misunderstanding. Nothing to worry about."

She glanced down at her hands. "Mrs. Smith was rather cool with me this morning, too."

He caught her hands in his. "Meredith, will you trust that I know what I'm doing? Cunningham will come around. So, what shall we talk about today?"

"I'm not telling you my name."

"How about we exchange information about our childhoods? For instance, I got my first hound when I was three. Lovely rascal, followed me everywhere. My mother hated him jumping onto her lap and licking her face."

"I'm not surprised. Did you not know how to train the beast?"

"I learned, but that is a story for another day. Your turn now. Did you have a pet when you were young?"

"Yes."

"And?"

She looked at him and fluttered her lashes. "He used to growl horribly at people who annoyed me."

Constantine laughed. "Well, I am grateful you no longer have the beast at your side as I plan to annoy you for some time to come."

"I'm not." Meredith turned to the window and leaned her head against the squabs. "I could have used his teeth a time or two in the early years. He never failed to protect me."

Constantine squeezed her hand tightly. It was on the tip of his tongue to press for more information, yet the beginning of a journey was no time to demand answers. He wanted nothing to spoil her mood. They had hours left in the carriage. Many more in a charmingly warm little inn he'd discovered on similar journeys. When Meredith faced his sisters, he wanted everything to be perfect. He wanted her to like them. After all, if she refused him the gift of her name and connections, his might be the only family she would have when they married.

Meredith let out a relieved breath as the carriage clattered into a small inn yard at an unmarked village. The trip so far had been slow and thankfully without incident, but despite their best efforts, the children had not always enjoyed themselves. She soothed the sleeping child in her arms as Maisy and Willow clambered out after Constantine. She forced herself to remember her lessons. Be calm. Be a lady. Yet if not for the sleeping child, Meredith feared she would lose her temper and shout at Constantine for keeping their final destination a secret. Her nerves were at their limit. Constantine would like seeing that.

His sunny smile when he poked his head through the doorway only increased her irritation. "The inn has wonderfully comfortable beds."

"You're not sharing mine tonight," she warned. She would remain with the children to teach him a lesson. Meredith did not care for surprises, and according to his hints, she had another day of not knowing their final destination. She did not appreciate being absconded to parts unknown. If their relationship was to continue, in any form, Constantine would have to cease planning further surprise events.

She wriggled along the bench to the door and slid Poppy into his outstretched arms. Constantine had been rather better equipped to deal with the girls on a long trip than herself, making up endless games and convincing them to nap. But then he'd likely done such journeys before and knew better how to keep his daughters entertained in confined spaces.

Meredith stepped out of the carriage after him and glared, little caring if anyone saw her do it. "Where are we now?"

"Another surprise." He urged her toward the inn. "Come inside where it's warm. Mrs. Lamb's company will soothe you after such an arduous day."

Constantine's attempts to tease did not improve her mood. She would… Meredith stumbled. In the act of taking a step, she had glimpsed something she recognized. The once-bold red paint on the inn door struck a chord of her memory. She glanced around her, trying to discover why the place felt familiar.

She glanced at the door again, at the lion's-head knocker placed squarely in the center, and her heartbeat slowed. Her legs trembled.

"Meredith?"

She gave her head a little shake to dismiss the coincidence and then stepped into the inn. She was imagining a resemblance to a place she'd been before. A gray-haired woman was waiting. "Welcome back, my lord. You must be tired from your journey."

Constantine smiled over the sleeping form of his youngest. "Two rooms for the night, if you please, Mrs. Lamb. The largest and warmest chamber for my daughters and their governess. A smaller chamber will be sufficient for myself."

"Of course, my lord." The lady reached for Poppy and led the girls toward the stairs. "Will you be staying long with the duke?"

A clammy chill had swept her skin. It could not be. She could not have returned her by mistake after all her efforts to avoid the location. Yet Mrs. Lamb's hair had grayed quite a lot in the intervening years since Meredith had last glimpsed her. She was almost certain it was the same woman. Meredith paused, holding on to the nearest object for support as she gathered her courage. "Will you tell me now where we are going?"

"Oh, very well. I suppose you'll discover the truth from Mrs. Lamb in due course, but we are going to see my sister, the Duchess of Romsey at Romsey Abbey. It's another half-day carriage ride ahead."

Meredith swayed and clung to the insufficient lifeline of the chair. *No.*

Constantine touched her arm. "What's the matter? Have you taken a chill?"

Meredith raised a shaky hand to her brow. Her skin was clammy; her breath came in short, fast pants. A chill was the only excuse she dared supply. "I must be," she said quickly. "Would you excuse me? I should tend to your daughters."

Constantine helped her to the bottom of the staircase, but

Meredith wished he'd not. Her heart couldn't take the strain. What she'd thought was possible was merely yet another nightmare. She shook off his grip.

"Let me help you?"

Meredith reluctantly raised her eyes to his face. "You know the Duke of Romsey?"

"Of course I do. I'm the lad's uncle and guardian."

Meredith swallowed past the lump in her throat. "You must be very proud."

When she moved up the stairs, he followed close on her heels. "I may have mentioned I have some fences to mend. I'm not expecting a warm welcome, truth be told, but I'm hoping having the girls with me will ease the way. My sisters are fond of the children. They are always inviting them to visit."

Meredith paused halfway up, her foot poised on the landing. "And why have you stayed away so long?" She took another step, hoping Grayling would keep a safe distance from her.

"My sisters have remarried and I'm not particularly pleased with their choices."

Meredith nodded and continued up, aware that Grayling followed close on her heels. The advertisements in the paper spun before her eyes. According to the newssheets, Grayling's sisters had married her brothers. Meredith had not wanted to believe such lies and she'd forced herself to forget what she'd read and not allow her curiosity to be stirred to investigate. At the door she placed her hand on the latch. "If you would excuse me, my lord, I should like a few moments' privacy. I'm not feeling the best, and the children need me."

"We all need you." His smile was a dagger to the heart. "But of course. I'll see you at dinner."

Meredith opened the door a crack and squeezed through. "As you wish."

She closed it quickly and leaned against the wood. Across the room, the three little hearts she'd grown to love were exploring the room and chattering with Mrs. Lamb. Three little girls with exalted connections. Connections that Meredith never wanted to meet again. She closed her eyes tightly and prayed for a way out that would save their tender hearts from breaking apart as hers was. Tomorrow she had to convince Grayling to travel on without her. Tonight she had to learn to hate him.

Chapter Twenty-Two

Morning bloomed bright and clear, making Constantine happy to leave the adequate inn behind for the superior comforts of Romsey Abbey. He glanced at the dining room door. What was keeping Meredith this morning? He'd risen at dawn feeling restlessness claw at his senses. He wanted to rush upstairs to see how she fared this morning, but given the way he'd introduced her to the innkeeper last night as his governess, he couldn't very well intrude. Meredith Clark had a reputation to maintain.

He pondered over her past decision to acquire a new name to suit the situation and marveled that such a plan had worked so completely. At no time had he suspected that anyone else doubted her background as a governess. They might now, thanks to Cunningham's spying, consider his governess had fallen prey to a seduction or seduced him. But Calista would never be discovered unless she met someone from the House when they finally moved in society as man and wife.

He drank the last of his coffee, pondering how he would sidestep any questions related to her similarity to the courtesan from the House. He couldn't very well keep Meredith locked away at Stanton Harold Hall. He hosted a hunt every year. Some guests stayed for weeks. When Meredith agreed to marry him, they would discuss and concoct a plausible history to spread about and divert any suspicions should she meet anyone she recognized.

At last the thud of tiny footsteps sounded outside. He took

two steps toward the door before it opened and Mrs. Lamb stepped inside. "Here we are."

The children filed in, Willow leading Maisy by the hand. Mrs. Lamb deposited Poppy on her feet. There was no sign of Meredith behind the innkeeper's wife, only his valet carrying the children's luggage. "My governess?"

"She asked me to give you this."

Mrs. Lamb passed him a folded piece of paper and he read it quickly. "Why was I not informed?"

"I'm sure she hoped to be well come morning, but she's not herself today and bids to be left behind. Took all her strength to attend the little ones' needs this morning. There's nothing for it but bed rest and time. If Your Lordship really needs her, my husband can deliver her in a day or so, if that's acceptable."

"Yes, I really need her, and a day or two is not acceptable." He called for his valet to come back. "Remain here with my daughters."

He would not leave Meredith. If she was ill, then they would simply not travel. He bounded up the stairs to the bedroom Meredith had spent the night in and knocked on the door. When he heard a muffled cough, he quickly let himself in. The room was cold and Meredith was huddled on the bed beneath the blankets. He could only see the top of her head.

Constantine rushed to her. Her skin was clammy. Her body shook. She was ill and he was a damned fool to have left her alone last night. "Darling, tell me how you feel."

Her face turned to his, and her eyes were puffy, nose red, and her voice shook when she spoke. "Dreadful."

He brushed damp strands of her hair back from her face. "I can see that. What can I do?"

"Leave me." She began to cough violently. "I'll recover in a day or so."

Meredith collapsed back to the bed and when she moaned, he clutched her hand. "I cannot leave you like this."

"You must,' she whispered. "Take the girls as far from me as you can."

He drew closer but she held out her hand to ward him off. "Stay away. I don't want to make you suffer."

He was suffering already. He felt helpless and utterly useless.

He'd not felt such panic since his wife had died. He couldn't leave Meredith behind. He would stay to take care of her. He stood and considered the room. "I'll add more wood to the fire."

Meredith pulled the blankets over her head.

When he was done, he hurried back to her side. "Have you eaten today?"

"I'm not hungry." She coughed again. "Just go."

He peeled back the blankets to see her face. "I'll never leave you."

Her teeth clenched and she pulled the covers tighter about her. "I don't want you to see me like this. Take the girls to Romsey. I'll recover in a few days and join you when I'm well. You cannot bring illness into the abbey and I will only get worse as the day wears on in the cold carriage. I'm sure the innkeeper will be glad of the additional coin to look after me. If you can spare it, that is."

"Of course I can, but I don't want to leave you in such a state. I would do anything to make you happy and take care of you. You need me."

"Constantine, be sensible." Her eyes met his, and the dark emptiness within made his heart ache. "You must go before you, too, become ill. You must think of your daughters. I could not live with the guilt should they lose you, too. What if they became sick? I'm so scared for them."

When she put it like that, Meredith made perfect sense. The young were very susceptible to infection and illness. But it would break his heart to leave her all alone.

"Go, Constantine." She pushed at him from beneath the covers. "I can take care of myself for a few days. I'll sleep and rest and join you as soon as I can. If you miss me too badly, you can always return without your daughters." She sniffed and held her handkerchief to her nose.

That was an excellent idea. He was not so far from Romsey that he couldn't travel there in a day and return. "Very well. I will take them to my sister and come back for you tomorrow."

"Good." Meredith closed her eyes tightly.

Constantine leaned in to kiss her lips and then thought better of it. He kissed her cheek, her clammy brow, and the backs of her fingers. "You rest. I'll pay the innkeeper handsomely to wait on you hand and foot. Oh, if only we were still at the Hall. Mrs. Smith would have you well in no time."

"If only we had never left," she whispered.

A tear trickled from her eye. Constantine caught it, his heart tumbling over. He'd never, ever expected Meredith to shed a tear. Seeing that she did because he was leaving melted him. He brushed his lips against hers. "I love you."

When he drew back, bleak, red-rimmed eyes stared at him. "Goodbye, Constantine."

He smoothed her hair one last time and strode for the door. Although her words had the ring of finality, he shook off the sensation. She was merely miserable with her ailment. He would return tomorrow and if she were not well, he would remain at her side until she was.

His feet might be as heavy as lead weights, but he had a responsibility to his daughters. He would pay the innkeeper well to tend Meredith while he traveled on to Romsey. Once there, he would make amends, meet the upstarts his sister had married, and return for Meredith as quickly as he could. Mercy was always begging for the girls to visit. She likely wouldn't mind having them to herself for a few days while Meredith recovered.

Decision made, Constantine found the innkeeper, paid for Meredith's upkeep, and gave strict orders she was to be checked on every half hour until he returned. Mrs. Lamb appeared amused by his fussing, but the money placed in her hands ensured she would not neglect Meredith.

He carried his daughters to the waiting carriage, brought his valet inside, too, for additional support, and gave the order to move off. As the carriage rumbled from the inn yard, he glanced up. Meredith stood at a window, watching their departure. He raised his hand, but if she returned the farewell, he never saw it.

The girls waited a whole five minutes before they understood Meredith was not with them. The first tear he expected. The hours of unrelenting crying threatened his composure. When Romsey finally came into view, he was desperate for reprieve.

An unfamiliar butler greeted him but appeared efficient in ordering the carriage unloaded and his men taken care of. He secured Poppy in his arms and led his daughters up the stairs. Mercy was waiting alone in the entrance hall. "Grayling."

"Your Grace."

She came forward. "Lady Willow, Lady Maisy, Lady Poppy. Welcome back, sweethearts."

Willow was the first to embrace her aunt, but he could see she wasn't as full of her usual enthusiasm for Mercy. His sister frowned when she stepped back quickly. "Come into the drawing room where it's warm."

Constantine followed her and took a seat where Mercy indicated.

"You are somewhat late, Grayling."

Willow perched beside him, and he said, "I am." There was no point beating around the bush.

"You have not written to explain your absence."

Maisy disappeared beneath a side table, and he replied, "No, I didn't."

"Do you have anything to say at all for missing my wedding?"

Poppy turned in his arms and hugged him, exhaling a little whimper of sound.

"I had other things on my mind than celebrating a poorly thought-out match."

Mercy glanced at his daughters, a smile ghosting over her lips. "I'm sure you'd prefer them escorted upstairs to the nursery for their governess to manage. Edwin will be so excited to see them."

Willow crowded his side. Constantine put his arm around her. "Unfortunately, their governess fell ill on the journey and remained behind at the inn we stayed in last night. We have had an up-and-down day so far. I'd rather not abandon them to the nursery yet."

"A new governess?"

Constantine smiled. "Miss Clark has exceeded my every expectation."

"Ill, you say. What is wrong with her? Do you know?"

"She must have taken a chill on the journey and sickened overnight. I would have delayed for her sake, but she was adamant the children should be taken away to safeguard their health."

"A practical woman."

A knock sounded on the door.

"A conundrum, in truth."

"Come in," Mercy called.

The door opened and a solidly built man stepped into the drawing room. The new husband. Dark hair, brown eyes, and mode of dress befitting his reported personal wealth. His expression was guarded but serious as he crossed the room. But when he smiled at Mercy, he revealed a pair of deep dimples. "Forgive the interruption, Your Grace, but I heard you had an important guest."

Mercy made a face. "At last. Leopold, I have the honor of presenting my rather tardy brother. Grayling, may I introduce you to my husband, Leopold Randall."

Weighed down as he was by Poppy, Constantine had trouble rising. He loosened his grip on his daughter to thrust out his hand. "Sir."

Randall's grip was firm and sure as they shook. "A pleasure, my lord." He glanced at the children next. "What pretty daughters."

He took a step back and seated himself in an armchair to one side. Constantine sat and rearranged Poppy more comfortably on his lap. He'd never known her to be so clingy, but perhaps the trip was more tiring than he imagined.

Maisy's head appeared from beneath the table, her eyes fixed on the newcomer.

"So, you're here at last," Mercy said. "How long will you stay? Long enough for Blythe to see you, I hope, and to introduce her husband Tobias to you."

"Actually, once I retrieve my ailing governess, I thought we might stay awhile."

Mercy and Leopold exchanged a long glance and then Leopold smiled broadly. "You see, there was nothing to worry over."

Maisy hurried across the room and, to everyone's surprise, crawled onto Leopold Randall's lap. She moved her head close to Leopold's and stared into his eyes. Leopold tried to look around her. "Ah… a little help would be nice."

Mercy stood with a laugh and lifted Maisy away. "Children always know who is kind. It's your dimples, my love. They reassure everyone you meet."

The man stood, shaking his head. "So you say. If you would

excuse me, I'd better return to work. Lord Grayling, a pleasure to meet you. I'll leave you two to catch up."

Mercy's eyes twinkled as she watched her new husband depart. "He had that same effect on Edwin when they met, and me as well."

"Are you trying to tell me you fell in love at first sight?"

"Not first sight, no." Her expression grew guarded. "First touch, perhaps. Let's go upstairs to the nursery. I think Poppy and Willow are falling asleep where they sit."

Constantine quickly glanced at the girls. "So they are."

When he stood, Mercy captured Willow and Maisy's hands and guided them toward the doors. "How will you manage without your governess?"

"I'm not sure, but it cannot be soon enough for Miss Clark to arrive." Constantine rubbed his jaw. "You know, Maisy doesn't usually care for strangers. She's more likely to remain beneath the table as come out."

Mercy started up the stairs. "Well, perhaps she saw something in his eyes that was familiar and comforting. Unfortunately, given her age, we'll always wonder."

Chapter Twenty-Three

When Meredith Clark had come into existence, there had been no knight to rescue her, no family left to care if she lived or died. She had been alone and frightened and unprepared for life's hardships. When she assumed the name Calista, it was to protect what was left of her dignity in the face of a terrible choice.

Names were important. Names defined who you were and how far you'd fallen in the world. In all her life, she had fought her identity. Her place in society and its suffocating expectations. With each new name she assumed, a little piece of herself had withered. Yet coming to this place had brought the past rushing back as if it had never been lost.

As night closed in on the rain-washed village, she pushed open the lych-gate and stepped into the graveyard, allowing the gentle hiss to lull her and its whispers to lure her closer to the crumbling grave markers. The thick grass cushioned her sodden footfalls, muffling her passage through the dead. Grizzled gray stone jutted toward the sky, angels and carved granite bestowing identity and position, even in death.

The rows of weeping headstones bore names and benedictions. Much loved. Sadly missed. Too good for this life. The poorer markers were no less poignant than the larger. She passed them all, stopping at one that bore no names. No identity and therefore no position to speak of. A simple stone edifice marked the passing of life.

Together in death was all it said along with a year.

Together but unknown.

Together and dead.

The woman known by many names save her own sank to her knees on the sodden ground, little caring if her carriage dress became as ruined as she was herself.

Names were important.

The couple buried here should have a name carved into their headstone. They deserved to be remembered for the life they had lived, for the sacrifices they had made, the love they had freely offered even as they guided their children to adulthood with determination to succeed and ignorance of the true danger. The headstone should say they had been loved and still were. That they were missed. That they were too vital to be taken away in an act of cold cowardice.

"Did you know them," asked a woman to Rosemary's right.

Did she know them? Not enough. No amount of time would be long enough, but she was glad they could not see what she had become. Tears burned her eyes, but she would not let them fall. When she did, she feared the avalanche of feeling would break her. She would not give in to her sorrows. She had already lost so much today. She would be strong, as she had always needed to be. "Did you?"

The gravestones blurred and she hastily wiped at her eyes.

The woman heaved a weary sigh. "I was not so fortunate. But I remember it as if it was yesterday. A sad case, indeed. I'd just moved here after my marriage when these two strangers were brought in for burial. I've always thought it sad that their loved ones never came to find them. If their family ever discovered the deaths we never heard, but without any information regarding their identity, there was no chance to write to inform them. I know the vicar did try."

Strangers? They'd had names. Rosemary surged to her feet and spun about. "Randall. James and Jane Randall."

Mrs. Lamb, huddled beneath a black umbrella, drew back at the heat in her voice. "So you did know them?"

Denial thickened her tongue. She had lived her life with lies to protect herself from discovery. To forget the nightmare of that day, the deaths she had witnessed, and the plans that had been set in motion for her future, had required many sacrifices. She, who had barely spoken one truthful word to a living human in a decade, did not want to lie. The habits she'd adopted for the sake of self-preservation were hard to break. Honesty had been the first virtue to be dispensed with. She swallowed past the lump forming in her throat. Didn't the dead deserve honesty? "Yes."

The woman nodded toward the distant vicarage. "He'll be happy to sign their names into the register and have the mystery solved. Perhaps it's not too late to inform their family. Do you know how they died?"

Splintering wood and the world turning over. Voices raised in anger. A woman's scream and pleas for help. Running fast for help, only to find it and be too late. Pistol shots bringing silence. "Yes," she whispered to the old woman. "Rosemary was there."

The sound of earth filling a grave reverberated dully in her ears. It was a sound she never enjoyed. She glanced beyond the graves to the distant forest and shuddered. This place was one reason she disliked the sight of gardens. Down beneath the prettiness of green and colored flowers was where the dead went at the end of days.

"Rosemary?" Mrs. Lamb remained silent as she studied her and then her eyes lit up. "If I remember correctly, there was a search undertaken for a girl a day after these bodies were brought for burial. I thought it rather odd, in fact, that the murderers were never pursued but a slip of a girl was. A considerable reward was offered for Rosemary's capture, but they never found her. We must write to say she's been discovered. We'd given up hope, but come. The vicar will know all about you."

"I'm not Rosemary." Hope for the girl Rosemary was certainly lost. She hugged her shawl tighter about her body and steeled herself to lie again. "I am simply recalling what a woman I met told me of the murders, but that was years ago. I've no idea where she is now or if she is even still alive."

The woman deflated somewhat. "Well, that's a spot of bad luck. I'd so hoped to solve the riddle. Randall, Randall. Are you sure about that? Lord Grayling's sister married into that family."

"Yes, so he told me yesterday." Rosemary spread her hands wide and held her ground, breathless with hope that her lies would be believed. "I'm sorry I cannot be of more help."

Mrs. Lamb shrugged and then her eyes sharpened on Rosemary's sodden clothing. When she had left the inn, Mrs. Lamb had still thought her ailing. "You're soaked right through. Oh, dear heavens. His Lordship will be furious with me. He left me with such a lot of instructions for your care. You must be a very good governess."

Mrs. Lamb hurried forward with an umbrella and attempted to shield her from further rain. "Come with me now, and let's get you back to bed where you belong."

She nodded but her soul was bleak. Rosemary belonged nowhere now save in memory. Her possessions at the inn were all she had left. She would need to reclaim them before she could plan ahead. Rosemary turned back to the graves one last time. The woman known as Meredith Clark would be gone long before tomorrow ever dawned. "Can you tell me when the mail coach will come next?"

"Tomorrow." Mrs. Lamb hurried her along. "But it doesn't run toward Romsey. Not from here, anyway."

Rosemary lifted her chin. "I'm not going to Romsey. I'm going anywhere else."

Mrs. Lamb spluttered. "Not going to Romsey? I cannot imagine His Lordship will be pleased to hear he's lost a servant after spending a pretty penny to keep you in comfort."

Tonight Rosemary would choose her new name, destroy anything bearing the name Miss Clark, and begin again as another woman without a past. No one would know that Rosemary Randall had walked the streets of this small village. If the stage came early, it would take her as far away as she could run. Somewhere she could become lost again.

Feet squelching with each step, she retraced her steps to the inn and let herself into her room. The emptiness battered her senses, the absence of Constantine and his sweet daughters was like the misplacement of a treasured object.

But Constantine was for Romsey. Brother of the duchess, uncle of the duke. A family she could never go near, despite the lies she'd read in the papers and heard tumble from his lips. Constantine was part of the great deception. Honey-coated poison. She couldn't trust him. If there was any truth in it, he would have attended his sister's wedding. He would have gone to protest the union in person.

But he'd stayed and shown his true colors. Not that she'd minded at the time. She would not lie to herself that he'd imposed on her in any way. Their time together had been all that she'd once dreamed for herself. A meeting of the mind and the body. A memory she would carry with her forever. For a brief, shining moment, she had felt she belonged before plunging back into the unknown. She'd almost felt safe enough to consider telling the truth. But if she had bothered with names and connections she would never have spent one night with Constantine in the first place.

He stood with the enemy.

She moved closer to the fire as she undressed, removing her wet things. Her hands shook so badly it took time to undo the first button. The rain had soaked her to the bone and she sniffed as her nose began to drip. The carriage dress Constantine had purchased was sodden and dirty, much like its owner. She spread the gown over a chair, knowing full well it would never be clean or dry in time for her departure in the morning.

There was nothing now to do besides choose a new name with which to introduce herself, catching what sleep she could. Weary to the bone, Rosemary crawled onto the mattress and pulled the bedding up to her chin. When she was safely away from here, she could think about what she'd lost. And mourn all over again. Calista, Meredith Clark, and the doomed love she had discovered, died tonight.

Chapter Twenty-Four

Constantine hurried down the main staircase of Romsey Abbey after saying goodnight to his daughters. He tried to ignore his bad mood. Since he'd arrived, he'd been scolded like a three-year-old boy with jam on his face, accused of coldness at dinner, and been questioned about the reasons for his daughters' low spirits. It wasn't his fault his governess had to be left behind and her absence had affected his tolerance of sisterly meddling.

He reached the bottom step and flexed his fingers.

It was time to lay down the law to this Randall fellow. His sister may have remarried a wealthy man, but he was a stranger to society. No one claimed to have had seen or met Leopold Randall prior to his sudden return some months ago. An unknown element would not be allowed free with the Romsey fortune and estates. He was here now and would examine what had been done and not done.

According to the servants, Randall ended his day in the ducal study and didn't leave it till close to midnight. He was sure to be there now, and Constantine was eager to establish some limitations. The first was that he was still the boy's guardian and would make all decisions for his upbringing. He would have final say on the boy's life and the estate finances. He wasn't about to let his sister's new husband rob the young duke out of his inheritance.

He pushed open the door without knocking. "Randall, we

need to talk."

The fellow's head appeared from behind the desk and then Randall rolled to his feet from the floor, brushing off his trousers. "How may I help you, my lord?"

"Let me make one thing clear."

"Oh?"

Constantine stopped before the neat desk and scowled. "Romsey belongs to Edwin. Everything and everyone living here is his responsibility. Not yours. Don't imagine for a moment that I won't be watching over him."

"Then he's a fortunate boy to have an uncle who treasures him." Romsey looked down and smiled at his feet. "That's very good, Your Grace. Now, where do your horses like to run?"

"There," the young duke's piping voice said.

Constantine moved forward to get a better look. The young duke lay upon the floor beneath the ducal desk, his finger pointing at a pencil-sketched map of Romsey. Toys were scattered everywhere between young Edwin and Leopold Randall's feet. Constantine looked at the other man curiously.

An apologetic smile flitted across Randall's face. "He's too young yet to make the decisions himself, but he's not too young to start learning about the estate. He's to have a riding lesson in the morning. Shall I inform the stables that you'll be joining him?"

"Are you not going with him?"

"Of course I am. After breakfast, Edwin spends part of his day with me outside if the weather allows and then he has riding lessons with the stable master, luncheon with his mother, and then lessons with his aunt in the afternoon. The whole house revolves around his schedule until he falls asleep at night. I'm due to take him up to the duchess in a moment, but he wanted to finish his game." Randall raised a brow. "Did you think I'd leave his care to servants and run the place as if it was mine alone?"

Constantine had. Randall had appeared the interloper when he'd arrived, interrupting his time with his sister and taking charge of the servants at dinner. The change from his last visit had set his teeth on edge. Mercy had run an informal household, but with Randall's arrival, it functioned like a well-oiled machine.

Leopold Randall might actually be a good influence on the

estate as long as he remembered who was to inherit it. He glanced down at the boy again and saw him rub his eyes. The young duke had a full schedule of activities bound to exhaust him each day. Thanks to Meredith's views on children and what they needed most, he understood a little better now that routine had value for all.

He skirted around Randall to crouch at the duke's level. "Good evening, Your Grace. Are you almost ready for bed?"

Although Edwin stared, it was clear to Constantine that he'd stayed away from the boy far too long to be remembered fondly. Although he was disappointed that his own nephew didn't feel comfortable with him, as his own daughter had behaved with Mercy, he held out his hand to help him up.

The boy surged to his feet and grabbed his hand. The shake was surprisingly firm for a child and the boy's eyes held his steadily. Was this the influence of Leopold Randall coming to the fore so soon?

He stood when the boy released him and assessed the man opposite. Dark wavy hair, cut a little longer than was the fashion in London. Steady dark brown eyes that saw everything but said little. A man of solid build and confidence in his abilities. He was struck by a sudden surety they had met before, in London or perhaps somewhere else in the countryside and he'd forgotten about it. He couldn't be sure of the time or place except for the nagging suspicion their meeting was recent.

Randall turned away, stepped carefully over the boy's toys, and began to shuffle journals on the large desk. "The estate accounts are now up to date if you'd care to inspect them, my lord."

Courteous, too. There must be something wrong with him. No man could be perfectly agreeable to give way to a mere child. The man was next in line for the title. There would be too much temptation to resist. "Was there an issue with them?"

Constantine took the journal Randall held out and leafed through the pages idly. He'd give Randall one concession, his entries were meticulously neat and detailed. The journals were possibly better documented than even his own. He whistled at the balance totaled on the very last page. So far Romsey was doing well under Randall's guidance. He'd still bear watching, though.

Randall shuffled and then bent to pick up a toy that was in danger of being stepped on. "They were woefully insufficient in the beginning. But a little effort and a few dozen late nights in this room have set them to rights. Her Grace is pleased with the work I've done."

Constantine looked at him slyly. "A wife should be pleased with her husband or she shouldn't have married him."

Randall threw the toy onto the desk. "Your point?"

"It's all very reasonable and convenient for you, isn't it? Marrying my sister, a duchess, and gaining a toehold in the abbey you could one day inherit. I'm sure you set your sights high for a reason."

"And what reason would that be?" Mercy asked from the door.

Constantine pivoted and took in her bearing. She had a mutinous glint in her eye that boded ill for getting to the truth. "He is the heir."

Mercy crossed her arms over her chest and scowled. "He would never harm Edwin. When he came, he never wanted to stay."

He glanced at Leopold Randall. "How cunning to make you believe in his reluctance."

"That's a dreadful thing to say. Leopold loves me and I him. Just because you prefer to avoid respectable women doesn't mean I am so easily swayed into a man's arms. I almost believed your story about the governess. Did she finally discover you never intended to marry her? How typical of you to seduce the help."

Anger trickled through him. Meredith was an incomparable, both in bed and out of it. And he would marry her one day. He wasn't keen to rush to that point and scare her away. "What did you hear about Miss Clark?"

"The girls talk of nothing else but missing her. Miss Clark this. Miss Clark and Papa that. Did you become bored with her and dump her at the side of the road to fend for herself?"

"Of course not," Constantine said quickly. Meredith was never far from his thoughts. "She fell ill on the way here, as I said, and wouldn't countenance further travel. I told her I'd return tomorrow once the girls were settled."

"So you say." Mercy scowled. "What, exactly, is wrong with her? Did you secure a doctor? A servant to attend her? Did you ensure she had funds for a physician should one be needed?"

"I..." Constantine tried to explain, but it was impossible to get a word in when Mercy had a head of steam going. He waited until her rant ended, waited a bit longer until she looked at him to speak.

"Miss Clark is a very private person. If she said she was unwell, then I believed her, but I paid the innkeeper handsomely to see to her every need. And yes, she is my lover. Anything else is for her and me to discuss."

But Constantine had to admit he wouldn't mind knowing Meredith a little better. Like her real name. Her obstinacy at sharing it was a constant irritation in their affair. He didn't believe he would be comfortable until he had it in his possession.

His sister touched his arm. "Don't tell me this one has gotten under your skin."

Reluctantly, he nodded. "She's different. But enough of me. This," he said and waved his hand about to include Leopold, "is completely different."

"Yes, it is. Leopold offered marriage rather than to continue our affair. And wipe that smug expression from your face. Our attraction was completely mutual."

"Really? Forgive me for not believing that."

Mercy stamped her foot. "Damn you and your suspicions. Can you not allow me to be happy at last?"

Grayling frowned. "You were happy before."

"No, I wasn't."

"What are you talking about?"

"Edwin." She threw her hands up into the air. "Did you know he had a weak heart before I married him?"

Randall scooped up the boy in his arms and moved him away out of hearing.

"No. Father was alive then and conducted the negotiations with the duke and Edwin. He seemed robust enough to me, but was he ill?"

"Yes and no. But two women, a wife and a mistress, were too great a tax on his stamina. There was no chance for an heir."

Constantine looked at the boy across the room and pointed out the obvious. "You have a son."

"I have a son." She moved closer. "But Edwin did not father

him."

He stared at his sister in shock. Mercy couldn't have gone that far to be a mother to gain an heir for the estate. But her defiant glare proved she may have done just that. He took a step back from her. "What the devil did you do?"

His sister shook her head a little sadly. "I did nothing. The duke arranged everything. If you had read my letters, you might have an inkling of his malevolence. His son had to have an heir by any means possible, even by blackmailing his own family to get one."

"Blackmail?"

"Blackmail." Mercy drew closer, her voice dropping to a whisper. "In return for his siblings' safety, the duke sent Leopold to my bed. That's why he will never hurt Edwin. Can you imagine anyone murdering their own child just to claim the title their flesh and blood already has?"

Constantine glanced toward the young duke, saw him laughing and smiling at the man playing games with him. There was a certain similarity in their features. The shape of the nose, the curl of their hair as they leaned toward each other over the game.

"The longer I look, the more I see. Leopold realized sooner than I did and still intended to leave us behind."

Hell and damnation. What else had he missed these past years? "Why did he stay?"

"Besides the fact that we love each other to distraction?" Mercy snorted. "Because of Edwin. Family means everything to Leopold. He didn't want Edwin to shoulder the responsibilities for this place alone. He stayed to guide my son when all he wanted from the start was to leave and continue his search."

"The missing siblings?" Constantine scowled. "I keep seeing those damned notices in the paper. Soon all of society will know and start to wonder what else is going on here. I shudder to think of the gossip the season will bring."

"We will weather whatever comes together. It is what families do. There is only Rosemary to find now." Mercy turned away and grabbed a handful of papers from the desk. She shuffled through them until she found one and handed it to him. "This is what we believe Rosemary might look like today. Leopold's sketches of his brothers were remarkably accurate, so we have hope someone will recognize her. Have you seen her? I asked everyone at the wedding with no success."

Constantine took the paper and stared down at it. At first, the face was that of a stranger. He held it out at arm's length before his face and then lowered his hand, placing it closer to five feet in height. He was struck by the familiar heart-shaped face and expressive dark eyes. Without color it was harder to imagine, but if those eyes were the color of whiskey and her hair was cut short, that sweetly deceptive face would usually show far more animation.

Meredith. Calista.

He shook his head. That couldn't possibly be right. If Meredith was in fact Rosemary Randall, and knew full well he was coming here, then she would never have stayed behind in that shabby village. It must be a coincidence.

He lowered the paper and found himself face-to-face with Leopold Randall.

The other man's eyes skewered him. "Do you recognize her?"

He handed the paper back, ignoring the thumping of his heart. When he returned to Meredith he would ask her about the similarity. Maybe she had a double. "I've never met Miss Randall before."

Leopold's nostrils flared and he held out the paper again. "That wasn't the right answer to my question. I asked if you have seen her face somewhere. Recently."

Constantine took the paper again. There was a definite similarity, but he couldn't believe Meredith was related to the Randalls. A woman in her position should have been overjoyed to acknowledge a connection to the Duchess of Romsey. Unless she was too afraid to come home to her family after the life she'd led. "Tell me about her?"

"We lost track of Rosemary ten years ago now. She'd been traveling with our parents and my brother, Tobias, when the carriage overturned. My brother tells me that our mother was injured in the crash and trapped in the wreckage. Tobias and Rosemary ran back to the nearest village to get help. When they returned, our parents' carriage was surrounded. Our parents were murdered where they lay trapped in the carriage, Tobias and

Rosemary captured. Tobias was taken to the docks and thrown aboard a ship. Rosemary was carried away, slung over a horse. We've found no trace of her."

Constantine pinched the bridge of his nose. "Describe her."

"A hellcat. A risk taker. She has a temper. Despite all our efforts, she either cannot or will not come home."

He stared at the drawing again. The woman who had graced his life with her vibrant energy for the past months, torturing him with pleasure beyond his wildest dreams, could not be this man's sister. "It makes no sense."

"It does when the Duke of Romsey, and possibly his son, were responsible for the deaths of our parents. They arranged the murder and our separation to keep us in their control, but Tobias unfortunately was too young to remember where he and Rosemary met with foul play and were parted."

"Is there anything else you can tell me?"

Mercy squeezed his arm tightly. "Constantine, what is it? Have you seen her?"

Constantine held Randall's gaze. There had to be something tangible to prove Meredith was not Rosemary Randall. "Does she have any distinguishing marks?"

"None that I'm aware of. However, I'm her brother and have never seen her without the modesty of clothes." He pursed his lips a moment. "Aside from a temper and a love of mean-spirited dogs, Rosemary was much like any young woman on the verge of coming out. She was rather fond of gemstones at one time. Garnets, I believe, were her favorite."

Constantine closed his eyes. "Meredith."

"What?"

"I fear the woman you are looking for goes by many names, but I know her currently as Meredith Clark. My governess."

"Your lover," Leopold Randall growled, arm hitching back.

The blow to his jaw, when it came, was well deserved.

Chapter Twenty-Five

Rosemary was dying. She was sure of it. As morning's faint light spread over the sleeping village, her stomach roiled again. She clutched the blankets against her chest as a moan escaped her and she prayed not to be sick again. It would be impossible to endure a long carriage journey if she was casting up her accounts every few minutes. This time she wouldn't have to call upon one scrap of acting ability to prove herself unequal to the challenge of getting out of bed. She'd feigned a poorly condition to make Constantine leave her behind, but now she truly was suffering. She had never felt this way before.

Mrs. Lambs voice came through the door. "Are you awake, Miss Clark?"

"Please come in," she croaked, grateful that finally someone had come. She was so tired of being alone and miserable.

"Here you are now, dearie. Got a nice cup a tea and spot of bread to soothe your poor stomach. These things can hit us hard, but you'll feel better soon."

"I couldn't…" Rosemary shook her head. "How did you know about my stomach?"

"I have ears. I've been listening to you retch since before the sun came up." Mrs. Lamb placed a small tray beside the bed. "Sit up now and I'll do my best to make you more comfortable."

With the Mrs. Lamb's help, she sat up and then leaned against the freshly plumped pillows. Meredith hadn't felt so cosseted in a long time. Mrs. Lamb pressed bread into her hands.

"Nibble this slowly."

While Mrs. Lamb took care of the soiled chamber pot, Rosemary looked at the hunk and then raised it to her mouth. She tried not to think of anything as she drew in a breath of fresh air. When her stomach roiled, she made the first bite very small.

She closed her eyes and swallowed the dry lump. Tears filled her eyes. How ridiculous to be laid low on a day she should be busy. She had to get up and dressed, pack her things, and start over. It had taken all night, but she had decided Mrs. Evelyn Lynch would be her new name. A pity she had no references to give weight to her claim to be a governess, but she could always say she was a mother and had lost her children to illness. That would be somewhat true. She would always think of Constantine's daughters as hers.

Rosemary opened her eyes to find Mrs. Lamb was watching her. "Tea?"

"Yes, thank you."

When the woman handed it over, there was pity in her eyes. "Like that is it? He broke your heart and left you behind."

"I'm not heartbroken." Rosemary quickly swallowed some of the tea and handed back the cup and saucer. The hot liquid did nothing to ease the ache and she slumped against the pillows, wishing Constantine had never revealed his connections. "I'm ill."

How annoying to remember Constantine so clearly now that he was long gone. The way he smiled, the way he was always trying to learn something new about her that she didn't want to reveal. How ridiculous to want to feel his hands upon her again and tell him the truth, given he was related to the Duke of Romsey.

They had no future together.

Mrs. Lamb sighed dramatically. "These lords can turn a girl's head so easily. They promise the world and leave your belly full. I thought Lord Grayling a little different by the way he fretted for your welfare yesterday. But I see my first suspicion was correct. When is the babe due?"

Rosemary stilled as shock set in. "I'm not with child."

"Oh, I think time will tell that you are. It may be cruel, but I could wave a raw mutton chop beneath your nose and make your stomach turn over. There is no sense pretending the worst hasn't happened."

Rosemary held her stomach as the mere mention of meat sent her nausea soaring.

Mrs. Lamb smiled kindly. "I can see a carriage in the distance, so I'd better return below. I'll send a tray up for you to consider if you're well enough to eat any of it in my absence and check on you again when they're gone, my dear. When I come back, we can talk about what you must do. For all his kind words yesterday, I doubt Grayling will be sympathetic. Forgive me for saying this, but he won't be marrying someone not of his level."

Rosemary pulled the covers up to her nose as a shudder filled her. "Never expected him to."

A babe changed nothing. She knew what to do to remedy herself of that condition. With no home, no future, she had only one choice. Constantine would never know.

He'd only wanted her for pleasure. She and Constantine were remarkably alike in that. When they'd met, neither had wanted more. Yet the longer they'd stayed together, the greater that pleasure had become. Even his children had been no barrier to her contentment. A contentment that ended when she learned his connections.

It was a shame she'd never see him again. He'd become the closest thing to a friend she'd had in a decade. She could think on that when this inn was a distant memory.

Rosemary climbed from bed and slipped into a day gown. She might not feel herself completely, but she had to be ready to get on that mail coach. The buttons on her gown proved a little difficult since she had to keep stopping when assailed by nausea.

When she was decently covered, she sat to fasten her half boots. As she lifted her head, the sounds of a carriage drawing up outside filled the room. Fearing it was the mail coach come early, Rosemary hurried to the window. The crest on the door blazed with the carriage owner's identity.

Romsey.

Rosemary picked up her skirts and ran.

"Are you sure this is the right place," Leopold demanded of Constantine as the carriage rolled to a stop in the sleepy little village he'd stayed in the night before. Being questioned so often, and in such a condescending manner, during the long hours of the night had removed any lingering guilt he felt over making love to the man's sister before they married.

Leopold Randall had no reason to scold him anyway after what he'd discovered about the young Duke of Romsey's conception. Only a fool would claim the higher ground. They had each lain with the other's sister before they ever intended to marry them.

Although Constantine would like nothing better than to scowl, he thought better of it. His jaw hurt like the very devil from the blow he'd received from his brother-in-law's fist every time he clenched it. "I always break my journey to Romsey here," he said carefully. "Another few minutes and you'll see her for yourself."

He cupped his jaw as pain spiked. Even talking a small amount hurt, and he was rather annoyed that no one else seemed the least bit concerned for his well-being. He could have lost a tooth. Maybe Rosemary would tenderly soothe him into a better frame of mind.

Spending the night in close quarters with three Randall men had not been the most comfortable night of his life. Although he hadn't argued, he had not been given much of a voice on the decision to return to the inn. He'd been spared a few precious minutes to tell Willow he was on his way to fetch her favorite governess and that had been all the concession he'd been given.

Yet for all the Randalls' silent scrutiny, he was rather glad they kept their questioning to a minimum, because he didn't think it fair to be accused of wrongdoing when Calista, Meredith, or rather Rosemary, had never had an honest conversation with him since they met. How was he to have deduced that the willful, wicked woman he'd made love to was a woman with an excellent pedigree, outstanding connections, and more suited to a ballroom than a brothel?

He'd never had her real name, although he had known that from the very beginning.

It took a brave woman to lie so boldly as she gave her body to yet another man. At least under the guise of being his governess, her family might be spared the knowledge of the rest of her past.

When the carriage steps were finally dropped, Randall was first out the door. Constantine followed, stepping out onto the familiar street. "This way," he called and then smiled at the inn's proprietor as he approached. "I've returned for my governess, Mr. Lamb."

"So I see." Mr. Lamb ducked back inside the inn, calling for his wife.

The brothers departed the coach and the younger one paled.

"Do you remember the place, Tobias," Oliver asked quickly.

The youngest Randall looked up and down the street and then he pointed. Dense smoke hung around the building he indicated. "We went to the smithy for help, the accident must have occurred some distance beyond that on the far side of the village. I don't remember much else."

Constantine's pulse quickened. Tobias's reaction was almost the same as Meredith's—curse his tongue, Rosemary—yesterday. Despite the lies and deception, he was rather keen to see her again. The younger Randall might believe they were near the scene of the crime that had robbed them of their parents, but Constantine wouldn't be satisfied until he heard the truth from her own lips.

His steps quickened as he hurried inside the dimly lit interior, and sweeping his hat from his head, he found the innkeeper's wife waiting, hands on her hips and a surprisingly hostile glint in her eye. "Back so soon?"

He ignored her sarcasm. "I've come for Miss Clark."

Randall burst through the door. "Where's Rosemary?"

The woman's brow rose. "Rosemary? There's no Rosemary here."

Constantine pinched the bridge of his nose. If Randall wasn't careful, he'd let everyone know Rosemary Randall was a fallen woman. He didn't think she'd appreciate that. "Miss Clark. My governess fell ill and wished to remain behind. The children would not rest until she rejoined them, so I've come to fetch her."

"You almost missed her. She didn't hold out the least bit of hope for your return. In her condition, I don't blame her." The innkeeper's wife shrugged. "Same room as last night."

Constantine pondered her words as he took the stairs two at a time, navigating the narrow staircase and hallway so he could reach Rosemary first. He pushed open the door and froze.

The room was empty. He glanced back into the hall and

determined that yes, he had come to the right room. The bed was still rumpled. "Rosemary?"

Leopold barged past him. "Where the hell is she?"

"As if I know." Constantine searched the room, wondering if Rosemary had adopted Maisy's habit of hiding beneath and behind furnishing.

He ducked his head to check under the bed and discovered her luggage had been stowed beneath. He dragged the case out and set it on the bed. When he opened it, everything he knew she owned was still there. "She cannot be far."

He strode from the room, shouting for the innkeeper's wife as he went. "You said we almost missed her and it seems we have. Where could she have gone?"

"But I just left her a moment before your carriage arrived." The woman frowned. "She was to catch the mail coach this morning, but it's not come yet. I'm surprised Miss Clark's out of bed, frankly. She's been casting up her accounts since before daybreak."

"She truly is ill? I thought perhaps..."

"You thought she'd what? Be all noble and run away before you came this way again? That she'd spare you the embarrassment of getting a bastard on her?"

"What did you say?" Constantine towered over her as dread filled him. Rosemary had once promised she could take care of any indiscretions and the thought of her plans filled him with fear. "Is she with child?"

"That is what I said, although she denies it's possible." Mrs. Lamb shook her head. "If she's not in her room, perhaps she's gone to confess her sins to the vicar. She's already visited the graveyard."

Their sins. He was as much to blame for what had happened between them as she was. He strode out the front door and onto the street. "Where's the vicarage?"

The innkeeper's wife pointed west. "That way. You'll likely notice the graveyard first. The house is beyond that, overlooking the valley."

Constantine stared up the street. Yesterday morning, Meredith had done the very same thing. *Rosemary, you fool.* The woman's name was Rosemary Randall, a woman with exceptional connections who had no need to bamboozle him with further misdirection. It would take him a while to keep that firmly in mind.

Her brothers jogged to catch up. "Where are you going?"

"To get her back."

He saw the graveyard first, bleak and cold. A reminder of the past for those who were left behind. He slowed his pace and allowed the Randall brothers to reach the vicar's residence first. Why would Rosemary have gone to the cemetery yesterday? He stopped dead in his tracks when the answer came to him. Because her past began here.

As he took a step toward the vicar's home, a flash of white linen amid the gray headstones caught his eye. He walked a few more steps and stopped behind an evergreen bush. Someone was in the cemetery. He peeked around the bush. Nothing moved. But he was certain he'd seen a body hiding there. A living, breathing one. Someone taking great pains to keep out of sight.

Slowly, he advanced into the graveyard, skirting large and small headstones while keeping his steps as quiet as possible. If Rosemary was hiding from them, he didn't want to scare her off. Who knows how far she'd run this time?

When he didn't see anything moving amid the grave markers, he concluded it might have been a trick of the light.

He took another step and stopped, eyes snagging on a patch of printed muslin. A muslin he recognized because he'd had the pleasure of removing it from his lover several nights ago. His pulse quickened. Meredith Clark had no reason to hide from him or from the occupants of a Romsey carriage. Yet the possibility that Rosemary Randall thought she did grew in strength. All those nights she would not discuss her past and the future came back to haunt him.

He should have tried harder rather than getting hard.

He should have teased and tormented until she'd told him her name.

"Is that you there, Meredith? Or is it finally Rosemary?"

The figure did not move immediately. The pause, he decided, was the woman stalling for time to come up with a story to explain her actions. Hiding wasn't something an honest or fearless person did.

She rolled to her feet and danced back several steps. Her skin was pale and shone with perspiration, but her eyes were fierce and defiant. She did not look the least bit happy to see him. "My lord, what a pleasure to see you again, and so soon. I was not anticipating your return."

"You were going to disappear again?" He took a pace forward. "Did you not think I would search for you, too?"

"The vicar hasn't seen her for hours," Leopold called as he strode through the graveyard, glancing left and right.

"There was no harm in asking," Tobias stated as the brothers hurried toward him.

Rosemary tensed, her hands curled into fists.

Could the brothers not see their prey? Constantine glanced around swiftly and guessed Rosemary was hidden from view by a very large mausoleum. A few more steps and she'd be discovered. Panic tensed her body until Constantine feared she would run for the distant forest and never look back.

He didn't want to lose her. Not when she might be carrying their child. Not when he loved her despite the lies. "Please," he whispered. "Be as brave as you have always been, Rosemary, and stay."

Chapter Twenty-Six

Constantine held out one hand. "Just meet your brothers. Give them a chance to prove your fears wrong. If not for me, then for my daughters. They need you."

Her eyes filled with pain, but it was too late for further pleas. Leopold saw her standing still and started to run. It all happened so fast. One moment Randall was poised to embrace his sister, the next moment he sailed through the air and crashed hard into the ground, breath leaving his lungs in a pained groan. While Constantine struggled to believe what Rosemary had just accomplished so effortlessly, Leopold staggered to his feet and faced Rosemary again. "Is that the best you can do, imp?"

Rosemary's eyes narrowed to dangerous slits and her head jerked around to keep track of the approaching men. Her posture was battle ready. All she needed were two daggers in her hands to make the image complete. When her gaze landed on him, her expression was so hostile that he took a cautious step back. This was a side of the woman he loved that he'd never imagined existed. Where was the woman who'd sung lullabies to his infant daughter? Had he known this woman at all?

Her eyes clouded with disappointment and then she straightened her shoulders and faced off with Leopold. "You're one of them now, are you?"

"There is only us, Rosie," Oliver said as he stepped between her and Leopold. "We are all that is left and there is no one to hurt you anymore."

Her hands lowered marginally but then she jerked them back up. "There is still the boy. Don't think I could forget he exists. If you take me back, I'll punish him for the sins of his father and grandfather."

"Then you would be punishing me and our father. He's my boy." Leopold sidestepped Oliver and surged forward to catch Rosemary.

But she was too fast. She ducked beneath his reaching arms, jabbed him in the ribs with her curled fist and danced behind a headstone, well out of reach of either brother. "Too slow."

"I'm not." Oliver vaulted the grave to reach her, but instead of trying to catch her, he swung his fist straight toward her face.

As Constantine lunged forward to save her, an arm clapped around his chest, preventing him from moving. Constantine struggled against Tobias's hold. "Let me go."

Rosemary avoided the hit, just barely, and found a large headstone to place between them. "That's new."

"It's a special occasion," Oliver told her as he shrugged his shoulders. "One must always try to throw one's opponent off-balance. Elizabeth will never forgive me if you come home sporting a black eye."

Tobias's grip firmed around Constantine's chest. "I wouldn't get between them if I were you. I learned my lesson when I was twelve. He'll be fine, I promise."

Rosemary eased forward. "What if you go home with the black eye?"

"Then I will have deserved it." Oliver lunged, caught her swinging fist, and forced her backward. Rosemary stumbled even while landing blows to his ribs with her other fist.

Constantine struggled. "I'm not worried about him, I'm worried about Rosemary. She could be hurt."

"She won't be, I promise. Oliver would never hurt our sister. Haven't you noticed he's only fighting with one hand? Makes it fairer that way. His longer arms give him an unfair advantage." Tobias sighed. "This bout is long overdue and probably a necessary salve for her pride. Admitting defeat is something she was never good at."

Constantine shuddered as Oliver raised his arm to block a

blow directed toward his head. How much more of this could a man stand before he fought back? "She *could* easily be hurt," Constantine hissed. "Didn't any of you hear Mrs. Lamb? She might be with child."

Tobias grunted. "Just the same. Stay out of it. Oliver will have factored her possible condition into his strategy."

Horrified, Constantine struggled toward Rosemary, but Tobias had a firm grip for one so slim. Tight bands of steel held him apart from the woman he loved and he was helpless to go to her aid.

"This should be interesting," Tobias said conversationally as Rosemary and Oliver sparred to and fro. He winced every time Rosemary connected a blow with her brother. Yet so far, the taller man had not connected once. He blocked and forced Rosemary to give ground. Rosemary's face was slowly turning red but Oliver wasn't even panting.

Leopold shuffled toward them, half bent over, holding his side as if he were truly injured. He glanced over his shoulder as Oliver grunted when struck in the center of his chest. "Damn, she's fast."

"And the sly fox appears to be slowly working her way toward the far doorway set in the stone wall. Excuse me. Keep Grayling here, will you, Leo? He's a little concerned about Rose."

Tobias released him and ran for the high stone wall surrounding the graveyard. When he vaulted it and disappeared behind, Constantine swore. "My sisters have married bloody circus performers."

He moved toward Rosemary, but Leopold blocked his path. "I'd rather you kept me out of that description. But never fear, Tobias promised Blythe never to let anyone see him do that anymore. Given this is an emergency, she'll forgive him soon enough."

Tobias appeared in the stone archway, arms crossed over his chest. When Rosemary saw her escape route had been thwarted, she renewed her attack on Oliver. Except that in her anger, she made a mistake. As she lunged to thump her fist into Oliver's unprotected ribs, he again stepped inside the blow and wrapped his hands about her waist. "Yield, Terror."

"No." Rosemary squirmed.

Oliver juggled her for a better grip as if she weighed nothing.

"Then up you go."

While Constantine watched in shock, the tall man lifted Rosemary above his head on her side. All five feet two of her was held stiffly in a rigid length.

"Put me down," she shrieked.

Oliver grinned up at her. "Are you ready for the next part? Remember how much you liked twirling?"

"Don't, don't, don't," she gasped. "I'll be sick all over you."

Oliver tossed her in the air once. "What do you think, Toby? Do we believe her, or should we continue our usual game?"

Tobias kept a distance, his expression wary. "It's your suit of clothes that will need cleaning. Grayling believes she's with child. Probably his."

"Of course it's his," Rosemary admitted. "Put me down, you brainless clod."

"And there is my sweet-tongued sister." Oliver grinned as he lowered Rosemary gently into his arms and held her there. "So the terror will spawn another. This I cannot wait to see."

Rosemary thumped his shoulder. "You're an evil man, Oliver Randall."

Instead of taking offense, Oliver laughed. "Elizabeth will never believe one disparaging word you say."

"So you did marry her?" In the blink of an eye, Rosemary wrapped her arms around Oliver. Constantine took a step in that direction but stopped when he heard sobbing. Leopold wasn't so timid. He strode the remaining distance, coming to a standstill before his siblings. He hesitantly placed his hand on her shoulder. "We've been looking for you, Rosemary."

Her head rose and she sniffed. "I know, but it's much too late to come home again. It would be better for everyone if you had never found me."

"Of course you can come home." Leopold pressed his hand to her hair. "You must."

When she wriggled to get away from the affectionate touch, Oliver lowered her gently to her feet and stepped back.

Rosemary scowled at her three brothers who'd formed a circle about her. "No one can make me do anything anymore. You must know, I am well beyond ruin. I'll only be an embarrassment to you all. You each have a family to think of."

All eyes turned accusingly at Constantine.

Yet he had a family to think of, too, and they loved this woman. A woman who would fight, and lie, and love more bravely than anyone he'd ever met. Despite what he'd just witnessed, his feelings hadn't changed one bit.

"Oh, leave Grayling be." Rosemary pointed to a headstone. "They're here."

All the brothers refocused on Rosemary. "Who's here?"

"Mama and Papa. Over by the wall." Rosemary moved off toward a headstone and the three brothers followed like obedient puppies, probably to be sure she didn't get away.

Constantine followed at a distance, wondering how hard the brothers would be to convince to let him speak to her alone. They appeared rather protective. Constantine had grown used to being with Rosemary whenever he wanted.

She stopped before a simple headstone and wrapped her arms about her chest. "They buried them here, the day after they were shot."

Oliver set his arm about his younger brother's shoulders while Leopold knelt. "Finding where our parents were buried is the last piece of the puzzle I never thought to have."

Rosemary stood alone, staring down at the grave silently.

Constantine waited until the brothers raised their heads from their study of the headstone and then he shrugged out of his coat. Rosemary would be cold. She was always cold. He advanced into the group and, ignoring their suspicious expressions, he wrapped Rosemary up. "You rushed out without even a coat."

Her smile was watery. "I had someplace I needed to be. Thank you."

"Anytime."

She stuck her arms into the sleeves and her hands into the pockets before lifting her chin to the heavens. "At least it is not raining today. I do hate to say goodbye when it rains."

Leopold caught his sister's face and turned her toward him. "If you are finished beating your brothers up, perhaps we could go back to the inn where it's warm. I'm anticipating Tobias will complain that he's hungry any minute."

A hesitant smile crossed her face and she looked away.

"Tobias was always hungry. Some things never change, I see.

I'm sure Mrs. Lamb can find enough to fill him and the rest of you before you go."

Rosemary caught up her skirts and headed for the lych-gate. Before she'd gone too many steps, she had a brother on each side, the younger trailing behind. No doubt making sure every avenue of escape was denied her. Constantine stared after them. Anxiety filled him. She wasn't coming back with them. No matter what her brothers hoped, Rosemary intended to remain apart from the Randalls.

But where did that leave him and his daughters, and the child she was expecting?

———◆———

Rosemary struggled against the vise-like grip Leopold had on one arm, determined to break free and stand on her own two feet. The stern face at her side made her heart ache so badly that she blinked back tears. Leopold looked so much like their father that she expected to hear his voice telling her to behave as a proper lady would. But the days when such a feat might be possible were far behind and could never be recaptured. She was what she was. Her brother didn't need to know just how far she'd fallen. "I see you haven't outgrown your bossy tendencies."

"I see you haven't been tamed."

"Hardly." Rosemary looked ahead toward the inn. She forced a sunny smile to her face. "Where would be the fun in behaving against my nature?"

His grip tightened. "None of us have enjoyed the past years. In fact, some of us were lucky to survive the duke's abduction to return."

Rosemary's pulse raced as Oliver moved closer. The sensation of being hemmed in was making her rather nervous of her brothers. One on one she could undoubtedly hold her own. But they'd grown to be rather tall and formidable opponents. She wouldn't be able to escape all three if they worked together against her. "Unless you are prepared to fight me again, I suggest you stop crowding me. I don't much care for the sensation. Or are you planning on abducting me, too?"

Leopold released her immediately. Oliver slipped his arm through hers. "Come now, Terror. You cannot fault us for giving you the greeting, the fight, you intended to have. I see you have improved your technique."

Rosemary tilted her chin to look up at Oliver. He'd grown so old. What had happened to him? He was pale and thin, his brown hair now as gray as Papa's had been before his death. At first, she'd feared fighting him. But after he deflected her first strike, she'd discovered her brother was deceptively strong. She looked ahead to the inn. "I had considerable incentive to remember your lessons. I won't run."

He laughed. "Elizabeth has suggested I should interact with people more often. See how well I'm doing, escorting my sister about on my arm? I am glad we cut our journey short or else I might have missed you. We eloped, you know. Is that not romantic?"

"I saw the notice in the paper."

"My wife's idea to bring you home."

"It didn't work."

"I could not help but notice that. She will be crushed."

Oliver was different. Admittedly, ten years had passed since she'd seen him, but he was decidedly more emotional than she remembered. She hoped it was Beth's influence. She'd always wanted her for a sister. "Where are you living?"

"Romsey Abbey. I've taken over our grandmother's wing and have been prying into every nook and cranny I can find. By the time I'm done, there will be no secrets left uncovered."

"His Grace should not care for that."

Oliver grinned impishly. "The boy is four. It is beyond his understanding at present."

"If he lives to reach his majority."

Oliver stopped dead in the middle of the street. "Did Leopold not tell you? The boy thrives. There is no chance of peril, save for his own stupidity. I trust Leopold and the family at large can instill some sense into the boy as he ages."

"If the duchess allows it."

"My wife will not only allow it but encourage it." Leopold squeezed her shoulders. "When you meet her you will see the truth and cease your mistrust."

"You married the Duchess of Romsey? I'll leave you to suffer the intrigues alone." She scowled at him. "How could you stoop so low? Surely there's someone nicer that caught your eye."

"Mercy was not cast from the same mold as previous duchesses. She is very different."

Rosemary folded her arms across her chest. She didn't believe that for a second. "I'm sure you'll be very happy together."

Leopold raised a finger. "We will all be very happy together."

Rosemary immediately understood his meaning and shook her head to end the discussion. "I will never go back."

"Yes, you will. I am the head of the family and until you marry your place is with us."

Rosemary pushed past him and started toward the inn. "My place is anywhere I choose. I'm of age and relish my independence."

She smiled at Mrs. Lamb as she stepped through the inn's front door. "Would you be willing to feed these gentlemen? They've traveled some distance and have a long journey ahead."

Mrs. Lamb glanced past her and then nodded. When Rosemary turned, Grayling was poised at the door, an odd expression on his face. Tobias loitered in his shadow. She shook off the nagging sensation her brother wanted a private word and made sure her elder brothers were made comfortable.

She took a place at the head of the table. Grayling sat at the far end. Tobias did not join them at all. She looked for him, but her younger brother was nowhere to be found.

As soon as Mrs. Lamb departed, Leopold resumed the discussion. "I left our wives behind with assurances you would come home with us. Will you make me a liar?"

"Hardly my doing when I wasn't consulted. I've no intention of setting one foot upon the estate." She spread her hands wide. "I do wish everyone the best."

"Rosemary," Leopold groaned. "I've no wish to fight with you. Not today. Not when we've finally discovered you and where our parents rest. Tobias, especially, will want assurances. His memory of the abduction still haunts him, I think. Are you not the least curious about what happened to us all?"

"No."

They couldn't have had a harder life than she'd lived. They

hadn't had to sell their body to ease the ache of their empty belly. They couldn't have wondered whether they would survive the night as she had more times than she could count. "I'm sure you're all safe and well at Romsey."

"They chained him," Leopold growled in a low voice. "Beat his flesh until he was scarred. It's a miracle he survived to come home to us."

Rosemary stared at her brothers. "Surely you jest?"

"Take the trouble to ask him for proof yourself rather than turn tail and run. It is Tobias's story to tell, not mine. I've seen the damage done with my own eyes. He can barely tolerate to sit inside a carriage, but as soon as he heard of your location, he forced himself to come and see for himself if you were the woman Grayling had employed." Leopold's mouth pursed in disapproval. "We've all suffered punishment of some sort at the duke's command. You've become a hard, unfeeling woman, Rosemary Randall, if you think you're the only one who's suffered. Mama, God rest her soul, would be ashamed of you for not caring."

"I'm sure she already is." It was better that they couldn't see what she'd become. Her parents had been keen to see her marry well. To be a lady at all times. Rosemary was not that. It pained her that her little brother had been injured. She glanced at Oliver discreetly. He seemed no different than before, but she had to wonder what punishment had been meted out to him and Leopold. Were they like her, scarred deeply beneath the surface and afraid to show how much?

Constantine stood. "Excuse me a moment."

Rosemary watched him go with a heavy heart. He didn't appear to be taking the news of her true identity very well.

When he was gone from sight, Leopold was quick to question her. "When did you meet him?"

If she told him the truth, would he leave her in peace and forget this nonsense about returning to Romsey? "He wasn't the first."

Her brother glanced down at the table. When his gaze lifted, his expression was bleak. "We'll remain until you change your mind."

Leopold stood and leaned over her. When he pressed a fierce kiss to her brow and strode from the dining room with long, determined strides, she hoped she would never see him again. It was best he knew as much of the truth as she could bear to share. She could never be considered clean again. Not wholesome. Not good. She had too much dirty laundry weighing her down to ever be what they wanted or expected of her.

Mrs. Lamb bustled over with two overflowing plates and set them down on the table. When she returned, she placed one before Rosemary. The panic she'd felt on seeing the Romsey carriage had subsided enough for her stomach to remember she was ill. The scent wafted to fill her nose and her nausea returned. She breathed through her mouth. Unfortunately, that didn't help enough. With a strangled cry, she bolted from the table and rushed upstairs to the rented room. She flung herself toward the chamber pot in the nick of time. The tea and scrap of bread she'd consumed earlier reappeared.

She closed her eyes as the spasms passed, willing yet another terrible day to end.

Chapter Twenty-Seven

———◆———

When Constantine reentered the inn after a short walk to clear his head, he discovered he was not the only worried man to grace the dining room. Two of the brothers were in deep conversation on the far side of the room. Several times the elder started for the stairs, but Oliver was quick to call him back.

Mrs. Lamb bustled over with a mug of ale and a plate of food and set them out on the table. "Something to whet your appetite, my lord?"

"Thank you, Mrs. Lamb. You're very good to me."

The look she gave him was tinged with distrust. "You returned. If you let her get away, I might not be so kind the next time you stay."

"Then I shall never let her go, just to keep your good opinion." Constantine didn't say it lightly. He'd had enough time to consider that her connections had no bearing whatsoever on his decision to marry Rosemary. The acquiring of her name was not the least bit important in the scheme of things. The woman was. He loved her, no matter what she called herself.

He sat beside Oliver Randall and took a long swallow of ale. The solitude of a short walk had also stirred his compassion. The situation was difficult for all of them. "Where is Rosemary now?"

Oliver pointed toward the staircase. "Upstairs. Tobias followed her to be sure she didn't run off again while we were eating, but I suppose her condition may hamper any plans for immediate flight. She couldn't stand the scents wafting up from the plate set before her, so the innkeeper's wife may be correct. Congratulations."

"Thank you." In the sudden rush of discovery, Constantine had managed to push the notion of being a father again to the back of his mind. To his surprise, he was not unduly worried about the birth. He was more worried Rosemary would take care of the matter without telling him and ensure she would never be in any danger.

Constantine picked at the food on his plate. He was almost certain he could convince Rosemary not to run away and to return to Stanton Harold Hall. But avoiding Romsey Abbey and her family was definitely part of her plan. He was torn in two. He had to prevent becoming separated from her again.

He cast a quick glance at Leopold and decided the man needed time to regain his temper before he discussed marrying his sister. Oliver was another matter. He didn't seem the least perturbed by his sister's recovery or her expectant condition. Constantine caught Oliver's gaze. It was almost as if sentimentality had no place in his life. Rosemary was like that at times. "Are you injured?"

A rueful smile flittered over Oliver's face as he tested his ribs. "Ribs ache, but no lasting damage."

What a strange response. Constantine set down his fork. "When Mercy and Blythe were young, the most I ever did to them was pull their braids. Did you make a habit of fighting with Rosemary? Is that why she distrusts you all?"

"You have to understand that Rosemary is different than most females. She always wanted to do what her brothers did and if we would not oblige, she found a way to do it anyway."

Constantine raised a brow. "Boxing?"

"Rosemary doesn't box. But she was popular with the local lads when she was young, and after one such fellow proved a bit too forward she wanted to know how to protect herself. I taught her without letting anyone know and she excelled at the vigorous activity. Her current fighting style has evolved in a way I never expected. She's limited, you see. Her shorter stature and the gowns society expects her to wear hamper her movements, so she's had to adapt."

"For God's sake, Oliver. She was supposed to have the education of a lady, not an assassin," Leopold growled.

Oliver leaned close to Constantine. "He's just annoyed that I won while he ended up flat on his belly with the wind knocked out of him. Elder brothers always like to be ahead of the rest of us."

Constantine found that offensive. "Do bear in mind that I'm an elder brother."

"Exactly. I gather you are completely in sympathy with his feelings."

Leopold scowled and resumed eating like a man preparing for battle. Rosemary was likely to give him one. Constantine had never seen a woman move as she had. He'd never known a woman to hold her own in a physical fight, either.

Leopold stood. "That's enough time."

Oliver pulled his brother back down to his seat. "I know what you intend and it won't work. She will not come peacefully and deep down, you know it. You cannot fault her for her fears. She needs time to trust us again."

Leopold looked set to argue but then shook his head. "She's always been pigheaded. I knew the moment I saw her that she hadn't changed."

If only they knew the ways Rosemary had changed, then perhaps they might have more compassion. As it was, only Constantine understood some of what had happened to her. He'd thought he'd have more time to learn the rest and gain her trust. But time and opportunity were fast running out. "Let me talk to her before you do anything rash."

Oliver shrugged. "It cannot hurt."

"Thank you." He nodded to Oliver, avoided eye contact with Leopold in case he had objections, and stood. "There are some things I should say to her in private before I rejoin my daughters at Romsey. I at least need to prepare an explanation for them."

Leopold's dark eyes bored into his. "If you hurt her, I'll never forgive you."

Now was hardly the appropriate time to become protective of Rosemary's feelings. "I never intended to."

Constantine climbed the stairs to Rosemary's room at the inn with a heavy heart. What could he possibly say to convince her she should trust him? She'd had good reason to run in the beginning, but her past, whatever that might entail, was sufficient to make her wary. He would have to make it plain that whatever she chose would be supported.

Tobias stood poised in the hall, hands in his pockets and a troubled expression on his face. Constantine approached. "Is she in there?"

"Yes, Rosemary is still with us, but I fear not for long."

He grasped the man by the shoulder. "If Rosemary will not remain, let me assure you her other personas are just as charming and challenging. Did she have a talent for the stage when she was young?"

"No. She is the same as she ever was." Tobias frowned. "You don't seem too concerned that she lied about her identity."

"I've known from the first time we spoke that she was not who she claimed to be. Your sister is a remarkably honest liar. Aside from the truth of her name and connections, I've always known her character. She's rather remarkable."

"You're in love with her?"

"Since the moment we met." He grinned. It felt very good to say that out loud and to a member of her family. Now he had to convince her that it was true still. "Are you the brother who smashed her toes during dancing lessons when she was young?"

Tobias scratched his head. "I'd hoped she would have forgotten that."

"I don't imagine she's forgotten very much of anything, and that may be the whole problem." He grinned at the other man's discomfort. "Excuse me. I should check that her stomach has settled now."

Tobias caught his arm. "Will you stand by her no matter what?"

"I'm still here, aren't I?"

Constantine moved toward the door. Although he knocked several times, Rosemary didn't answer him. When he tested the handle, he found the door was unlocked. He let himself inside, prepared for Rosemary to have disappeared through the window. A small lump was curled up on the floor beside the chamber pot. He rushed across the room and eased Rosemary into a sitting position.

"That's no place for a lady to be."

Discontented eyes glared at him. "I'm not a lady."

"Are you sure? Because you have all the necessary parts in your possession. In fact, I'm very fond of seeing them in my bed."

After a moment, Rosemary spared him a reluctant grin. "I do enjoy your sense of humor, Constantine. All right, help me up so I might find my dignity."

Since she weighed next to nothing, she was on her feet in a moment. Constantine encircled her waist carefully. "The floor is no place for a woman in your condition."

She frowned. "I never expected to fall so soon, but as we discussed, it's not your concern."

"It is if that's my child in your belly."

She set her hands to her hips. "Of course it's yours."

"Then I get to talk about the fact." He brushed the back of his fingers across the front of her gown. "How long have you been feeling ill?"

She grabbed the hand skimming her belly and held it out of the way. "Today."

"Then I haven't missed much." He smiled. "I promised to take care of you and I fully intend to be at your side every moment of every day."

Rosemary moved away from him and sat on the edge of the bed. "There is nothing for you to worry about."

"I will always worry. It's in my nature." He shifted to sit on the edge of the bed and took her hand lightly in his. Her knuckles were red and likely tender. "So you are Rosemary Randall?"

"I haven't been Rosemary Randall for some time. That young girl is long gone."

He lifted her hand to his lips and kissed each tender knuckle. "I feel sorry for your brothers then."

"Oh?"

He cupped her cold fingers between his hands and blew a warm breath across her skin. "They will miss getting to know how wonderful you are."

Rosemary snatched her hand back. "It's best that they don't. They know enough already and I cannot bear to see their opinion of me brought lower. In time, they will understand and accept my absence. They can stop placing those plaintive advertisements in the paper and get on with their lives."

"That first day you brought my daughters to my study, you saw the notice begging you to come home. How long have you known your brothers were searching for you?"

Rose shrugged. "Months. Long before we ever met."

"So you did not care to answer them?"

"I never said I didn't care. I tried to write once."

He shook his head at her stubbornness. "That's not what Leopold believes. I've never seen a more shattered man. You're breaking his heart."

"The duchess will console him," Rosemary said bitterly.

"Not in this. There are limits to even my sister's ability to divert one's attention. He will regret this day all his life. Can you live with that? Can you walk away, knowing it was you who hurt them so badly?"

Rosemary flung herself off the bed and stalked to the window. "You don't know what you're talking about. You barely know my brothers."

"That's true. But I know a little about you and I would be the poorer should we never have met. Are you afraid?"

Rosemary stilled. Her hands clenched into fists. She spun about. "I am not afraid."

"I see that despite the discovery of your name and connections, some things never change. You really do have a dreadfully short temper. I do enjoy the fire in your eyes."

Her eyes narrowed. "I'm no different and that is the problem."

He sighed and stood, stopping close enough to set his hands on her arms. "If it's any consolation, I will be at your side every moment should you return to Romsey. If they have a problem with you, then we can leave together."

"Why would you do such a thing? She's your sister."

"And you are just as important to me and my daughters. You are my governess. The one my daughters cried hours over in the carriage yesterday. You cannot discard our feelings so easily. You made us love you."

Rosemary's eyebrows shot up. "Love?"

"The girls certainly do. Who else would tell them stories and help them remember their mother? None of the other governesses I hired could be bothered to keep her memory alive. Only you did that for us. I can never show you enough gratitude."

Rosemary stilled. "I'm sure that you can figure something out."

His lips curved into a smile at her challenge. "There are many ways to prove you are adored. All of them required you to not run away. There will never be enough hours in the day to learn everything about you, but I promise to start now."

Rose frowned. "Forgive me, my lord, but I'm not feeling very energetic right now."

"I know. You're carrying my child." He caressed her face gently. "Back to bed for you."

He swung her up into his arms, crossed to the bed, and settled her comfortably on it. Rosemary didn't protest or say he wasn't needed, and that gave him hope. He added a blanket over her legs to ensure she stayed warm and tucked it closely around her.

Rosemary caught his hand in hers. "Thank you for understanding."

"I don't understand anything, Rosemary, except that I hope you will not dismiss my feelings as easily as you do your own family."

"Surely you can see I have my reasons."

"Some, but they're not enough in my opinion to make me accept them. Mrs. Lamb mentioned you planned to leave this morning, before I returned."

Her gaze dropped from his. Her hands twisted in her lap. "I planned to be very far away before you discovered I'd gone."

He stood back. "What do I tell my daughters?"

"What do you usually tell them when you misplace a governess?"

He took a deep breath to keep his frustration in check. "No matter what I say, you will never believe you're more than that to me."

"I cannot be more. Society expects—"

"Society's expectations can go to hell. I want you."

"Really?" Her brow rose. "And what if my services came at a price?"

"I'd pay any sum you named and more."

"I'm certain that is not true. For instance, I doubt you'd do what my brothers would expect should they learn our affair was to continue."

"Are you afraid they'd suggest we marry?"

"I'm not afraid of that."

"Neither am I." He leaned closer. "In fact, I had intended offering for you before I even learned your real name."

"And you've come to your senses now? I'm not surprised."

"No, I decided that since I was your present to yourself when we first met, and you clearly enjoy making decisions for me, that you should ask for my hand in marriage. You do like to be in charge. Why stop now, hmm?"

"That's ridiculous. Gentlemen of the *ton* do not ask a whore to marry them."

"I would never use such a vulgar term for so tempting a wench as you." He grinned at her stubborn expression. "Since that isn't the case here, I feel it only fitting that you should do the honors."

"You'll be waiting a long time."

"Then I will wait." There. He'd thrown out the challenge. It was up to Rosemary now to be brave and accept there was far more between them than mere lust.

She rounded on him. "Have you taken leave of your senses? Why would you want me to be your wife?"

"The question is why I shouldn't. I know enough about you not to have made the decision lightly. I would have spoken of the subject before, but I thought I had ample time to convince you when we returned from Romsey. At the moment, I'm sure you're planning to disappear the moment my back is turned."

Rose didn't deny it.

He leaned over the bed, getting close enough that she pressed back against the headboard. "Why don't you explain to me why you are an imperfect candidate to be my wife and perhaps I will reconsider."

Marriage or not, he really wanted to be the one she confided in about her past. "Convince me I'm wrong about you."

Rosemary licked her lips. "You were not my first."

"I'm not a fool."

"Not even my fifteenth, truth be told."

No surprises there. "How many? Do you know the number?"

"I ceased counting at seventy-four."

"Hmm, a goodly sum." He glanced at Rosemary. "Tell me about the first."

Her eyes closed and Constantine ached to pull her into his arms and tell her not to. Yet he would know her secrets. All of them.

A shudder shook her slender body. "I was sixteen, alone and afraid and so desperately hungry that I'd begun stealing from farmhouses. One day I wasn't quick enough in leaving. I'd lingered to straighten my hair when I spotted the lady of the house's hair comb. How foolish that decision was. Her husband caught me and made me earn what I'd taken."

The cold, emotionless retelling caused gooseflesh to rise on his nape.

"And what did you think of me when we met?"

A sad smile crossed her face. "When I saw you, I thought to spend a night with a man purely because I wanted to."

"I did pay Mrs. Cohen well for your services the next morning."

"I didn't do it for the money, or the bet. I just… wanted to touch you."

"As did I." He moved closer. "A lucky coincidence for my daughters. They have grown in confidence and contentment since you came to live with us."

"Children are easy to please. They do not see the wickedness behind the hand that guides them."

"You're a little hard on yourself. You did what you had to."

She set her hands to his chest. "You're not listening to me."

"I'm listening. I'm sorry about the farmer who caught you and every other man who took advantage of your desperation. It was more or less what I expected. Everyone has baggage in their life."

"Have you slept with so many men?"

He grinned. "No men at all. But women, that's another matter."

As he hoped, her eyes brightened with possessive fire. "How many?"

He laughed then and caught her face between his hands. "Shh, now, little vixen. I'd no idea you'd be so jealous."

Her arms twined around his neck and she looked up at him with a fatuous expression that belied her mood. "How many were there, Constantine?"

"One hundred and three wenches, not counting you or my wife. I've kept an accounting of such matters from the beginning."

She stared hard at him. "That's a lot."

"I was a wild young man sowing my oats as my father once put it." He shrugged. "I had nothing like your explanation to make my behavior understandable. You sold your body to survive."

Constantine brushed a stray strand of hair from her cheek and tucked it behind her ear. "Rosemary. A name that finally suits you. I promise you, I do not hold your past against you. I thought you the bravest woman I'd ever known even when I didn't know your real name or connections."

He could sense her wavering and took advantage of her distraction. He dipped his head and pressed his lips to hers, savoring the sweet passion of her lips. His pulse raced as her arms tightened about his neck. He kissed her passionately, as if this was the first of many. He hoped so because he feared he would never find another lover like her. He wanted to imprint her on his soul and make them inseparable.

He eased back eventually and met her gaze. "If the price of keeping you in my life means a permanent break with Romsey, then I will do so without reservations. I would make any sacrifice if it meant you would share my life. All you have to do is trust me."

After a long moment, Rosemary's chilled fingers slid across his open hand and captured him in a tight grip.

Chapter Twenty-Eight

<hr>

Rosemary studied the far horizon as the sun set behind a thick bank of clouds. If not for Constantine's hand firmly clasped about hers, she would have fled the carriage and given up this foolishness. Ahead lay Romsey. A place she despised. The only bright spark on the horizon was seeing Willow, Maisy, and Poppy. They were adorably innocent and, according to Constantine, utterly miserable again without her.

The carriage rattled over the small bridge and revealed the looming bulk of the abbey in the distance. She squeezed Constantine's hand, but the panic she expected had left her. She felt no anxiety at being so close to the cause of her suffering. How strange. The sight didn't fill her with the same dread that sometimes invaded her dreams. The abbey appeared perfectly ordinary in the daylight.

She eased her grip on Grayling and leaned toward the window. The last time she had been here she had been a girl of sixteen and easily impressed with the grandeur of her surroundings. But beneath that pristine exterior was a purpose that had filled her with revulsion and anger.

The main doors opened and servants trouped out to line the front stairs in wait of their arrival. Behind them came three women and one small boy. It made for a pretty picture, but the ones she longed to see were not on the stairs yet.

She lost sight of them at the curve of the road. Her eyes flew to Constantine's.

"Courage." He kissed her hand, as he had done every time she had doubted the wisdom of acceding to her brothers' wishes on this journey.

When the carriage drew to a halt, Leopold, Tobias, and Oliver clambered out first, hurrying up the stairs toward the women. Constantine waited a little longer before he released her hand and stepped out. Heart pounding hard, Rosemary considered ordering the carriage to take her away without him. But she'd agreed to come, on the condition that he would help her leave exactly when she wanted to go, without argument or persuasion applied to stay beyond one further hour.

She climbed from the carriage unassisted and faced the front of the abbey. Rosemary lifted her face to the façade and inspected the ducal residence. This time, the structure failed to impress. She'd seen enough of the world to overlook the trappings of wealth. What mattered most lay beneath the polished exterior.

She smiled quickly at Constantine to reassure him that she wasn't afraid anymore and moved toward the servants, rather surprised that they were led by one face she knew well.

Eamon Murphy stepped forward and smiled through the tears in his eyes. "Welcome home, Miss Randall."

She frowned at him. "Oh, do stop blubbering, Eamon. I haven't had the least reason to be cross with you for the last decade. But... there is always tomorrow, I suppose."

Eamon laughed then and the servants all twittered a little nervously.

Leopold came down a few steps, the young duke holding his hand tightly. "Your Grace, may I present my sister, Miss Rosemary Randall. Rosemary, I am so happy to introduce you to the sixth Duke of Romsey."

Rosemary, standing on a lower step, had the perfect position to be eye to eye with the boy. She leaned close to inspect him and then looked closer again when he grinned happily. Green eyes, but his face bore no resemblance to his supposed father. That man had possessed a narrow nose and delicate chin. There was nothing delicate about this boy.

Suspicions rising, she glanced at her brother in confusion. The boy had dimples. Only their side of the family was cursed with the blasted things. In truth, the boy looked like… Leopold.

She straightened and scowled at her brother. "You might have told me."

"Actually, I did. You're as bad as Oliver, you know. He never listens either." Leopold drew her to him with a laugh and hugged her. "You see. There's nothing to fear anymore. May I introduce you to everyone else?"

When she was released, her brothers had surrounded her, forcing Constantine to the outskirts of the group.

"There's no need," Beth said as she barged between them and pulled Rosemary into her arms. Her grip was tight and infinitely familiar. "I've been waiting for my sister all my life."

After a moment, Rosemary had to loosen Beth's grip. "Dearest, you're crushing me."

"I'm just so relieved to see you back home where you belong." Beth laughed and drew back, wiping the tears from her eyes. "Come and let me introduce you to Mercy and Blythe. They're dying to meet you."

Rosemary was led past her brothers and taken to two ladies standing a little apart from the rest. The elder of the pair was utterly stunning. Dark hair, brilliant green eyes like the young duke's. Rosemary searched for signs of deception and found none in her open expression.

"Welcome to Romsey, my dear. Leopold has told me so much about you." Even the Duchesses voice was beautiful.

Rosemary refused to curtsy. She just couldn't. She inclined her head instead. "Your Grace."

Constantine's fingers threaded through hers and gripped her hand tightly.

Her Grace's eyes brightened with merriment. "I always rather thought we'd get along and you've just done the one thing to make that true. Just so you know, I don't tend to follow the rules; I'm a terribly informal duchess and possess many more unforgivable vices that society undoubtedly gossips over. Oh, and I should warn you, I'm fond of matchmaking."

The duchess's gaze drifted to the man holding her hand, her eyes shrewd. Rosemary was certain the woman was busily plotting to make her brother propose a marriage between them. She almost laughed. Constantine wouldn't propose. He was waiting to be proposed to. "Then that makes you the perfect Duchess of Romsey. Did you know the old duke intended for me to marry his son, your first husband?"

Her Grace nodded. "That is what Oliver suggested to us on his return. Edwin wasn't a cruel man, Rosemary, but I can understand you wanted to make your own choices. I admire that."

Tobias strolled over and placed his arm about the other woman. "Rosemary, meet Blythe, formerly Lady Venables and my wife. The woman determined to reform me and the only one who might have a chance."

"Reformation is impossible and you know it, sir." Blythe smiled at her husband affectionately before meeting Rosemary's gaze. "It is very good to finally meet you. I hope you will stay so we might become better acquainted."

Rosemary made a noncommittal sound. Everyone was being so nice, so pleased to see her, and she didn't know quite how to behave. However, Tobias's wife appeared to be kind and she didn't want to be at odds with her youngest brother. He'd been so hesitant with her so far. "Congratulations to you both. I hope you will both be very happy together."

A light snow began to fall and Leopold shooed everyone inside. The king at work with his subjects. She shook her head at how everyone still listened to him. As children, his bossy tendencies had driven her to rebel against him as much as to her parents' expectations. Even Constantine passed through the door without looking back.

Rosemary remained where she was and stared at the gaping black maw of Romsey's open front door.

Warmth slid over her hand then and she looked up into Tobias's face. "Is there space left for me in your affections? I tried to get to you, but they were so strong," he said quietly.

Rosemary's heart broke. The hesitant smile on Tobias's face was so painfully familiar that she started to sob. His long arms wrapped around her, holding her tightly against his chest. When she moved her hands over his back, she detected odd lumps covering his skin beneath the linen. He had been whipped. When he stilled, she buried her face in his shoulder and cried her heart out.

How could anyone have hurt her brother? He was the kindest

and gentlest of them all. He rocked her gently and handed her a lacey scrap of handkerchief that clearly belonged to his wife. Rosemary released Tobias and quickly dabbed at her tears. She never cried. At least, she never did where anyone could see. At least she had waited until the inhabitants of the abbey had returned indoors.

Feeling foolish, she raised her head. Tobias's gaze was as watery as her own. He pressed his forehead to hers. "Thank God you're here, safe and sound. Any longer and Leopold would have had a seizure. His temper has not improved with age."

Rosemary grinned. "I noticed that."

"I was almost sure you had." He glanced toward the door. "It takes courage to cross the threshold."

She gripped Tobias hand. "The boy."

"You saw it faster than I did." Tobias sighed. "Of Leopold's making. There is no one left to have our revenge on. That moment passed with young Edwin's first breath. Do you still enjoy sweet treats, Rosemary?"

"Of course."

Tobias nodded and patted his stomach. "Then you'll enjoy Romsey. Mercy has a sweet tooth. I always enjoy my visits."

"You don't live here?"

He chuckled. "No. I live at Harrowdale with Blythe. I'm not suited for society, but I visit often."

Rosemary sighed. "I'm not suited for it either."

"Then you'll have to be like me and learn all over again." He left her then, standing on the stairs alone with only the falling snow for company.

The same feeling of desolation she had striven to ignore for the past ten years came back in full force. She didn't want to be alone anymore. She wanted what everyone else had.

The first step was the hardest. She reached the very threshold and paused as she looked inside. Constantine was waiting on the black-and-white tile, a smile tugging his lips. The cold opulence of Romsey faded in the face of his warmth. But to get to him required all her determination. She raised her hand to touch the wood frame. Not a dream. Not a nightmare.

Using the door as leverage, she pushed her way inside and walked to Constantine.

He cupped her face. "That wasn't so hard, was it?"

"You truly don't know what you are talking about, do you?"

"Not a clue, but I'm sure you'll educate me eventually." He glanced up. "I'm on my way to see my daughters. Should they ask, will you be visiting with them today?"

"I am their governess."

His lips pressed together as if she was testing his patience. His hand fell away from her skin. "If that is all you wish, then I will give you leave to spend as much time as you need with your family. They are in the library."

She followed his progress up the staircase, half of her longing to follow. But she'd come back to put the past into its proper place. Rosemary peeked into the library and was instantly struck by the easy camaraderie of those gathered. Leopold and his bride were reading the newssheet together and talking over the events inside. Tobias had laid himself out on a long sofa, his bride cradling his head on her lap as she read a book. Even Oliver was there, scratching out words on a sheet of parchment. At his side was a boy Rosemary hadn't met yet and Beth, gazing fondly at the pair.

All around her, everyone had a place. Everyone had their own concerns to occupy their time. None of them spared a glance in her direction. She backed away from the doorway.

If this was what she'd come home to, she need never have bothered. Didn't they want to question her about her life? Didn't they want to hear from her own lips the indignities she'd suffered?

Rosemary rocked on the balls of her feet, disturbed that there would be no inquisition. It was as if they didn't want to speak of her past. As if they didn't care. Did it not matter to them that she was not the woman she should have been? She turned away from the library and slowly made her way up the staircase. Was it really that easy to ignore what she'd done with her life before Constantine?

A maid gave her directions to the nursery but she would have found it anyway, given the ruckus ahead.

Maisy screamed and Rosemary hurried toward the sound.

"Now, Willow, don't do that."

Willow started to cry. "She pinched me."

"Maisy, sweetheart, don't hurt your sister."

Poppy began to wail.

"Dear God, this is intolerable. What the devil is taking that woman so long? Doesn't she know we need her desperately?"

Rosemary nudged the door open with her foot.

Constantine stood in the center of the room, Poppy in his arms, middle child wrapped around his legs, and the eldest attempting to remove her sister from her father's legs by pulling her hair. The young duke watched from a corner, a servant hovering at his side. The girls hadn't ever been so badly behaved. Did everything have to fall apart as soon as she'd turned her back? She stepped through the doorway. "Who is desperate?"

Constantine looked her way with relief. "Me. They were about to come find you."

The children stopped their crying and fighting, staring at her with huge eyes that never failed to melt her heart. They might not be her flesh and blood, but to Rose they were kindred spirits.

The baby wailed and all but threw herself from Constantine's arms. His scramble to hold on to the slippery bundle made Rosemary laugh. She took the child. "Shh, little lamb. Here I am."

The other two girls joined their sister until Rosemary was hampered from moving an inch by all three sets of arms. She touched each one gently, brushing their curls from their hot faces and listening to their complaints. After a few moments, they calmed down and simply hugged her. Rosemary smiled at her charges with pride. Just a little bit of attention went a long way with them. They were the easiest of children to manage.

She raised her face to see the young duke watching them in silence. The resemblance to her brother was so strong that she couldn't possibly bear him any ill will. He might be the Duke of Romsey, but there was a chance he could grow into a good man. Hopefully he would do a better job of treating the wishes of others with more respect than his predecessors.

When she looked up into Constantine's smiling face, her heart tumbled over, and her legs grew weak. He reached out to touch her face with his warm fingers. When she pressed her face into his hand, he winked. "Now do you know where you belong? You're the woman we've all been waiting for."

Chapter Twenty-Nine

———◆·———

Constantine prowled his bedchamber, frustration growing at his lack of success. Yes, he was happy that he'd brought Rosemary home to Romsey. Her brothers had congratulated him on convincing Rosemary and as they'd talked after dinner he'd realized they hadn't expected him to succeed in changing her mind. He didn't tell them what the bargain had been. If he had, he feared Mercy and even Blythe would have been upset over his plans.

He shook his head as the clock on the mantel chimed another hour since Rosemary had disappeared. Had she always been so stubborn, or had circumstances been responsible for her utter self-reliance? The problem with Rosemary was she still held back just enough so that he could never be truly sure if she was with him or not.

The only thing he was sure of was that his daughters had her undivided attention. She'd been more mothering toward them than any governess they'd had these past years. She treated them as her own, and Constantine didn't mind that at all. But he was their father and couldn't be left out. He wanted some of Rosemary's attention from time to time. He feared he might have to wait his whole life for that.

He was pleased she hadn't tried to take his late wife's place. In fact, Rosemary mentioned her several times during the day. It was as if she knew they all needed those memories to forge ahead in life without Augusta standing beside them.

However, the second part of his plan had failed. Rosemary was determined to remain his children's governess and that meant he had to keep a respectable distance. Never mind that her stomach would soon grow large with his child. He still wasn't sure if he'd convinced her to keep it.

Constantine slipped his jacket from his shoulders and rubbed his jaw. It ached less than it had and he was relieved. He'd been an idiot to allow Mercy to winkle out the information about his lover. His only defense was that he hadn't known she was Rosemary Randall, sister to a man who punched as if he held lead in his hand. He gently tested his jaw again.

The door closed behind him. "Are you in pain?"

He glanced toward the voice and found Rosemary inside his room, robe wrapped tightly around her delicious body. She looked so tempting that his heart skipped a beat. "Some. How is your condition this evening?"

"What condition?" She came closer and caught his face in her hands and inspected the slight bruise forming on his jaw. "Who did this? Leopold, I assume."

Constantine winced. "He seemed rather protective of your virtue."

Rosemary snorted and released him, her hands falling to the ties of her robe. "Too late for that. The girls are asleep finally and it's time you were abed. I realized you must have come straight back to get me. I'm flattered."

Constantine jerked his eyes away from the white nightgown that was revealed as Rosemary parted her robe. Damn woman. She knew exactly how well she excited him. "I never wanted to leave you in the first place if you remember, but you were very convincing. I won't be so easily led again."

He sat on the edge of the bed and fought her allure. "Are the children happier now?"

"They are angels, as I keep telling you. Really, Constantine, if you cannot handle them at this age, then how will you get on when they make their debut? Do you intend to lock them in their rooms and deny them suitors?" Her robe fluttered from her fingers to the floor.

He groaned. "I'm trying not to think about that as it's not for many years to come. When the time does come, you decide who is worthy or not."

"Children age in the blink of an eye."

"So do their fathers."

A smile tugged her lips as she inched her nightgown up her legs. She struck one out, toe pointed, and teased him. "Won't you come play with me tonight?"

"This is my sister's house and your large and very easily irritated brothers are close by. I'd rather not fight them all if we are caught together in an intimate moment."

She dropped her gown and set her hands to her hips. "What we do when alone is none of their business."

"Rosemary," he said as he crossed the room and picked up her robe. "I can understand why it is they are protective. I have sisters. I would not be happy if they had carried on under my roof before marriage as we have under mine."

"This is different. You know what I am."

He drew her against him. "I know that you are too important to me to ever risk your reputation again. Can't you see? Our affair must end."

"What? Don't be ridiculous. You asked me to ask you to marry you. Do you take it back?"

"I do think we should marry and I've given you every encouragement to ask. If I were to ask you now, I still believe you would refuse. I can only conclude that you don't love me as deeply as I love you. I would do anything you wanted just to make you smile."

She scowled. "I do love you."

"Really? Well, that's a relief. I hope I'm not old and decrepit before you take pity on me. It's marriage or we go back to how things were before Christmas. Celibacy for both."

She snatched the robe from his hands and stormed to the door. "You'll regret this."

The door slammed behind her and Constantine shook his head. He already missed her like the devil, but it was well past time to do the honorable thing. If she didn't marry him, he didn't know what he could do about the babe she carried. The scandal didn't bear thinking about when society found out his governess was big with his child.

Yet he wouldn't punish his daughters by forcing their beloved governess from his home. That would be cruel. The only thing he could do once he escorted them back to Stanton Harold Hall was beg her to marry him each and every day. He shuffled back to the bed, falling onto the mattress and drawing the pillow over his head.

The door banged open again. Constantine didn't bother looking to see which brother had come to beat him up because Rosemary had just been in his bedchamber.

"All right," Rosemary said, a decided reluctance in her voice. "I refuse to be celibate ever again. My lord, would you do me the honor of taking my hand in marriage? I promise to love, honor, and obey your every command for all the days of my life."

"I'd be honored." Constantine tossed the pillow aside and raised his head. "Every command?"

She threw her nightgown on the floor and crossed the room naked. When she crawled over his body and sat over his hips, her smile turned cunning. "As long as you obey every one of mine."

The thing he liked best about Rosemary was that she wasn't anything like his late wife. Bold, bossy and determined to win any challenge. He'd never had a dull moment in her company and couldn't imagine one in their future. "I'd be delighted to. What is it that you want?"

She caught his hands in hers and threaded their fingers together. "I dislike the rooms the children sleep in."

"Oh," he said, frowning that her first demand did not involve him. "What do you propose as a solution?"

"There are a set of rooms not far from your own. I should like them to sleep nearby so they will always be close to us."

Constantine wasn't against the idea, but he waited a moment before nodding. "What else?"

"Miss Cunningham may have the makings of a fine maid, but she's not the best around the children. She should have other duties elsewhere."

Constantine sat up slowly and wiped a hand over his face. "As my wife, decisions about household staff and duties will be for you to decide and see implemented. I will not hold to past habits if you have other ideas on how best to run our home."

Rosemary's face grew thoughtful and she eased off his lap,

coming to rest on her hands and knees. "You're tired. Into bed with you."

Constantine didn't want to argue with her. Now she'd asked to make their relationship official, they were as good as married in his mind. She wouldn't change her mind. When she drew back the covers, he flung himself between them, but before sleep claimed him, he patted the space beside him. "Come to me, my love. Let us spend tonight in each other's arms."

The bed dipped and a chilled, slender body cuddled up against him. In the flickering firelight, Constantine thought he might actually have everything he needed. The woman curled up against his chest sighed contentedly, hands clutching him possessively. "Do you really not mind what I've done?"

"Rosemary, there is nothing you can say that will drive me away from you."

"There might be one."

Constantine hugged her close. "What more is there that I do not know?"

"I detest condoms. I refuse to have relations with you again if you insist on wearing one."

Constantine laughed and then clenched his jaw as it ached. "I think we can dispense with that if you are certain you want me."

"Good. Because the last night we lay together, I snooped into your possessions and found the blasted thing. I burned it."

"Well, that settles that." She'd taken the decision of protecting Rosemary out of his hands. The strange thing was, he really didn't mind that she'd taken the matter over. Even if he had the condom, he would debate its use as a preventative measure. Yet if she found it so uncomfortable, he wouldn't inflict it on her. "Rosemary, could I ask a favor now?"

"I suppose you could."

"If there is any other possession of mine that you do not like, could you at least talk to me about the matter before you allow your destructive tendencies free rein?"

Rosemary wrapped her arms about his waist. "You can keep Rothwell and Lady Farnsworth as friends."

Constantine stilled. "About Arabella?"

"Still worrying?"

"Well, yes. Of course I am." He swallowed. "Please tell me she is not going to throw herself at some reckless rogue who will abandon her after the first dance, so to speak."

Rosemary began to laugh. "Oh no, she's not going to be taken advantage of. That's not her plan at all."

"So there is a plan? Is she going to marry again? If so, I should make a point of warning her away from Rothwell. The man has a reputation and he was rather inquisitive about her on his last visit."

Rosemary kissed his chest. "Don't worry; they say reformed rogues make the best husbands."

He tossed Rosemary onto her back and pinned her to the bed. "Does that apply to reformed Randalls?"

"I doubt it. We Randalls were born to break the rules. There's not much that can tame us." She smiled wickedly. "But I don't mind if you keep trying."

<h1 style="text-align:center">Epilogue</h1>

———◆———

Rosemary Hunt, Countess Grayling to larger society, eased into a chair and accepted the bundle from the housekeeper with a contented sigh. She had been lady of the manor for close to seven months and at last she had everything she'd ever wanted. A devoted husband, children, and comfort. But most of all, she knew in her heart where she belonged and whom she belonged with.

Mrs. Smith peered out the window and scowled. "He's finally returned, my lady?"

Rosemary smiled at the revenge she was about to inflict on her husband. Until now, she had not found a suitable opportunity to repay Constantine for their surprise trip to Romsey nine months ago. But a perfect solution had fallen into her lap today and she wasn't about to squander the moment. Everything was ready. "And not a moment too soon. I thought I might have to resort to violence to keep my siblings at bay."

"They love you, my lady." Mrs. Smith's eyes softened. "As do each of us at the Hall. I am sure I even glimpsed a tear in the corner of Cunningham's eye at your news."

Rosemary caught the housekeeper's hand and squeezed. "I could never have found my place without your help. Can you please make sure my husband does not linger belowstairs overlong?"

"You have my word." The housekeeper bobbed a curtsy and hurried for the door. Just as she reached for the handle, it opened and Constantine strode in. Windswept and out of breath.

Rosemary would like nothing better than to rub her hands in glee, but they were rather occupied at present.

"I'm sorry I was so long," he said quickly as he flung his hat to the far corner of the room. "The tenants over by the mill were celebrating. Their daughter has just become engaged and they insisted I share in the celebrations."

"Did you pass along my congratulations?"

"Of course. They sent along their best wishes for the coming birth."

She stifled a laugh. "Did they? It was kind of them to remember me."

"The estate talks of nothing else. I've had every woman I meet reassure me, but you know I will still worry about you."

"There's no need." Rosemary smiled at the bundle in her arms. "Don't worry about changing. There's been a slight alteration in our plans for the evening. Why don't you come tell me how clever I am?"

Constantine's footsteps grew closer and then stopped a few feet away. "How did you…?"

Men were so predictable. She'd have to tell Mercy that Constantine was every bit as shocked as they both expected him to be. The sudden labor and fast delivery had thrown the house at sixes and sevens. "Oh, it all happened in the usual way. I won't bore you with the details."

He came closer and fell to his knees at her side, staring in stunned amazement at her lap. "When? You were sleeping peacefully when I left."

Rosemary lifted her gaze away from their son and cupped his cheek. "Obviously in the intervening hours."

Her husband blinked rather foolishly. "I wanted to be here."

"Well," Rosemary said, "this little man had other ideas. He was born very quickly. It seems I must take after my mother in that. We each were faster than the last to present ourselves. Tobias reminded me just last night that Mama barely made it to the birthing chamber before he appeared. Have I surprised you?"

"Beyond belief." Constantine leaned in and kissed her full on the mouth. "You are the cleverest, most beautiful, most ingenious woman in the whole world."

Rosemary nodded. "That's more like it. Would you like to hold your son and heir?"

Her husband gulped nervously but took his son from her arms

with the skill of a man used to such tasks. She leaned back against the headrest, admiring the man she'd married and the warmth of his smile. She'd chosen well the night she'd stolen him for her own pleasure. He treated her gently and allowed her the liberty she craved in most things, but most of all she just liked to be near him

He looked up. "What will you call him?"

She grinned. "I thought you might claim that privilege."

Constantine bit his lip as he gazed upon his son. "James, of course, after your father. Peter, after mine. James Peter Hunt. Do you like it?"

Tears filled her eyes. "That was exactly what I would have chosen."

Constantine glanced around at the sound of a giggle. "Are our daughters here?"

Rosemary nodded and crooked her fingers toward the bed. "They wanted to see your reaction to meeting their baby brother. Come out, my little darlings."

Three pretty faces appeared from beneath the tassels of the master bed and hurried across the room. They crowded their father and new brother, their little fingers caressing James Peter Hunt's dark head of hair gently as she'd shown them.

"He cries a lot, Papa," Willow confessed with a sad shake of her head.

"See, he's looking at you." Maisy giggled. "He gets cross."

Constantine rocked James a little until he settled again, his smile proving him utterly besotted with their son. "If that's the case, he must have inherited a good portion of Randall blood."

Rosemary met Constantine's gaze over the heads of their children and her heart filled. The girl's fascination with their new brother was simply adorable. After a moment, the girls drifted back to her side, and to her delight Willow climbed into her lap and lay against her shoulder. Rosemary brushed the girl's hair from her eyes and cuddled her close. "What do you think of him?"

"He's perfect."

Rosemary touched the girl's cheek and then Maisy's and Poppy's too. "You are all perfect, and all mine. Never ever forget that."

Willow kissed her cheek and scrambled off, leaving her arms free. Poppy climbed onto her lap next and when Constantine placed James into her other arm she juggled the two together.

With luck, this wouldn't be the end but only the beginning.

Acknowlegements

Each book I write begins as a single idea that won't leave me alone, taking months to craft until I'm prepared and willing to share the story with others. This series has been a labor of love and determination and I'm so pleased my wild Randalls have found their way home.

For my extraordinary editor Anne Victory, my deepest sympathies for the burden you carry in correcting my mistakes. I do not know what I'd do without you. No really, I've no idea. Don't go anywhere, ok?

The amazingly insightful and talented Laurie Schnebly saved me when faced with what seemed like an insurmountable problem in promoting this last book. Bless you for your rockin publicity skills and the generosity of your time.

The Wild Randalls series began over two years ago now and I'd like to thank the people who have brainstormed with me, shared their expertise and generally held my hand when I couldn't find my way: Julie, Melissa, Michelle, Tamara, Suzi, Sandra, Tammy, Amy and Angieleigh. You're all incredible ladies. Thank you so much for being in my corner when I needed you.

And last but in no way least I want to thank my awesome husband and our sons for allowing me time alone to write, edit and promote my stories, for eating cheesecakes to celebrate my milestones (that one was a burden), for understanding that 'mum needs to write' isn't a joke but her career, and for delivering endless cups of coffee while I'm working. I love you so very much.

An Accidental Affair

Chapter One

Being good was a damned nuisance. Merrick Bishop, Lord Rothwell, steered Lady Harrison away from curious onlookers for a moment's privacy.

When they were alone and safe from prying eyes, Louisa's eyes lit up with mischief. "I thought you came to my ball to further your search for a wife, Rothwell?"

"I did." He sighed at her suggestion that he was after more than just information from her tonight. Louisa might be very lovely and have curves enough to tempt a man away from honorable intentions, but she had connections he needed to make use of first. Merrick wanted a wife this season, not a potential scandal. He'd put the decision off long enough. He was thirty and at an age when the future, not just his but others, preyed on his mind. "There is still much you can tell me about my quarry. What did you discover?"

She smiled at him fondly and ran her hands over his forearms. "A pity it must be so, but I agree it is high time you married. With your connections and wealth you should have had even the most cautious of fathers lining up to offer up their daughters for marriage to you by now."

He frowned. "That has *not* been my experience. I only need one." If he wanted to find himself the right sort of wife, then he needed access to information about the candidates and their families before he approached them. Louisa had her ear in the right circles, and the wrong ones too. Merrick cast an anxious glance along the hall, hoping no one was lingering close enough to overhear their conversation. He didn't want to ruin what he'd started before he'd truly begun. "Where is your husband tonight?"

"Oh, the card room, I imagine. You know how he is when there are high stakes involved. Except"—her brow furrowed and her head turned toward the hall door—"he did seem rather interested in the guest list, so I think he may have his eye on someone I invited tonight. I do hope it's not one of your possibilities."

Merrick studied her face, wondering if Louisa had it in her to be the least bit jealous of another woman. "Does that disturb you? That he might be meeting with a lover of his own even now?"

She made a face and then laughed. "Only if he chooses someone I dislike. I do not like to share with my enemies."

He laughed along with her, but he wasn't the least bit amused. Marriage was a serious business. When he found the right woman, Merrick would not share. He knew his own mind well enough to believe that when he found a woman who matched his criteria and married her, he would be entirely possessive about her company. "Tell me."

Louisa's gaze softened. "It is as you feared."

He cursed under his breath. "Why?"

"I'm not entirely sure." She frowned. "The old rumors about your father's frequent dalliances are circulating again, as well as whispers of your own more recent affair with that dreadful actress. I warned you anyone who named herself after fruit would be trouble. But she has cried so convincingly over the loss of your affection and everyone thinks you were a monster to her."

Merrick scowled at the memory of his last affair with Josephine Peach. He was not sorry to have ended things as abruptly as he had. "I found her in bed with not one but two grubby stage hands when she'd claimed to be indisposed for dinner. I brought her flowers for heavens sake to brighten her bloody room."

"Well, she is an actress and they do lie for a living." Louisa shrugged. "Couple that with your new interest in balls and even attending the odd picnic, and your behavior has taken on a wholly different light than what you wished for. I imagine every father with a daughter fresh to the marriage mart is watching you closely, and they don't believe you intend to marry. It's no wonder there's a chill greeting you."

Merrick slumped against the wall. "I'm nothing like my father."

"I know. We've been friends a long time and that is why you have me on your side. I'll help ease your way into their good graces, though I'm not sure how much good it will do. You'll have to prove you have honorable intentions, at least for a while."

Lady Harrison eased closer, her hands caressing his chest fleetingly. "So, the Howard chit is rumored to prefer books to balls, and there is Lady Cecily, who seems meek and mild at first glance, but she has more spirit than most beneath the well-polished exterior."

She paused for a moment, thinking. "You also asked about Miss Milne's family. Her father has built a reputation as a shrewd businessman, thanks in no small part to the weight of his pocketbook, though that also makes her less appealing when compared to other young ladies coming out this year. The girl is quiet but always the first to supper. Nerves, I expect. Some women eat when they are anxious. She will regret that later in life, I believe."

Merrick nodded. "The Howard girl clings to her mama's skirts at balls and will not leave her side, so we have not spoken more than a few words." He would never consider Lady Cecily, though he did not mention that to Lady Harrison because he didn't care to fuel the gossips as to his reasons. Miss Milne was a possibility, though with her common background and lesser connections, she had not been invited to tonight's ball. Louisa's remarks about her appetite did explain why he could never find her at other events she attended though. He'd avoided the supper room in the hopes of striking up conversation away from prying eyes. He wasn't keen to single out any one woman yet, but if he wanted to speak with Miss Milne, he was looking for her in the wrong places. "Thank you for the information."

"It must be rather tedious to court a proper girl, given your past preference for naughtiness. Everyone expects you to continue as you always have, and there have been more than a few long faces this season, I can tell you." Louisa's gloved fingers curled around his. "You should stick to your own kind, Rothwell. You want a wife with an adventurous manner, not a frumpy mouse who'll clear the sideboard in one sitting. I think Lady Cecily deserves a longer look. She has come into her own in terms of fashion, thanks to her aunt's excellent influence. If you would simply tell me your exact requirements the pain might be done already. You're holding back something, I can tell. If I knew all it might make finding the right wife for you easier. I hate to see you unhappy and I know just the way to make you smile again."

Her hand slipped lower to brush across his groin, tempting him away from his plans for the night. A romp with Louisa would do his body good, though getting caught in an affair, no matter how fleeting, was the surest way to lose ground. The ball underway was in part a way to help him find a wife. He had spoken with Lady Mary tonight, though he still had doubts they would suit. Her mother and father had seemed ill at ease when he joined them, almost frightened, which he found utterly ridiculous. He did not make a habit of seducing virgins, though it was highly likely he would end up married to one. Observing Miss Milne's behavior around others would require planning on his part and would await another evening.

"What I want precisely is my business to know." Merrick eased back from Louisa, offering an apologetic smile. "I do appreciate whatever advice you can offer, my dear."

She pouted. "Whoever you marry had better deserve your skills in the bedchamber. You will find you sacrifice much freedom in a marriage."

"That is true." And it was also not. The lady he married would be the one to sacrifice much. The rumors of his father's misdeeds had plagued Merrick his entire life. His mother had fled society eventually, humiliated and hurt because it was all too true. Once Merrick married, he feared that his wife could be subject to the same sort of speculation.

Yet he needed a son—a legitimate heir to take responsibility for the estate and all those who depended on him.

So in return for taking him on, and the burden of his father's legacy, Merrick would make his own pledge. Fidelity. His wife would be the only one to bear his children. There would never be a bastard child bearing his likeness. He would not cause the same pain as he had witnessed in his parents' marriage. He had told no one of his thoughts on the subject because in truth, he expected to be disbelieved. However, he had come to the decision that the woman bound to him for the rest of her life deserved the same consideration. "I should return to the ball."

"A pity." Louisa's gaze searched his, and then she smiled, proving there were no lingering hard feelings about his unavailability for a romp in the foreseeable future. "There is a dinner at Lady Berry's this week. I shall endeavor to have you invited so you might meet Miss Milne in simpler surroundings. Her parents will be guarding her as carefully as usual, which would get in the way of any seduction, but I am sure your charm alone will win her over the dinner table." She looked up at him from under her lashes. "And if you change your mind and want my company in private, I'm only too happy to oblige."

"Thank you." Miss Milne was at the top of a short list. There were still questions in his mind about her nature to be satisfied, and although she stirred no great passion in him now, Merrick had no doubts he could bed her successfully if they married. He had scant enough new information for tonight, but what he had would have to do.

Louisa flicked her fingers in an intimate wave and departed, leaving Merrick to make his way slowly back to the ballroom. As he returned, he mused at the gamble he was taking in confiding in Lady Harrison and placing so much faith in her information. The one thing in her favor was that she was no friend to his wider family, having locked horns with his aunt, Lady Penelope Ford, on several notable occasions.

Louisa was also very critical. She frowned upon indiscretions in the very young and unmarried set, an amusing contradiction for a woman whose dalliances were as scandalous as any he'd heard. But not for the first time did he fear that the names she'd supplied him were what she might want in his wife and not what he needed. It was clear she expected him to continue their assignations once he was married. It was altogether likely the names she'd provided were for women whose morals matched hers and who would turn a blind eye to indiscretions.

He caught the eye of a servant and secured a cup of punch. Not his favorite beverage, but his aim was to appear innocuous and no threat to a good woman's virtue. As always when he thought of a good woman, his eyes turned to one in particular. Tall, slim, and perfectly poised. Arabella, Lady Farnsworth, stood well above those around her, wrapped in pink, tasseled muslin and a feathered turban hiding her pale hair. He had a slight acquaintance with her through a mutual friend, but while he knew much about her from shared confidences, he had actually spoken very little to the lady. Arabella might be a widow, but she wasn't the kind to invite a gentleman to get to know her better.

She was much too straightlaced to give him more than a cursory glance when they met. Judging by her frequent high color, his reputation with the ladies made her distinctly uncomfortable. She would never give him the time of day, so Merrick kept a distance and enjoyed the view from afar.

He frowned now though, his eyes flickering to her unexpected companion. What the devil was she doing in Lord Parker's company again? Her niece, Lady Cecily, a debutante whose behavior bordered unacceptable, wasn't even there to be paraded before the man. Parker, an older bachelor like himself, might have the distinction of being received everywhere, but there was something about him that didn't sit well with Merrick. He wasn't worthy of standing so close to the very respectable Lady Farnsworth, but Merrick couldn't pinpoint why.

"Ah, Rothwell." A pleasant male voice interrupted his musing. "Are you making the rounds again tonight?"

He turned to find Lord Louth, an earl he'd not spoken to in close to a year, looming beside him. Louth was extremely tall and broad and well-muscled. He dwarfed most gentlemen and tended to keep to himself. Merrick shook hands with him. "I seem to be. I'm surprised to see you here tonight."

An unhappy grumble left Louth. "Keeping up with recent events."

Merrick glanced at his face and laughed. "Your mother's suggestion?"

"Something like that." His gaze scanned the room slowly, as if looking for someone. His next words confirmed he was. "Have you seen Taverham of late?"

"Last week, I think. Passed him on Bond Street. Why?"

"Was he with anyone?"

"Only Lord Acton and his widowed sister. They're thick of late, and I wouldn't be surprised if Taverham is ready to give up on his wife's return and find a new one."

"That's what I heard, too." Louth smiled grimly. "Well, so good to see you again. My thanks again for the lease of your Yorkshire property."

"My pleasure." Merrick grinned. "Did you and your lady friend enjoy the winter there? I'm told it's quite lovely if one doesn't leave the bedroom."

"I don't know." Louth scowled . "The lady threw me out in a fit of temper the very first night."

He hurried off, leaving Merrick to puzzle over that final remark. After all the trouble Louth had gone to in leasing the property and practically begging for absolute discretion, he must have blundered quite badly to not spend even a single night with the woman.

He faced Arabella again and froze as Lord Parker, being taller than the lady by several inches, cast a lascivious eye over Arabella's perfect breasts. The man was practically drooling over her. In fact, as Merrick watched on, Parker's hand rose to play with the tassel hanging from her loose-fitting sleeves. The touch was protracted, and yet Lady Farnsworth did not slap his hand away.

Merrick took a moment to suppress his surprise and then checked the room to see if anyone else had noticed the proper Lady Farnsworth being seduced so publicly. Unfortunately, Louisa had noticed. Her little fists were clenched tightly at her sides, her eyes narrowed. Louisa certainly wasn't the sort to guard the virtue of another lady, so he was convinced she wasn't outraged on Lady Farnsworth's behalf. Was she engaged in an affair with Lord Parker too?

A cunning smile flittered across Louisa's face, and it seemed a distinct possibility she was engaged to some degree with Lord Parker. When she glided slowly toward Arabella and Parker via a circuitous route, Merrick moved to better view the encounter, heart sinking with dismay. Louisa clearly had no love for the situation and Lady Farnsworth seemed unaware she was in the line of fire. It wasn't in Louisa's nature to make a public spectacle of herself, but as she had told him on more than one occasion, there was always a first time for everything.

However, when Louisa insinuated herself into the conversation, Arabella engaged her in a protracted conversation, leaving Parker at a distance from the pair and largely out of the conversation. Indeed, they spoke so exclusively together that when Parker went on his way, neither paid much attention except to bid him farewell. Perhaps he'd been wrong about Louisa and Lord Parker. But whatever the situation might be, it seemed Arabella's knack for avoiding awkwardness with other women was as strong as ever. Her ability to appease others was a skill she employed effortlessly. No matter what happened around her, Lady Farnsworth continued on as if any untoward behavior had never happened.

About Heather Boyd

Determined to escape the Aussie sun on a scorching camping holiday, Heather picked up a pen and notebook from a corner store and started writing her very first novel—Chills. Eight years later, she is the author of over thirty romances and publisher of several anthologies too. Addicted to all things tech (never again will Heather write a novel longhand) and fascinated by English society of the early 1800's, Heather spends her days getting her characters in and out of trouble and into bed together (if they make it that far). She lives on the edge of beautiful Lake Macquarie, Australia with her trio of mischievous rogues (husband and two sons) along with one rescued cat whose only interest in her career is that it provides him with food on demand.

You can find details of her work and writing at
www.Heather-Boyd.com